The Bells of Saint Clements

A work of fiction with a strong historical content

Michael Alty

Published 2014 by arima publishing

www.arimapublishing.com

ISBN 978 1 84549 620 3
© Michael Alty 2014

Printed and bound in the United Kingdom

Typeset in Garamond

Swirl is an imprint of arima publishing.

arima publishing
ASK House, Northgate Avenue
Bury St Edmunds, Suffolk IP32 6BB
t: (+44) 01284 700321

www.arimapublishing.com

Chapter One

The Cenotaph in Whitehall, London, Sunday 11th November 2001

It was precisely eleven o'clock when the chimes of Big Ben could be heard striking from within the huge clock tower looming over the Houses of Parliament in Westminster. The distinctive booming knell of the clock's hourly bell was hammered, the sound reverberating down the crowded esplanade of Whitehall to herald the annual and respective two minutes silence to commemorate the dead of the First World War and subsequent conflicts fought inside and outside the shores of Great Britain.

Those who were fortunate to have had the ability to stand in the crowded thoroughfare of Whitehall stood still for the statutory, albeit obligatory recommended time, whilst, others, namely veterans could be seen seated in their wheelchairs looking down from a better vantage point to observe the numerous wreaths of poppies which had been deposited around the base of Sir Edwin Lutyens 'empty tomb' by the Royal British Legion. The Poem 'For the Fallen', by Robert Lawrence Binyon; the thought provoking beauty of the words capturing the true spirit of remembrance and a poignant reminder of those who made the ultimate sacrifice was ecclesiastically and audibly orated by The Lord Bishop of London before the last post was sounded:

"They shall grow not old, as we that are left grow old:
Age shall not weary them, nor the years condemn.
At the going down of the sun and in the morning
We will remember them."

Following the extreme quietness when, not so much a cough or splutter was heard, the reveille was sombrely played by a distant bugler to softly awaken the crowds from their moment of deep thought. Seeing the old and bold, the Chelsea Pensioners dressed resplendently in their red tunics and three-cornered navy blue hats and rounded capons; their much cherished campaign and gallantry medals shining brilliantly in the morning sunlight as they marched proudly, albeit carefully, to the pipes and drums of the impeccably tartan-clad Scots Guards. It was indeed a

3

memorable sight and, as always, enough to raise the hackles of any onlooker, military or otherwise.

Standing a few feet away from Downing Street, and facing the Cenotaph was a league of elderly gentlemen, who, in the past had been members of the Foreign Office, namely the MI6. The tall and sprightly ninety-year old Rear Admiral, Sir Steven Halewood CBE. KCB, retired, was wearing a dark blue crombie overcoat, black leather gloves and a rather elegant, albeit, a much worn brown trilby hat. He was standing to attention behind a grey steel barrier with his hands firmly resting on the top of a neatly folded umbrella placed upright directly in front of him. Sir James Brown MBE, a small but stocky eighty-nine year old retired gentleman and another ex MI6 officer was standing next to him to his right, head bowed to honour his long gone friends and colleagues, the brave and courageous. Standing to Halewood's left was an eighty-nine year old veteran of MI6's inner circle called the 'the Circus', Commander Edward Greaves MBE, highly distinguishable by a black patch covering his left eye, and standing to his right was the man with the silver hair, ex MI6 'scalp-hunter', eighty-eight year old Colonel Brian Woodruff MBE. For some of those men, it was to be their last stand.

Whites Club, St James's, the same afternoon

'They say, in one of the newspapers, that if the Americans were to build the twin towers again in New York, they would be more architecturally sound.' Greaves pointed out as he twirled a silver fork around in order to inspect it.

'With all due respect, Edward, there are times when you speak absolute tripe!' Brown intervened quickly, 'you try telling that to those three and a half thousand innocent men and women who lost their lives just two months ago, and besides, you of all people should realize, what you read in sleazy downmarket newspapers is not always and not necessarily true, and another thing, as you know very well, there is nothing wrong with the cutlery in this club.' he added.

'I'll ignore that, James; you've always been an absolute radical, but this is neither the time, nor the place, I may add, for your personal prejudices to raise their particularly ugly heads and I still use my Dictaphone.

'You don't need your dick to phone anyone, and I would suggest you put it away, preferably back inside your trousers.' James said, now laughing like a hyena; the others: Ha! Ha! Ha! Ha! Ha...

'I have an amusing story to tell you,' Steven Halewood put in, once their laughter had subsided, 'which I might add, is quite true. Shortly after the war, in 1946 in fact, as you know I had a posting in Malta. My secretary at that time, an English woman called Emily Gresham who was somewhat eccentric, preferred to be known as Gershy.'

'Is this the amusing part, or is there more to come?' Sir James asked him, impatient for him to get on with what, judging by the sarcastic expression on Halewood's face, was giving every indication of being prolonged indefinitely.

'Patience, dear chap.' Halewood said, clearing his throat, 'Gershy', who incidentally was in her forties then, had lived in Malta for eighteen years, although she said she could never quite remember how long. So, I asked her one day when, to be honest, I had nothing better to occupy myself with, "how do you get off the island?" She quickly replied by saying: "Usually in the morning sir!"

An immediate repetition of Ha! Ha! Ha! pervaded the packed restaurant.

'You'll be saying next, Edward, a disaster of that magnitude won't happen again!' James said cautiously.

'This is serious, James,' Edward replied convincingly, 'we're here this afternoon to discuss what we, our country, are going to do about the next dramatic development in Afghanistan.'

'I agree.' Admiral Halewood said, sitting at his usual table with the three surviving members of his exclusive wartime team around him.

'It's that damned Osama Bin Laden,' Brian Woodruff said with a concerned look on his face, 'we've got to find him before he and his fuzzie-wuzzies strike again, and next time it could possibly happen on our doorstep.'

'You mean here in the heart of London, Woodruff.' Sir Steven replied, leaning forward in his chair looking surprised at what Woodruff had just suggested.

'Yes, I mean just that.' Brian said, as he looked around before lowering his voice to reduce the sound to a more discretional level.

'We are supposed to be retired gentlefolk now.' Sir James put in, smiling broadly.

'Retire! Retire! My dear boy, we shall never retire; officers belonging to the Foreign Office, Royal Navy and Army never retire!' Admiral Halewood replied angrily, banging his fist down on the table, dismissing Woodruff's insistence for everyone to talk quietly.

'The desk warriors always seem to have a reason not to do something in case it damages their promotion prospects or taints the government's decision on matters of security, that's how it is, and I'm afraid to say, it has always been so in our department,' Brian said reluctantly, 'but, it is vitally important we, the last of the 'Martians' and 'Bull Ring' masters act now.' he added.

'The Home Office, The Ministry of Defence, or indeed the Metropolitan Police would not be interested in listening to what we old cronies have to say.' James said getting up from his chair to find five minutes of much needed solace in the gents' cloakroom.

'No need to worry your head about anything, Woodruff old boy.' Halewood said patting him gently on the arm. 'The *Met* will have pre-empted this, and the boys in blue will sort any terrorist threat out as they have always done in the past, and as for that Bin Laden fellow, the Special Air Service (SAS) have already got him in their sights.'

'Does this Osama Bin Laden fellow make washing machines and spin-dryers as well?' Commander Greaves asked the Admiral.

'Why do you ask that, Edward; is this another one of your silly little jokes I have had to put up with for years?'

Before Edward was able to explain that he and his wife had just purchased two Laden appliances from Comet, the waitress interrupted to take their order for lunch.

The lunch consisted of three courses: a half avocado filled with *crevette* rosé and a seafood sauce, or alternatively a huge portion of French *pâté forestier*, followed by lamb cutlets, roast potatoes, broccoli and a delicious gravy one could die for. The dessert, a more than generous serving of Apple pie served with a choice of either ice-cream or custard was a speciality of White's exclusive restaurant. A vintage bottle of claret was shown to Admiral Halewood by the wine waiter for his approval before it was transferred into a highly polished glass decanter and placed in the centre of the table; a Havana cigar and a large balloon of brandy was complementary that day.

After Woodruff had politely excused himself to go and listen to Mozart in the gentleman's cloakroom, James surreptitiously asked Halewood and Greaves if they were any further forward in their quest in solving one of the biggest mysteries on the island of Malta.

'No, not yet.' Halewood replied shaking his head and sighing at the same time. 'But we still have time.' Greaves confidently put in.

'Somehow, I don't think so; time Steven, has become an expensive commodity.' Sir James said to them knowing they had come up against a brick wall and it was only a matter of time before they could be pushing up daisies. 'And did you know, Edward,' he continued. 'You have an uncanny and remarkable resemblance to the portrait of Captain William Longhorn, Royal Navy, which at one time was on the drawing room wall in Bradley Hall.'

'Yes, I have heard this from Melanie Bradford-Jones during the war,' Greaves pointed out and keeping a watchful eye on the time. 'I would have thought, Admiral Lord Nelson would be more befitting and furthermore, he didn't end up inside a dustbin.' he added.

'Melanie was one of Britain's best secret agents and, it is a great pity she couldn't be with us this afternoon.' Halewood said, his tear ducts beginning to rapidly fill up.

'Here, here.' Sir James replied sympathetically. 'We didn't know in 1962 she was going to be pushed in front of a London Transport Bus directly outside the British Russian Embassy.'

'I never did get to the bottom of that.' Greaves said without thinking properly.

'Well, from what I am told, you and quite a few others did.'

It was just after three when the Festival of Remembrance came to an end. The four just men made their way out of the club and to get into the taxis which were waiting outside ready to take them home, with the exception of Sir James Brown, who preferred to freeze and return home by public transport namely the Number 91 Crouch End bus from Trafalgar Square, watching in mild amusement as the others sped off extravagantly and regally waving one behind the other.

My name is James Brown, no relation to the singer, songwriter, I might add, but there were times in my life I wished I was. I live in an exclusive high-rise three-bedroom apartment in London; number 167 Russell Court, Bloomsbury, with my wife, Mary, whom I have adored immensely for the past fifty-five years of marriage to her. Mary and I live just a stone's throw away from Russell Square and just around the corner, in Coram Street, we have our local pub, named the, 'Marquis Cornwallis' which the breweries profess to be the 'in-place' in Bloomsbury. We collect our state pensions from Russell Square Post Office every Friday morning and then pop along to our favourite coffee shop on the ground floor of the Bedford Hotel to enjoy a pot of their delicious Darjeeling tea and chocolate muffins; our loyalty card has been punched so many times since our first visit, we cannot remember the number of free beverages we have been given since then.

I was born at No 13, Odo Road, Dover on the 15th April 1912; the same morning the *Titanic* sank, which I suppose is historically correct because, according to my mother and father, the news of the disaster came as a tremendous shock to the community and the port of Dover. In later years, some of the books I read on the subject, especially when I was a student at Trinity College, Cambridge, and studying history and learning how fifteen hundred people, poor and not so poor, passengers and crew, lost their lives early on the same morning I was born. As a teenager, I can remember attending the local fire brigade social evenings on a Saturday where we played pass the parcel, musical chairs and other silly games prior to us quick-stepping around a small room in front of the bar. My father was the chief fire officer in Dover, Kent and little did we all know that in 1939 there was to be another war looming on the horizon. In 1942, following the allied intervention I can recall travelling down from London to Dover by train and then going to the American supper parties which were at that time held in Dover's High Street town hall. Everyone brought their own food and shared it with the other guests, the dancing sometimes being interrupted by the deafening sound of the air-raid warning.

It was on VE Day on the eighth of May, 1945, when Churchill waved to the crowds in Whitehall and broadcast to the nation that the war with Germany had been won; it was there among the crowds of people, I met my wife Mary for the first time. We were standing together, directly opposite to Horse Guards Parade and joining in with the expected euphoria of the Victory celebrations. Mary looked delectable in her worsted grey pin-stripe suit; a knee-length skirt, straight, with a box- pleat and a long jacket with two slanted pockets; the wedged-heel shoes with the artificial snake-skin straps, wrapped around her slim ankles were to me quite erotic, her black stockings adding to this vision of loveliness and, one I will never forget. Her hair was quite short, in keeping with the fashion at that time; now, it's a little bit longer and has a stylish blue rinse.

Mary Jane Fuller, a Civil Service clerical officer from Holborn, West London, worked at the Admiralty building in Trafalgar Square, and it was on the tenth of April the following year we tied the knot in the Parish church of Saint Etheldreda's, Ely Place, Holborn and just a few minutes away from her parent's newsagents, tobacco and sweet shop in High Holborn.

My tenure with the Foreign Office had begun some years earlier when I was twenty-six, after becoming a member of the Metropolitan Police force and then moving on to New Scotland Yard in Whitehall. It was August1938 when I was approached by MI5 and asked to join them. After I had been given my new terms of employment by the military intelligence authorities, I agreed to accept their offer and it wasn't long before I was poached by MI6's so-called talent spotters because of discovering a couple of bent coppers at the Yard.

I had already phoned Mary on my mobile and was now making my way towards the bus stop in Trafalgar Square via the two Ship & Shovell pubs in Craven Passage, and this is where I sat down amongst a gathering of

British Legion revellers who would insist on buying me a pint of Badger Ale. It was probably my medals which impressed them and not the man; I couldn't wait to get on that god-forsaken bus. I was standing next to the ornate wrought iron fireplace looking up to admire the magnificent portrait of Rear Admiral of the Red, Sir Cloudesley Shovell, the controversial seventeenth century Captain of HMS Prince when I saw, sitting alone, at the far end of the lounge, a rather sinister looking man whom I thought, must have been in his late eighties, and was occasionally glancing over in my direction. I felt I had seen him somewhere before but I couldn't remember where, or when it was; this conundrum began to bug me as I walked back down Craven Passage, crossing over Craven Street and then past the Sherlock Holmes pub in Northumberland Street leading up towards the Strand.

The bus came along at four-thirty and I was just in time for the driver, an Afro-Caribbean gentleman to wave me on to his bus without me having to pay. I thought: these medals are working wonders for me today, but, tomorrow will be another story when I try to put one of them into a parking meter!

I was sitting in the lower deck of the bus on the left-hand side where I could see quite clearly the Pakistani souvenir shops, the Turkish take-away kebab houses and the Italian Pizza Huts as I looked out through the window. It was when we stopped outside an Italian restaurant in Aldwych I suddenly remembered who the pub 'Spy Guy' was, and the secretive events which had happened more than sixty years ago. This man, whom I had seen just fifteen minutes earlier, had been an Italian wartime MI6 agent called Ronaldo Donatello, code name the Condor; both names derived and attributed by me. A cold and nervous shiver ran down my spine, plus an element of fear, when suddenly it occurred to me he could be on my tail, and, in which case I could be living dangerously once again; this time, in the twenty-first century. My immediate reaction was to pull up the collar of my dark blue crombie overcoat, adjust my black Australian bush hat before sinking down inconspicuously on to the red plastic seat, firmly gripping the lapels of my coat tightly together, all too aware I was probably looking like a man who had just undergone major throat surgery.

*

Bloomsbury, London W1

I got off the bus directly outside the London Pub next to The Royal National Hotel in Woburn Place, Bloomsbury. Feeling rather unsteady on my feet, I attempted to cross the busy road adjacent to Coram Street and, after seeing my life flash by me on the bus a few minutes earlier; I was then nearly knocked to the ground by an emergency ambulance travelling at high speed from its headquarters in Herbrand Street or the famous, Great Ormond Street hospital near to Russell Square.

Going into Entrance 'B' of Russell Court was indeed refuge and, as I made my way towards the lift to take me up to the third floor, a voice said: 'Good evening, Sir James.' the concierge, William Walton greeted me.

'Good evening, Walton, it was rather cold in Whitehall today.' I said, before removing my black leather gloves to induce some sort of circulation back into my hands.

Walton came out from his cubby-hole and remarked: 'I would have liked to have been at the Cenotaph this morning, Sir James, and I could have worn my General Service Medal which I received for my tour of duty in Aden; nineteen sixty-six it was, sir, thirty-five years ago, and indeed how time flies.'

'How right you are Walton, how right you are.' I replied, before he pressed the button to summon the lift.

The warmth and glow from the artificial log fire was instantly pleasing when I opened the door to our apartment. Mary was sitting cosily on the settee and had just finished reading the intriguing book written by John Le Carré, 'Tinker Tailor Soldier Spy', for the umpteenth time and, once again, she had been trying to understand the novelist's complicated but not so incredible story.

'Don't bother to take your coat off, James,' Mary said, tossing the book on to the coffee table directly in front of my favourite wing-backed armchair, 'I would like to visit the book fair in the Royal National's

Galleon Suite and then, perhaps, we could have a couple of drinks in the cocktail bar.'

'Do you really think this is a good idea, Mary?' I said, dismissing the thought of a much welcomed cup of tea coming my way. 'Anyway, the stall holders will have started to pack up because the fair closes at five-thirty.'

'This is the best time of the day to browse around, and as you very well know, James, one can always pick up a bargain; the bookcases in your study are full of them.' she emphasised, looking up towards the clock on the mantel piece.

'Okay, Okay, we will go over the road to the Royal National in Bedford Way, if it makes you feel any better for doing so, Mary.' I said with a big sigh. 'It's not as if we have to walk very far.'

'Going out again, Sir James?' Walton said to me; the question, I think was possibly directed to my wife as well.

'Yes, Walton, we are both going out, and I may be away for some time.' I replied, quoting Captain Lawrence Edward Grace Oates's famous statement and, at the same time trying delicately to infuse an element of wisdom into his brain.

'He never came back.' Walton said, opening the glass doors for us.

'Who never came back?' I asked inquisitively.

'Captain Oates of the Antarctica, of course; apparently, he crawled out of his tent one night in 1912 and didn't return, it was a funny business, if you ask me.'

'What was funny, Walton?' continuing to question him before Mary intervened and lowering her voice said: 'Come on, James we are going to be late; you know you are always like this when you have had a few drinks.'

I suggested to Mary that a nice cup of fresh coffee wouldn't have gone amiss and, as for Walton, he is probably right this minute drooling over a copy of the Mayfair magazine I had seen opened at the centre pages behind his desk.

'Do you know, James,' Mary said, looking over her shoulder at me as we drew closer to the edge of the pavement, 'I really don't want to hear about Walton's particular interests in the female form and,' she added and, perhaps fortunately for me, knowing my wife extremely well and recognising the teasing smile hovering on her lips, I knew where she was going to come from next, 'as far as your wish for a re-vitalizing cup of coffee, I'm sorry, but that will have to wait until we get back home. And, as for the magazine you saw, what about the copy of Titbits I found underneath the bed several years ago, James?'

With Mary by my side we negotiated the traffic in Woburn Place, it was I suppose like a film being run in the fast forward mode and then being quickly reversed as we attempted to cross that dangerous and busy road.

In the hotel's forecourt there were three coaches: one from Naples, Italy; one that had just brought forty-six Japanese tourists from Heathrow airport and the other which had travelled from Osnabruck, Westfalia in north-west Germany. My immediate thoughts were: I bet they are really enjoying themselves in there, sitting in the lobby with glasses of mineral water and scratching their heads when they receive Scottish five-pound notes included in their change from the bar. It wasn't so surprising when I learned later that when a couple of these people had turned up at the Albert Hall the previous evening for the annual gala, the Festival of Remembrance, they were turned away for not being in possession of a ticket. Perhaps many of their voyagers were probably wishing it was seven o'clock when they could escape from the hotel in a regimental sort of way, only to fall asleep in one of the theatres in the West End.

Mary and I entered the Galleon Suite where the book fair was being held and there was no sign of it starting to close; in fact, it was bustling, very warm in comparison to outside and we had the impression the stallholders didn't want to go home. It was when we were passing a pile of dusty old books and an encyclopaedia which could have been printed by William Caxton himself, I saw an elderly man standing at the far end of the room browsing through *"Mein Kampf"* by, Adolf Hitler, the leader of Nazi Germany; the book I had seen and held two minutes earlier. I later recognised the man to be Herman Klaus Schneider, a German double agent whom MI5 and MI6 successfully turned in 1942 by threatening to harm his family. I thought this to be absolutely bizarre when two people from my past were to turn up simultaneously; Ronaldo Donatello and Herman Schneider had certainly conjured up my imagination, this time to the extent of extreme paranoia and nervousness, knowing both of them had, and could still be, working together.

Mary was standing at a nearby stall and had managed to find an old copy of Mrs Beaton's cookery book and seemed generally interested in buying it, but that was until the seller became greedy and wanted an absolute fortune for it. After joining her at the stall, she remarked: 'I know my cooking isn't all that special but, you never complain, do you James? And, at my time of life I don't need Mrs Beaton to show me how to make a better omelette. The book is far too expensive, James; I used to work for the Civil Service, I didn't own it!' I agreed with her that the book wasn't a good purchase and then went on to tell her there was nothing wrong with her Spanish omelettes with delicious sauté potatoes and asked could we go home?

'Really, James, there are times when you can be terribly selfish.'

'In what way, Mary? I've made a perfectly reasonable suggestion. I would really like to go home now.'

'You do not understand, do you; in fact, you are behaving in an extremely strange way and why,' she added, 'do you keep looking over my shoulder in that furtive way. There are times, James, I don't understand you. What is on your mind, James?' she emphasised, looking concerned as she held on to my arm, 'you look as if you have just seen a ghost.'

'I have, as a matter of fact;' I replied nervously and making a supreme effort not to look across the room, 'two in one afternoon.'

'Perhaps, we should give that drink a miss.' Mary said angrily, folding up the empty green plastic Harrods bag she'd hopefully brought with her, and leading the way, stiff-backed, to the door.

'What culinary delights are you serving up this evening?' I asked her, thinking this could be my last supper, as we took our lives into our hands once again in trying to cross that busy road.

'Sausages, egg and chips,' she replied, and I knew then, I was being systematically, albeit temporarily, relegated to the proverbial dog house.

It was bitterly cold as we walked hurriedly towards the delectable looking Greek restaurant which normally has tables and chairs conveniently placed on the pavement for passers-by to fall over. The Bureau de Change next door, and on the corner of Coram Street, looked equally enticing, inviting American tourists to exchange their hundred dollar bills into a currency which no one living outside the shores of Great Britain can understand. It is when they have expended all of their money they find it necessary to take out a second mortgage on their home before buying a cheese and pickle sandwich in Leicester Square; the tourists probably wonder why they ever bother to visit London in the first place. And, being a total cynic, pulling up the collar of my crombie, the Japanese should take first prize for the worst trolley bag wheelers in the world, because this morning I didn't know whether I was going to be mowed down by two micro nip-over people from Tokyo as I continued to venture along Woburn place towards Southampton Row to collect my *Sunday Times* newspaper.

I was in the bedroom fiddling with my old train set, an American ASP 9 mm automatic pistol which I had taken out from within one of the fitted cupboards. Mary, without me noticing, walked into the bedroom and saw me loading a full magazine into the weapon's pistol grip, and then when I made it ready to fire, she said, sounding more sad and pathetic by the second: 'I thought you had put your toys away for good, James? It would seem you are still living in the past; your mind is so complicated and such a puzzle, my dear!'

It was then I knew Mary had finally understood the plot in the novel and was probably comparing me to George Smiley.

'I was only joking about your dinner,' Mary said, touching my arm gently, 'and it's hardly an excuse for killing me, is it?' she added.

'Don't joke with me.' I said to her, 'I have heard enough jokes for one day thank you very much.'

'Kiss me, James; kiss me, as if it were for the last time.' Mary asked passionately.

This was now sounding like a cross between Beryl Reed and Ingrid Bergman all over again and then I started to think: is my wife really sending me up or could it be just my imagination. When we were both back in the lounge, Mary went one step further by playing "Moonlight Serenade" by the Glenn Miller Orchestra, and that was when I really began to become concerned about my future well-being.

'Remember when we used to go to the Odeon cinema in Leicester Square, James and...'

'That was a long, long time ago, Mary,' I pointed out as we waltzed slowly around the room waiting for the Andrews Sisters to walk in through the door at any moment. After the floor show had ended we nostalgically sat down next to each other in front of the glowing fire place when Mary began to question me about the events which had happened during that afternoon and I started to tell her...

Chapter Two

'At 0200 hrs, Mary, on the night of 18 May, 1942 a fascist spy called Caio Borghi, also known as Carmelo Borg Pisani and other things, of Senglea in Malta, and Lorenzo Giovanni Marino, alias, Rolando Donatello, an Italian British MI6 agent from Naples, with a code- name "Condor", rowed ashore from an Italian torpedo boat to the cave at Ras id-Dawwara, 2.5 km; approximately one and a half miles north of Dinghli Cliffs which are situated on the southwest coast of Malta. Pisani was a Maltese fascist sympathiser educated on a scholarship in Rome. To feed his ideology and repay his moral debt he volunteered to recce the defences and supplies prior to the planned Axis invasion of Malta, 'Operation '*Herkules*', but the sheer cliffs above him were impossible to scale, and within forty-eight hours, all his rations had been washed out to sea. However, Donatello made it to the top because of his recent mountaineering skills which he had learned from the British army's Special Forces prior to their departure to enemy-occupied Norway when their mission had been to destroy the huge gun emplacements in Bergen and secret heavy-water establishments constructed in the mountainous countryside, near the town of Stavanger.

'Dinghli cliffs, Mary, and I'm trying to describe them; they are the highest point in Malta and fall two hundred and sixty metres to the sea. From here, the Mediterranean appears to begin, even when the white foam angrily whips the indigo and wine-dark ocean below. The cliff road stops alarmingly at the precipitous edge. The track, to the left, eventually links back to the village of Buskett, four kilometres out of Rabat on the road to Dinghli and is overlooked by the infamous and illustrious Verdala Castle; an elaborate palazzo, disguised as a castle. Following Pisani's frantic efforts to attract the British patrol boats Pisani was arrested, and subsequently confessed. The British hanged him, you know, he was only twenty-eight and this was on the twenty-eighth November in 1942, as a spy, and for being the main participant in acting as decoy, creating a diversion to allow Pope Pius V11, the Vatican and his administrative officers, to jettison and temporarily deposit several tons of Nazi gold on to the island by Italian navy E boats.

'Lorenzo Giovanni Marino, however, was an Italian army officer and along with several hundred of his fellow officers and men, had been captured by The British eighth army along the desert wastes of Alexandria eight months prior to the battle of El Alamein. For some Italian prisoners of war it was to be an indefinite period of internment in a dowdy camp on the outskirts of North Berwick-on-Tweed, east coast of Scotland, but then for, Captain Marino, it wasn't long before he was faced with a pressurized ultimatum by British intelligence. He had no choice, Mary, but to conform to their wishes before being released, but what a price he paid for his freedom. I don't think you could possibly imagine just how much, but the British MI5 intelligence agents were using ruthless tactics to *turn* ordinary Italian army officers into spies. Furthermore, MI6 special agents were threatening Captain Marino by harming his wife and two children and destroying his house in San Giovanni a Teduccio, which is east of the bay of Naples, if he refused to carry out the mission.

'Meanwhile, Herman Klaus Schneider from the really picturesque town of Osnabruck, Westphalia, Germany and a member of a German Spy network called the *Abwehr* was arrested in the West End of London by New Scotland Yard on the sixth of April 1942. He had been recruited by the Gestapo and the *Sicherheitdienst*, or SD, the intelligence wing of the SS, and the Nazi Party. Code-named "The Rottweiler", by his handlers in Germany, Schneider became a professional German agent and had been forcibly sent to a special school in Hamburg to learn how to become a spy in the war of secrets. His ruthless team of handlers were based in Hamburg and they methodically trained him to look and behave like an Englishman. We trained him methodically and he was quickly turned into a double agent, behaving like a true German and had the code-name "The Hare". This may sound bizarre to you, Mary, and judging by your puzzled expression, I don't think I'm wrong. Anyway, the chief instructor was an Oxford University graduate, specialized in psychology and sinister undercover activities. The tutor taught Schneider and his spies to create an aura of respectability in Britain by opening Post Office savings accounts and to have healthy bank balances, also to join the local

Liberal Party which the SD considered in their so-called wisdom to be an advantage.'

'This is all too complicated for me, James, a bit like the book by John Le Carré,' Mary said, shaking her head and giving me the impression she was finding my story extremely difficult to believe, 'and, the two foreign guys,' she went on. 'Lorenzo what's-his-name and, Herman the German, they were working for you?'

'Yes, I'm afraid so.' I emphasised, placing my hand on the top of hers and patting it gently to alleviate her nervousness of what I had just told her.

'But James, you threatened both their families and surely that is inexcusable, isn't it?'

'Principles do not pay the mortgage, Mary,' I said, sounding like Lord Kinnock, speaking to the European Parliament when he had to pay a small increase for his gas and electricity. 'and, I personally, had nothing to do with that sort of thing; it was the scalp-hunters', the cash and carry heavies' responsibilities, and they were under orders from 'C', the Controller.'

'Can you tell me James,' Mary asked and I could see by the way she was looking at me she really wanted to know, 'where is the gold that was deposited on to the island of Malta; where did it come from, and why was it put there?'

'If I knew that, Mary, I would certainly have to kill you.' this time I was sounding like the irresistible James Bond 007, on Her Majesty's Secret Service.

'That's not very nice to talk to your wife like that, James Brown.' she said, giving me a thump in the chest with her elbow. 'There's time yet, you know, to change your favourite lobster salad into something quite inedible.'

'I was only joking, Mary, you should know that. I love you very much.' I said to her with feeling, knowing whatever I was about to receive for my dinner, I should be truly thankful to her, "Amen".

Mary turned up our mini hi-fi stack system; the CD was still Glen Miller and was now playing "I know why, and so do you". This was when I asked her: 'Sing to me, Mary, as you used to.'

'Oh, no, James, I can't sing.'

'Just sing, Mary.'

After the delicious dinner, consisting of Campbell's cream of mushroom soup, Sainsbury's specially packed lobster salad and a Waitrose crème caramel, Mary and I retired into the main lounge and once again sat down cosily in front of the fire.

'Would you like to watch some television this evening, Mary, or would you prefer to see one of our videos; 'Notting Hill', you like that because Hugh Grant is in it.' I asked, looking around for the handset; the gadget almost invariably, disappearing down the side of the settee. Having retrieved it with a great deal of huffing and puffing I was about to point it at the television screen when she said:

'No, James, what I really would like, is for you to tell me more about what you were, and what you did, during those war years before we met.' she asked adamantly.

'Well, Mary, we are going to be in for an extremely long night if I am to tell you everything.' I emphasised shaking my head. 'Do you really want to know all about this retrograde stuff?' I added.

'Yes.' was her reply.

'Are you sitting comfortably, Mary, now I shall begin by telling you: Before the Second World War, the Germans had installed two spy networks in the UK (the *abwehr*). The *Abwehr*, German military intelligence and the *Sicherheitdienst*, or SD, the intelligence wing of the SS and the Nazi Party, and one of the authors of the 'Final Solution' was Reinhard Heydrick who was assassinated in Prague, Czechoslovakia in 1942. The *Abwehr* chief was called Admiral Wilhelm Canaris, a known anti-Nazi; he was executed on the 9th April 1945 as one of the *Schwarze Kapelle* conspirators who had tried to assassinate Hitler in the *Wolfschanze*, the Wolfs lair, his East Prussian headquarters, in July 1944. However, the new head of the SD's military wing, like 'C', had become unbeknownst to the authorities that he was another member of the *Schwarze Kapelle* and loyal follower of Canaris; his incompetent Nazi attempts of espionage were extremely inept, you know. Also, the Germans sent agents to

Britain who could not speak English fluently and knew nothing about the country. They were supposed to mingle with the large population of foreigners who had fled Nazi persecution.

Pope Pius VII was the Pope during The Second World War. He became the Pope in 1939 and was one of the most controversial pontificates for centuries. Pius VII had been accused in recent years of taking far too supine an attitude to Nazi brutality and of doing nothing to alleviate the sufferings of the Jews. In October 1939 he displayed a supreme lack of appreciation of what was happening in Europe. But, when my book is published, Mary, I am going to put the record straight because I know that the Nazi gold which had been stored in the vaults of the Vatican was destined for Malta, via Sicily. The gold which had been extracted from Jewish inmates who had been interned and murdered in the concentration camps, such as; Auschwitz-Birkenau, Bergen-Belsen, Mauthausen, Treblinka, Dachau and Sorbibor was made into ingots, embossed with a swastika and put into the vaults of the Vatican, and that, Mary is an indisputable fact. The gold was to be returned to the Jewish people.

The Vatican – the administrative offices of the Vatican City has an area of approximately 109 acres in the centre of Rome, surrounding Saint Peter's and is the smallest state in the world. Part of the 'army' of the Vatican is made up by the well-known Swiss Guards, organised by Pope Julius11 in the early 16th century. Their black, red and yellow striped uniform was allegedly designed by Michelangelo or Raphael; historical records remain unclear about this. The secret archives of the Vatican and the grand corridor of the library which, incidentally, is reputed to be the longest room in the world, hold collections of books, priceless paintings, sculptures and fine art which are probably the finest in the world; this secular authority of the papacy, whose direct administration once covered about a third of Italy.

The spectacular German victories of 1939 and 1940 convinced Mussolini; dazzled by Adolf Hitler, that the moment had arrived otherwise he might be too late in sharing the spoils of war.

My part in all of this, Mary, is very clear; I was on His Majesty's Secret

Service. MI5 was, and still is, the counter intelligence organisation in Great Britain and Northern Ireland, working secretively for the Home Office and New Scotland Yard's Special Branch. Meanwhile, MI6 under the control of the Foreign Office, and together with a special sector of MI5 called the XX ('Double Cross') Committee became another secret organisation, entirely ruthless in their methods and tactics. The job of the XX Committee was to turn German and enemy agents into double agents and their offices were in Battersea, which is as you know in south London.   In wartime years Churchill's headquarters was called the London Controlling Section, under Colonel John Bevan and Lieutenant-Colonel Sir Ronald Wingate and they worked closely with ('C'), the Controller.

At this time, the MI6 unit was covertly based in London's Oxford Street and were known as the Martians; their job was to piece information together, most of which had been gathered from GCHQ, the Communication, Observation and British Surveillance and Communication Headquarters at Bletchley Park.'

'You may very well have to kill me, James for asking you this question again,' Mary said as the anniversary clock on the mantelpiece chimed twelve o'clock, midnight. 'Why was the gold put on to the island and where is it?' she added.

'The gold was intended to be secretly handed back to the Jewish people by Pope Pius V11 without Mussolini knowing, but, unfortunately it disappeared soon after it arrived on the shores of Malta and, to this day nobody knows just where the hell it is.'

'You don't really believe James; those two guys have come to London, of all places, and after all those years to get at you. I really think you are becoming paranoid; for goodness sake all of this happened almost sixty years ago! You are tired; let's go to bed.'

Chapter Three

The digital alarm clock which wakes Mary and myself up gently with soft music and people singing quietly in my ears came on at seven-thirty precisely; however, on that Monday morning we were very nearly blasted out of bed with the aid of a tenor saxophone.

'It's main-stream jazz they are playing, James.' Mary said, turning over and burying her head underneath her pillow.

'Well, they should play it more up-stream; preferably, Kingston-upon-Thames, because it is doing my head in.'

'Now, James, there's no need to take it out on the radio station just because you've woken up in a bad mood.'

'I would sooner listen to, Freddy what's-his-name, Mary; you know the, guy who has a name like something from a laboratory.'

'You mean 'Queen',' she said, informing me of something I didn't know about the Royal Family, 'and by the way, his name is Freddy Mercury; he was born in Zanzibar, you know.' she added, her eyes peeping out from under the pillow.

'I knew, as soon as I saw him he came from another planet.' I replied cautiously, knowing full well Mary was a big fan of his.

'There's no need to be unkind, James.' she said, and this time turning her back on me. 'He couldn't help the way he behaved and Freddie was only forty-five when he died.'

'He was a good singer, I will say that my darling, but he always looked as if he couldn't afford to buy a shirt.' attempting to climb out of bed with the emphasis on trying to find my spectacles.

'James! Do you have to? You are so graphic at times.' Mary said to me, used to my off-the-cuff witticisms.

'But let's face facts,' I said to her, 'anything is better than this crap.' muttering to myself.

'Best foot forward, James.' she said, as she does every morning, knowing her cup of tea is imminent and will be delivered personally by her favourite Joe Waiter.

I was still wearing my Douglas tartan dressing gown when I brought

Mary's cup of Earl Grey into the bedroom. She was asleep and making peculiar noises with her nose, sounding like a hog playing a high-pitched flute. I placed the cup and saucer quietly on top of the bedside table so as not to wake her, but then she stirred, gently opening her eyes and said to me softly:

'You are a good man. James, I was dreaming of when we went to Buckingham Palace for your investiture in 1953 and the young Queen Elizabeth, how beautiful she looked when you were kneeling down in front of her to accept the knighthood. It was the second time we had to go there and I can remember, how proud I was in 1946, the year we were married, when King George V1 presented you with your MBE and, then afterwards, we went to the Hotel Russell by taxi for afternoon tea; how romantic it all was.'

'Yes, I too can remember, as if it were only yesterday.' I said, remembering all too clearly when my valuable tenure of service was terminated. Those series of undercover events working for the 'Circus', the code name for British Secret Intelligence Service, are as vivid today as they were then. I can recall it was on a Monday, the 23rd of September in 1946 when I was forced into retirement by a Christ Church College Oxford academic who later became involved with Cold War espionage in Russia and Czechoslovakia. I left the 'the Circus' with a big fat pay cheque and a pension for life with the proviso I signed the Official Secrets Act for the hundredth time and kept my close mouth firmly shut.

For a while, I missed my cosy office, secretively hidden away on the second floor of 'The Gown Shop', in London's Oxford Street; the 'Singer' sewing machine and a headless tailor's dummy displayed in the centre of the window and the handwritten 'Closed Gone for Lunch' sign which used to swing drunkenly behind the glass-fronted door adding to the ruse. I was thirty-four and it was no surprise I was accepted as an English and mathematics school-master at Saint Bartholomew's Proprietary School, close to the City of Winchester. Sir Winston Churchill used to call the "Twenty Committee" (XX Committee; the tangle of plot and counter plot, ruse and treachery, cross and double cross, true agent, false agent, double cross agent and interwoven in a texture so intricate as to be incredible and yet true.

The spy-masters handling the agents and double agents of the Second World War were considered to be an unusual breed of people and most of them still alive today, would not dispute this and, as Churchill put it, they have "corkscrew minds". The spying game tends to attract people who are distinctly off-plumb, eccentric nonconformists with shifting loyalties and peculiar imaginations; espionage encourages make-believe and 'the Circus' is no good without an impresario, or indeed its performers. I can recall asking my immediate boss, Halewood: 'At what time does the performance start, sir?' his reply being: 'At what time can you turn up?'

I was one of MI6's double-agent case officers and have always believed I didn't fit into any of the categories Churchill described with great eloquence in his memoirs; it was because of this I didn't wear the prescribed Gieves & Hawkes of Saville Row penguin suit on my first visit to Buckingham Palace.

All these ancient memories were coursing through my brain and mentally, I was achieving nothing, suddenly realizing I was hungry.

Mary and I were sitting down at the breakfast table facing each other; a box of Kellogg's cornflakes traditionally placed next to the condiments; salt and pepper, HP Sauce and Heinz Tomato ketchup bottles in the centre. She makes both of us a full English breakfast every morning consisting of bacon, eggs, tomato, Bury black pudding and baked beans, cooked to perfection, before I journey along Woburn Place to collect my copy of 'The Times' newspaper from my regular newsagent's shop on Southampton Row. It was while I was munching my way through another piece of buttered toast and an over-generous spoonful of golden shred marmalade, she said to me: 'I was reading the holiday section in 'The Sunday Times' supplement yesterday, James, and I saw an advertisement which seems to be a bargain. It's for one week in Malta; the price is only five hundred pounds per person and it boasts a three-star hotel in Valletta, including transfer fees, half-board with waiter service and many excursions too, even a day trip to Popeye's village; now isn't that wonderful?'

My immediate thoughts were, great, just great, that's what I didn't want to hear after seeing those two foreign double agents from my past and with whom I had been involved in the dangerous operation, 'Cliff-hanger'. I was also thinking of Halewood and Greaves who were given the chop; axed from the secret intelligence services in London soon after the war and then seconded to the Admiralty building, the *Auberge de Castile et Leon*, the British forces' headquarters in Valletta, Malta. It was only yesterday I saw these people I said to myself.

'And when does this holiday take place, Mary?' I asked, wiping my mouth with an egg-stained napkin and getting up from my chair.

'A week tomorrow, the flight is on Tuesday the 20th November, James.' she said enthusiastically and then confidently pouring herself another cup of tea from our much-used Lipton's teapot. 'It will give me the chance to buy a new summer dress from Marks and Spencer in New Oxford Street.' she added.

'We are practically into winter, Mary and the climate in Malta can change quite considerably during the month of November; it can rain and be very windy indeed.' I replied, trying desperately to change her mind.

'I don't care, James. Can you remember the last time you and I went on holiday? It was five years ago to the day when we went on a Shearing's coach excursion to Bournemouth. What I can't remember, James was when I was supposedly hit on the back of my head with a crazy-golf ball on the first day and had to go into Poole hospital.'

'Yes, I can remember it very well, Mary,' I said, wrapping my red silk scarf round my neck and fastening the buttons of my overcoat, 'It was fortuitous I knew an off-duty chap from the Ambulance Station in Herbrand Street to bring you home that day.'

'Don't be long, James,' she called out to me as I reached the front door, 'you know I get worried about you crossing those busy roads and perhaps, when you get back from the newsagents, you can book the holiday to Malta on-line.'

'Oh, very well, if it makes you feel better, I will succumb to your wishes.' I replied, shaking my head with the utmost displeasure.

It was just after nine when I made my way out from the apartment and was confronted by the young, Lucy Vicente, our Portuguese maid from Lisbon. She is employed to help Mary around the house, and occasionally, as an added chore, prepares a rather nondescript Atlantic type of salad for our lunch consisting of different coloured peppers, lettuce and red tuna fish.

'It's cold out there, innit, Sir James? You are not going out in weather like this, are you?' Lucy said, brushing away a flurry of snow from her black-quilted Michelin-man jacket.

I replied, saying: 'Someone has to go and find out what's going on in the world.'

'Yea, yea, I suppose you're right; well I better start work, time is getting on, innit?'

'It always does, Lucy.'

The concierge, William Walton, greeted me as I stepped out from the lift in the entrance hall by saying eloquently in his east end of London accent: 'Good morning, Guv; it's been snowing this morning, bloody useless stuff, snow, you know, no good to man or beast.' and then he continued with his weather forecasting followed by: 'Captain Scott of the Antarctica had a lot of this stuff to deal with when he tried to reach the South Pole, but the poor man, he never made it, did he, sir?'

I thought to myself, as I went out, does this man never have a day off?

I passed by the bus stop where the No 91 for Trafalgar Square had temporarily pulled in, and it was there I saw the Deutsche Reise bus manoeuvring slowly out from the Royal National Hotel's forecourt. I was standing to the right of the distinctively red London Transport Bus gazing across the road, trying to comprehend the enormity of this monstrous apology for a people carrier. The coach was the same one I had seen the previous day with a grey Germanic Gothic-type inscription, 'Helmut Gosselin Reisen', painted in bold letters along the side and the address on the boot which read: 43, Lubecke Strasse, Osnabruck, Westfalia, Deutschland. The red bus moved off quickly to enable the coach to straighten up and follow on from behind and at that precise moment I noticed Schneider glaring down at me from behind one of the semi darkened windows.

The small flurry of snow had stopped and, amazingly, the sun began to shine down Woburn Place on to Russell Square. It was twenty-past nine when I walked past the Hotel Russell in Southampton Row to reach the newsagents to collect my *Times* newspaper and then to buy some well deserved sustenance from Mister Patel, namely a Kit Kat, before making my way back home. Mr Patel is the kind of Indian gentleman you would have liked to have befriended had you been accosted by a hungry tiger somewhere in the Punjabi delta. His leathery moon-cratered face, resembling a half-baked poppadom staring over the high glass counter, and with jerky head movements likened to an out-of-sync pendulum, saying to me: 'Just in time for the rush, Sir James, Oh, yes, just in time; the commuters are coming, unquestionably.'

I've always had to remind Mr Patel, for commuter belt, read conveyer belt and this morning was no exception. At times, life was so predictable, it was downright boring.

On my arrival back home, Mary took hold of my overcoat, gloves and scarf and then said in her usual everyday voice: 'It's a joy to see you have your daily quota of reading material, darling; keeps one occupied and stops one from bothering me in the kitchen because, today, as you know Carol and Steven are coming to visit us for afternoon tea.'

'Yes, I haven't forgotten, Mary, it's been on my mind ever since I got up this morning,' I said, staring at my little girl's photograph on the sideboard wearing a long white chiffon wedding dress and standing next to her, a big footed, larger-than-life constable, Steven Bailey, who in my opinion was a trifle naive in 1969 when he became bobby attached to High Holborn Police Station. I jokingly call my fifty-six year old son-in-law, Rumpole; he doesn't like it, but then I often say to him: 'if the cap fits, wear it.' Since his retirement from the Police Force two years ago, Steven has spent most of his time employed by the gaming authorities, inspecting fruit machines in and around London, making sure the mechanisms are not fixed and that the cash isn't misappropriated or ends up inside the turn-ups of someone's trousers. Mary and I have three grandchildren; Christopher who is now the grand old age thirty-one, Barbara twenty-nine and Jonathan twenty-seven, and together with our five great-grandchildren, it is nearly all happy families, however, sadly for Mary and myself, with the exception of Jonathan who is currently going through an acrimonious divorce. Meanwhile, Carol who lives in Kensington Road, Knightsbridge works for Selfridge's in Oxford Street and has done since the children left school. Her forte is buying shoes, handbags, soft leather gloves and accessories for women and men alike, if they want!

While Mary, with Lucy in attendance, occupied themselves, exercising their culinary skills resulting in mouth-watering smells emerging from the kitchen, I took the opportunity to browse through the holiday section of *The Sunday Times* supplement. After reading the advertisement on Malta, I came to the emphatic conclusion that Mary's idea of relaxation and having to meet Popeye wasn't a good idea. I remembered what Halewood had said to us jokingly the day before, how easy it was to get on to the island but, so difficult to get off; his joke was as funny as having a broken leg. It was then I asked Mary to join me in the lounge to discuss the situation because it was now beginning to drive me round the bend.

'What did I tell you, James? I told you not to bother us in the kitchen!' Mary said angrily, wiping excess pastry from her hands with a tea-towel.

'I know,' I replied, trying to sound contrite, 'but how about a two weeks holiday in India, we can visit the Taj Mahal and take in Jaipur and Delhi; they have wonderful restaurants too.' I added hopefully, but not all that hopefully.

'We can go directly across the road for a curry, James.' Mary put in. 'Will you just be a good boy, darling, and get on to your computer and book the holiday in Malta before we all go completely round the bend.'

'Yes dear.' I replied, and recognising I had no choice, going into my study to turn on my computer to check if any e-mails had come in while I was out trekking in the wilds of Bloomsbury.

There was one e-mail from Greaves saying: "Don't go down into the woods today, the teddy bears are having their picnic", which was one of our coded messages we used during the war to alert our fellow colleagues of dangerous situations. My immediate thoughts were, Edward's hackles were being raised too and there could be a possibility he was also being tailed.

I booked the holiday to Malta in record-breaking time and within minutes I had closed down the computer and, having walked out of the study to go into the bedroom I found my Panama hat and white safari suit in one of the wardrobes. This was when Mary appeared in the open doorway and said: 'You are going on a week's package tour to Malta, not on safari or a big game shooting expedition in South Africa.'

'I know, dear,' I said, beginning to get somewhat journey proud. 'I am quite looking forward to the idea now.' I added.

'See, James, I knew in the end, you would come round to my suggestion, you always do, don't you, darling.'

After saying: 'Yes dear' at least four or five times, I proceeded to tell her that I saw Herman Klaus Schneider again on my way to collect my newspaper. She said: 'James, can't you leave the war alone. It's in the past and that's where it belongs.'

*

At half-past five the door bell rang loudly; it was Carol and my intrepid son-in-law, Steven.

'Hello, Dad.' Carol said as Lucy took hold of her camel coat to deposit it in the hall. 'Did you have a good Remembrance Sunday? We did, didn't we Steven?'

'Well yes...' Steve replied, before he had the chance to elaborate on what could have happened to them the previous day.

'Don't tell me; your Aunt Peggy came to visit you and she had one sherry too many.' I asked.

'No, it was nothing like that, dad, it was to do with a couple of "Al-Qaeda" terrorists who were picked up by the police in Kensington High Street.' Carol pointed out excitedly, 'we saw it all from our lounge window. They had machine guns, smoke grenades and everything.' she added.

'Who had the weapons, the terrorists or the police?' I asked.

'The police forces' special SWAT team, dad, it was really exciting!'

'Don't bother to take off your coat, Steve.' I said, nervously. 'We shall both be going out to the pub in a minute.'

Mary reminded me it would be Carol's birthday party on Saturday. I told her there was no need to remind me because, having just forked out twelve thousand pounds to buy madam a brand new Mini Cooper to cruise around Knightsbridge, I was hardly likely to forget.

'Come on, Rumpole, let's go to the pub,' I said to Steven, who up to now had said absolutely nothing since he came into the apartment. 'I think I've had enough problems these last couple of days to last me a lifetime.'

'And don't be long.' Mary said folding her arms and trying to impress Carol in the manner she's been doing for years, 'Lucy and I haven't done all this baking for nothing.'

On the way out I said to Walton: 'What pearl of wisdom are you going to come out with this afternoon?'

'Well, Sir James, it's funny you should say this but...'

Chapter Four

It was around four on Saturday the 17th November; my little girl's birthday, when I parked the Rover as near as I could to their house in Kensington High Street. The weather was atrocious: torrential rain with the additive of thunder and lightning accompanying us as we scurried beneath my trusty old umbrella to Carol and Steven's house with the green door.

Aunt Peggy, Mary's eighty-nine year old sister, had already arrived by taxi from Greys Inn Road. She was helping herself to a large glass of whisky and, judging by the ashtray beside her, halfway through her second cigarette when we walked into their spacious lounge from the hall. She had, for a number of years, been a literary agent, spending most of her days in a tiny office in Drury Lane, perusing through unwanted manuscripts from would-be authors and script-writers; the real garbage, as she used to called it, ending up in the nearest dustbin because in her so-called professional opinion, it wasn't even worth returning. However, Peggy's only claim to fame was when she received a letter from Steven Spielberg asking her not to bother him again. I can remember the day when Mary and I were married; my sister-in-law, who then looked like a taller version of Mary Pickford, sang: "The White Cliffs of Dover" before falling off the stage in the reception room; that distinctive excruciating voice is still ringing clearer than ever in my ears. It was so embarrassing for Mary's father when they found out she had drunk more booze than the entire guest list put together.

The next to arrive was the apple of my eye and first grandson, Christopher, his beautiful wife, Beryl, and my three great-grandchildren, Susan, Olive and Shirley. My grand-daughter, Barbara, turned up late with her husband, Jackie, and my two other great-grandchildren, Peter and Stanley, having been held up in the traffic between Kensington Gardens and Kensington High Street. Meanwhile, my grandson, Jonathon, a young army officer, having gone through yet, another painful ear-bashing from his twenty-six year old American wife, Sue-Ellen, had told Carol a few days earlier that he preferred to be on his own in London during that particular weekend and then return to another type of mess in Browning barracks, Aldershot, the following Monday. Jonathon has always been full of surprises and Carol's birthday party was to be no exception when he changed his mind and turned up around six o'clock.

In addition to the family, there were in attendance, a few of Carol's colleagues and friends from Selfridges and her keep-fit class in the Bayswater Road.

The savoury things were being handed round by Steven, the 'chef', on an all too familiar solid silver tray; the very same one Mary and I gave them as a wedding present some thirty-two years ago. Steven was trying his best to off-load his home-made sausage rolls and things on sticks to the guests who much preferred the slices of pepperoni pizzas which had been delivered by way of a souped-up motor bike, courtesy of *Pizza Pasta Pronto Express*. Meanwhile, Mary was helping Carol in the conservatory sorting out the coca cola cans, bottles of lemonade and numerous packets of different flavoured crisps to keep the children occupied until they were distracted by the piece de resistance, namely, Carol's birthday cake illuminated by fifty-four candles.

Freddie Mercury began singing, "It's a kind of magic" as more burnt offerings, sausage rolls, chicken tikka masala, deep-fried Samosas and curried to death onion Bhajis came out from their crematorium in the kitchen. I was beginning to think I was sitting in the 'Kismet', my favourite Indian restaurant around the back of New Oxford Street and this was because of the exotic smells permeating throughout the lounge. I was half-expecting Steven to emerge from the kitchen looking like a Punjabi waiter. Whatever possessed Carol to combine English, Italian and Indian food for her party nibbles was beyond me, but, I have to say it was different and the lavatory became the busiest and most popular room in the house. The noise bellowing out from the mini hi-fi stack system was automatically turned down by Steven who rigorously pointed the remote control in its direction. Mary, now wearing a colourful apron, was holding the huge birthday cake in both hands as she cautiously brought it into the lounge from the conservatory. Everyone in the room sang "Happy Birthday" to Carol and then afterwards received a more than generous piece of stodgy food which I later learned had started its life on the shelves of Marks and Spencer. The juke-box had been turned up again and it was Stevie Wonder's turn to sing: "Happy Birthday to You"; the kids who, up until now had been reasonably controllable, were behaving badly, and running around like wild animals. The 'Rolling Stones' were next to add to the party madness by singing "Honky-tonk Woman"; this was when I sought solace in the back garden with the aim of smoking myself to death on a more than overdue Rothman cigarette. From Carol's beautifully tendered garden I could hear the dulcet tones of Simon and Garfunkel singing "Bridge over troubled Water" sweetly coming out from one of the top windows of the conservatory; I thought to myself this tune was so apt because of what was happening to me.

At five-minutes past six the door bell rang loudly in the hall. My grandson, Jonathan who had just parked his much-cherished Morgan in Victoria Road was carrying a bouquet of roses and a gift-wrapped birthday present for his mother as he walked through into the lounge. He kissed Carol on both cheeks before wishing her happy birthday and then said to me: 'Hello, Grandpa, how are things in the retirement business?'

I answered by saying, 'Not going particularly well at the moment; the stock market, as you already know, has fallen flat on its face once again and according to Robert, our financial advisor, things are on the downturn and this is why your grandma and I are travelling to Malta on Tuesday for a short holiday to relieve some of the stress. It is a known fact that laxatives of profit, eventually shits itself. And what about you, Jonathon, how are you coping in the Parachute Regiment?'

'I have my ups and downs like everyone else,' Jonathan said, referring more to his parachute jumps on Salisbury Plain than to his temperament. 'When I'm not wet-nursing some of the lads in my platoon after wreaking havoc and ransacking the town, I then have to contend with repetitive barracking from Sue-Ellen at the weekends. She doesn't like army life, sir, and says she wants to go back to New York at the earliest opportunity, which for her, means on Tuesday.' he added.

'Sorry to hear that, Jonathan, but you are only twenty-seven.' I said reminding him of his age, career and the forthcoming birthday party Mary and I were arranging for him.

'Yes, but I feel old in comparison to the young lads in my company,' he continued to tell me. 'they are as fit as a butcher's dog, grandpa, and can run faster than a gazelle with a thunder-flash up it's backside; I just wish there was something else for me to do other than to sit around waiting for another war to begin.'

'You haven't lived until you have found something worthwhile to die for.' I said to him, not knowing exactly what it meant after hearing the phrase being mentioned by one of my MI6 colleagues back in the old days; 'Live and Let Die', that's the kind of phrase I would have used, I think.

'And what's that supposed to mean, grandpa?'

'I don't really know.' I replied, shaking my head like a demented buffoon, while continuing to put my foot in it by saying: 'The army must have spent a great deal of money training you because I can remember when you were just a skinny little boy wearing short trousers.' this was when he retaliated angrily: 'I'll have you know, grandpa, what you see now, I achieved by my own efforts and energies, and it was definitely nothing to do with the army.'

'It can't be much fun, Jonathan, knowing you could end up being the fittest corpse in the ground.' I put in cheerfully.

'You know, grandpa, a man is incomplete until he is married, and then, he is finished.'

I immediately took offence to that uncalled for statement which was hardly original, but retaliated by saying, it was fortunate his grandma didn't hear him say that because she would have gone crazy and furthermore, if it wasn't for us he wouldn't have had the privilege of standing next to me.

I quickly ended the conversation knowing full well that if we had continued I would have lost a grandson forever. It was in the dining room I offered him one of my Havana cigars; he quite rightly refused by saying they were not conducive to his health and mental efficiency. Meanwhile, my sister-in-law, Margaret, commonly known as Aunt Peggy, continued to disgrace herself when she began singing: "Cigarettes and

Whisky and Wild, Wild Women", having consumed far too much alcohol. We called for a taxi to take her home and according to Barbara, who kindly volunteered to escort her home told us when she returned, the cab driver broke down in tears and had to stop outside Holborn Station because Aunt Peggy would insist on giving us all a rendition of "Don't worry be Happy"; this was the last song he wanted to hear having just buried his mother in Brompton Cemetery two days previously. Barbara arrived back in Kensington Road by way of the Underground after paying dearly for Margaret's outrageous antics, and then, to add to the story, I learned later Margaret had lost the keys to her flat and Barbara had to call for a locksmith from Covent Garden.

Jonathan said to his mother, he was truly sorry he had to leave the party so early; the reason being he had another engagement with a friend in the West End. Before he left the house he said to Mary and me: 'I will see you both at Christmas,' I replied by saying to him: 'you know Jonathan, Christmas takes hypocrisy to its maximum and I sincerely hope we will all see you at Christmas.'

'You will grandpa, you will, but I'm not so sure about Sue-Ellen; I have recently been complaining about her laughter lines, I wouldn't mind but, she's not in the least bit funny.'

At seven, with the exception of the children, who were occupied with their Nintendo games and watching the Simpsons on television, it was time for us all to sit around the huge mahogany dining table in the adjoining room. We were all wearing ridiculous party headgear and with me, in particular, donning a large cardboard pirate hat complete with a skull and crossbones motif emblazoned on the front. Mary was wearing a Red Cross nurse's cap made out of paper and this probably reminded her of when she was in the FANY, the First Aid Nursing Yeomanry, during the war. There were twelve of us seated at the table, each one of us looking just as ridiculous as other members of our family and Carol's guests. I think the pink bishop's mitre took first prize for being the most outrageous when later, Roger, the husband of Carol's friend and colleague won an extra scoop of strawberry ice cream.

Steven, appropriately, was wearing a real chef's hat resembling an over-sized pancake leaning to one side on the top of his head. He looked like your regular pizza guy, a typical Joey Panzani when he brought piping-hot Nan bread, poppadoms and assorted pickles into the dining room; the main course being his speciality, turkey Korma with yellow basmati rice which he and Carol had spent most of the morning preparing in their ultra-modern kitchen. Afterwards, I complemented Steven on his gastronomic expertise, telling him it was worthy of gracing the pages of a 'Michelin Good Food Guide', and then I continued to ask him where he learned to cook such delicious Asian meals, he replied by saying that it had been in Holborn Police Station of course, where else! I told Rumpole, if he were to exchange the Italian chef's hat for a turban he would make an absolute fortune in Kensington High Street.

The 'BEE GEES' were now screaming at the top of their voices: "Night Fever" and the noise was beginning to effect the little grey cells within my brain. I asked Carol if she wouldn't mind turning the sound down to a more acceptable level because the guy with the long hair and big teeth is quite obviously in pain. She told me they all have big teeth and long hair, dad and, which one in particular was I referring to? I replied by saying: 'The one who sounds like he's got a problem inside his 'Y' fronts!' Carol, totally disgusted by my witticisms conveyed to me that I was so guttural at times but, she has learned to live with it.

Barbara congratulated me on my knowledge of the heavy-metal band singer, 'Meatloaf' and after I had made comments about his portly stature and how he made lots of money from making people deaf, she went on to say: 'You know, grandpa, it's absolutely amazing how you, at eighty-nine, could possibly be so knowledgeable about pop music.' to which I replied: 'Quite simple my dear girl, it was part of my job to tune into radio stations.'

It was now Rick Astley's turn to give us all a headache with his song "I'm never going to give you up" and this was when I continued to enhance everybody's knowledge by saying he has been in and out of his plumbing business in Wigan more times than Dracula gets out from his coffin.

My grandson, Christopher, the architect of the family was seated next to Beryl and directly opposite to Mary and myself. He leaned over and said to me: 'I believe you have just written a book grandpa; am I in it?'

'Yes, I have written a book and, no, you are definitely not in it; does this answer all of your questions?' I asked, attempting to make a move from where I was sitting to go into the garden to have another cigarette.

'What is the book all about, sir? Barbara's husband, Jackie asked inquisitively.

I made it quite clear that the book was a novel about the Second World War; the contents of which happened a long time ago and way before they were all born.

'Not the bloody war again, dad.' Carol said when she reached over the table to collect some of the dishes and plates prior to them going into the dishwasher. 'Isn't it about time you hung-up your boots and forget.'

'How can we ever forget, Carol?' I remarked, bringing her into the real world before adding: 'If it wasn't for our allies, the British armed forces and us gentlemen in the Foreign Office, we could all have been eating Frankfurter sausages and listening to "Lily Marlene" or worse, this afternoon.'

Jackie, the practicing solicitor and the so-called egghead of the family said concernedly: 'Point taken, sir, I have never liked Frankfurter sausages and as for that Lily Marlene, wasn't she in the Eurovision Song Contest last year?' I conveyed to him privately that there was a large cavity in his education which needed to be rectified.

'Frankfurters are a good idea for our Christmas party,' Steven put in enthusiastically; 'German Bratwurst sausages, Wiener schnitzel, Black Forest Gateaux and Lowenbrau beer and that will be fun, won't it?'

Mary and I looked at each other with strange abandonment and then came to the conclusion, Steven, my son-in-law, was not a full box of matches and quite a few crumbs short of a biscuit and I was tempted to say to him: 'Before you bring over a bunch of Bavarian slap-dancers from Munich, don't call us, we'll call you,' but I didn't.

The conversation continued with Beryl saying to Mary and me: 'Mum has just told us you are both going to Malta next week on holiday, and as you know Christopher and I went there for our honeymoon. The holiday turned out to be a complete and utter disaster when, during the first week, I was stung by a jellyfish and Christopher disappeared down a hole in the pavement breaking his ankle, and then to make matters worse, after several visits to the hospital we had no choice but to stay in the hotel and fester around the swimming pool for two whole weeks trying to put an escape committee together with other holidaymakers.'

I thanked Beryl very much for sharing her Grand Maltese Experiences with us and then said: 'I don't think Mary and I will be going swimming in the Mediterranean at this time of the year and, furthermore, I will be extra vigilant looking out for potholes in the pavement.'

'It was precisely eight-thirty when we decided to say goodbye to Carol and to her friends and family. Everyone was in the hall when Mary and I were being shown out of the house; this was when Steven said: 'What is that noise I can hear?' I replied by saying, 'it was my hip; funny things hips, old boy.' Mary, was not amused by my clever excuse for not having been to the toilet before leaving and I didn't want to upset Steven by saying he may have contributed much towards me having to undergo a potential hip operation.

Chapter Five

Gatwick Airport, Tuesday morning 20th November 2001

The check-in desks were busy with journey-proud passengers patiently waiting to off-load their baggage before proceeding to the departure lounge. It is from this area, the travelling nightmare began for Mary and James when they went through various security checks to determine whether or not they had any explosive devices, such as bottles of water, whisky, lotions, perfume, deodorant and shaving foam contained within their hand-luggage. When all of this upheaval has been finalized and Mary's padded bra had been reformed into its original shape and James's trousers pulled up from around his ankles having been told to remove his leather belt, one would say, they could really start to enjoy their holiday when identical articles which had been taken away from them some minutes earlier were on display in the duty-free and coffee shops.

Mary and I were no worse for wear having been subjected to this necessary manhandling process and it seemed like we had just arrived at the finishing line in the London Marathon. I can remember the sweet smell of expensive perfume permeating around the departure lounge and fresh aromatic coffee playing havoc with my nose as we looked out through the windows watching the aeroplanes taking off and landing. It was when we were sitting in the bar area enjoying a little liquid refreshment; namely a large Scotch on the Rocks, we saw Sue-Ellen sitting alone reading a copy of a 'TimeOut' London magazine. We immediately walked over to her and I surprised her by saying: 'Good morning, Sue-Ellen, fancy seeing you here!'

'Yes!' she said, answering nervously. 'I'm going back home for a few weeks to see my mom and dad.'

'But your home now, surely, is with Jonathon.' reminding her of her marital relationship and duties which are to be expected from an army officers wife. 'Jonathon tells me you don't like the army life and can't wait to go back to America.'

'That's what he told you, is it?' she replied with tears in her eyes. 'The truth is, he has found himself another woman, grandpa, and there's no room now for three in this marriage. It all started to go wrong eighteen-months ago when he came back from Sierra Leone and unless our baby was born holding a SA80 assault rifle in both hands and a parachute on its back, he wouldn't be at all interested.'

'I'm truly sorry Sue-Ellen, really sorry.' I said, putting an arm around her shoulders to reassure her that Mary and I had every cause to be concerned.

'I am expecting a baby in May; a little boy, and it's a great pity Jonathan won't be around to see him.' Sue-Ellen told us emphatically.

It was eleven-fifteen when the passengers on flight BA 460 to New York were called to the departure area and it was at this point Mary began to cry when Sue-Ellen got up from her seat, picked up her travel bag and walked away.

*

It was around four pm local time when the Air Malta AIRBUS 320 touched down at Malta's International Airport following a three hour bumpy ride over the French Alps where we were subjected to high winds and terrifying life-threatening turbulence. It was raining, albeit warm, but the climate was not what Mary and I had expected from an island positioned slap-bang in the middle of the Mediterranean.

'The flight wasn't all that bad, James.' Mary said to me as we walked one behind the other down the steps from the aeroplane on to the pot-holed tarmac.

'It wasn't my fault I fell in the aisle and ended up sitting on the lap of Mr Dom Mintoff's personal colleague and spin-doctor when I was caught unawares on my way to the toilet.' I quietly told her. 'The seat of my pants, Mary, was a mess, completely covered with squashed meatballs in tomato sauce and was not a pleasant sight; I knew the BOSS after-shave I bought from the duty-free shop would come in handy.'

'Yes, I could smell the oregano, and by the way who is Mr Dom Mintoff when he's at home?' Mary asked as we walked towards the bus to take us on to arrivals.

'Who is Dom Mintoff, who is the Hon. Dom Mintoff?' I said, trying to catch up with her as we walked hurriedly trying to avoid the showers. 'He is only the leader of the Malta Labour Party and was the country's longest-serving prime minister.' I added.

'And how do you know he is Mr Mintoffs personal colleague and spin-doctor?' Mary asked with an air of disbelief.

'Because after he had given me one of his business cards, telling me who he was, I gave him one of mine and, it was at this point it was his turn to visit the toilet.'

'Nice one James,' Mary said with a wicked smile on her face. I knew then I must have been doing something right.

When Mary and I were standing close together on the bus holding on to those plastic handles which could instantaneously turn one into a monkey, I said to her: 'Happiness is a journey, you know, not a destination.'

'Yes, I do know that.' Mary replied looking down inside the side pocket of my travel bag. 'You read it in Air Malta's Sky Life in-flight magazine, didn't you?'

'Well, yes, amongst other interesting things like what one is supposed to do if one is approached by a shark on the picturesque Marina Promenade in Marsascala or having one's bag snatched in the heart of Paceville.'

'And just what is one supposed to do in situations like that, James?' Mary asked.

I replied by saying to her: 'If you have read the article in the magazine, why are you asking me the question?'

'Because, James in my copy some of the pages were torn out.'

Mary and I completed the entry cards before having our passports thumped with an illegible immigration stamp by a wary and unsmiling Maltese official. The baggage claim, along with passport control was equally, an unwelcoming anachronism and nightmare when we couldn't recognise our trolley bag as passenger luggage careered around the carousel at ninety miles an hour, disappearing behind a rubber flap like coffins destined for immediate cremation. Eventually, I managed to push myself forward into a prominent position in order to grab the bag before it decided to do another time-consuming circumnavigation of the airport. I can recall a customs officer standing at ease watching us as we walked past him pokerfaced to go into the Welcomers Hall.

There were taxi drivers, baggage handlers and scruffy looking guys holding up placards made from the sides of cardboard boxes in an attempt to find the tourist whose name had appeared on them. We spotted our man immediately:

'Mister Brown, are you Mister Brown?' he asked with an apology for a genuine smile.

'There's only one.' I insisted but, then later, had to eat my words when I discovered there was more than one passenger with the name Brown travelling on the same flight from Gatwick.

'Here, let me take your bag and then I will drive you to your hotel.' he said to us before showing us his shiny black Datsun which probably hit the road sometime in the late nineteen-sixties.

'And what's your name?' I asked him, knowing what the answer would be.

'My name's Charlie; Charlie from Birkirkara.' came the reply as he momentarily looked back from the driving seat.

'Are there many tourists in Malta at the moment?' I asked, inquisitively.

'It's very quiet.' he replied, looking up towards the roof of his taxi and taking his hand off the wheel for a second to gesticulate to God about the weather.

It was when we reached Ghallis Rock on the coast road between Sliema and Bugibba I mentioned to Charlie that it seemed a long way from Luqa Airport to Valletta.

'But you are not going to Valletta, you are going to the New Dolmen Hotel in Qawra.' he said shrugging his shoulders as if he couldn't have cared less.

'I think there has been a mistake,' I said to him. 'we are staying at the Hotel Broadlands in Valletta.' I added.

When we were approaching the Kennedy Grove Camping Site after leaving Salina Bay, I knew Mary and I had made the mistake by getting into the wrong taxi.

At precisely half-past five, Charlie delivered us to our hotel, the Hotel Broadlands, a traditional hotel in a great position on the edge of the city commanding one of the highest points in Valletta. The breathtaking views of the sheltered creeks of 'The Three Cities'; Senglea, Vittoriosa and Cospicua were in evidence overlooking the famous Grand Harbour as we journeyed along Floriana, Valletta's immediate tree-lined suburb.

Mary followed me as I opened the large glass-fronted door which led into the reception area guarded day and night by a blue Amazonian parrot. The hotel had the appearance of a castle built by King Arthur and, together with a musty smell emanating from the ancient stone walls, I was half-expecting a Knight of St John to come charging down the marble staircase at any moment. The huge mahogany Maltese railway clock, mounted on the wall behind the desk had stopped some time at a quarter-past six and had never been wound up for reasons only known to the hotel. Anthony Vella, the receptionist who was wearing a clean crisp open-neck white shirt and shiny black Terylene trousers, leapt out from his position behind the desk to help us with our bags. He said to me, apologetically, when Mary disappeared inside the tiny toilet, the size of a broom cupboard, to relieve some of her stress, that on occasion transfer taxis and mini-buses taking tourists to their hotels almost invariably get it wrong and then he went on to say:

'That's Malta for you, Mr Brown.'

'My real title is Sir James Brown.' I told him, just to put his all important records straight after he had man-handled my passport, which had, until I had arrived on the island, been in perfect and pristine condition.

'Well, in that case, you will have to be upgraded and be allocated one of our more generous and better rooms on the first floor, namely room number twelve,' he said, hovering nervously behind his desk looking and behaving like a character from the Muppet Show. 'The room has excellent views overlooking the Square and the Auberge de Castille et Leon. It's a pity you couldn't have been here to meet one of our more important guests, Sir Rupert Dandruff-Wilson; he was, for a number of years, a member of the British Consulate here in Malta, you know.'

'Yes, I did know that,' I replied, comparing the time on my watch to Big Ben upon the wall directly in front of me and thinking the hotel must think it was still British summer time. 'And where is he now?' I asked.

'He checked out half-an-hour ago and was taken to the airport by Gino Baldacchino.' Anthony quickly explained and then put my mind at ease when he said the white powdery substance on the floor was cement caused by Joseph banging into the walls with his bath.

'And who is Gino?' I asked, assuming he was another one of those taxi drivers who almost invariably get it wrong.

'He's the manager, the big boss man and this is his sister, Zhara, coming down the stairs from the office; she is a secretary in the hotel. Dinner, Sir James, is served in the restaurant on the fifth floor from six-thirty onwards and tonight's speciality is Maltese Lamb Shanks in Maltese red wine sauce.

Joseph Mizzi, the hotel's 'Monkey see Monkey do' service and odd-job man was carrying a bath on the top of his head when we were eventually presented with the keys to our room.

'Who is that, and what is he doing?' I asked Anthony.

'Oh, that's Joseph underneath there,' Anthony explained laughing. 'He's carrying a bath and is heading towards the lift; he often does that.' he added.

'Thank you so much Anthony for welcoming us to your hotel but I think my wife and I will take the stairs, they seem to be much safer.'

'I'll get Joseph to bring up your luggage, Sir James.' Anthony said.

'Once again, thank you Anthony.' I said and muttering under my breath: that's the least he could bloody do as Mary and I started to ascend the marble stairs to God knows what.

The key was turned twice to unlock the door to let us into our room; it wasn't entirely Fort Knox but it became less secure after Joseph was called in the following Sunday morning to let us out. We missed the notable Sunday market in Valletta because of our being banged up for two hours after breakfast and then Mary and I were then in urgent need of some liquid refreshment, namely, a large gin and tonic outside the Italian Café Cordina in Republic Square. All of this was promulgated by me, having to shout loudly through the keyhole to Anthony who was doing his best to console me; however, it hadn't been my intention to buy rusty old nails, nougat, or bars of teeth-shattering peanut brittle toffee from the market, anyway.

The bedroom was spacious and it was exactly as Anthony had described it, in a great position, an imposing old palazzo, near to the Square and the Auberge de Castille et Leon. Most importantly, it had a bathroom and toilet en-suite and a remote-control television which was positioned high in one corner to receive CNN and BBC world news should Colonel Kaddafi and his Libyan mates decide to break into our bedroom sometime during the night.

I opened the two widows to allow some much needed fresh air to penetrate the room. The unmistakable smell of paint emanating from the recently decorated stone coloured masonry began to play havoc with my over-sensitive nostrils and this was when I decided that the bottle of BOSS after-shave lotion I bought in the duty-free shop at Gatwick Airport was one of my better purchases as the day wore on. The light was fading fast when I looked out from our bedroom window over the Square and towards the salubrious Valletta Waterfront and the Chapel of the Flight to Egypt by the Holy Family. I saw hushed yachts gliding back into the harbour as bells began to toll reminding church-goers not to be late for the six o'clock Angelus and reminding me that after almost five-hundred years since Valletta's heyday, Malta is still rooted in its religious past. While I was in the bathroom I called out to Mary to ask her what was on television to which she replied: 'You can either watch Bin Laden, George Bush or Rodney Trotter.

'Who is Rodney Trotter?' I asked, poking my head around the door after applying lather to my face from a shaving stick which somehow escaped being confiscated.

'He is the young man in "Only Fools and Horses", you know, James, the comedy programme starring David Jason as the unscrupulous Del Boy.'

'Ah yes, I remember now, he was the one responsible for me choking on a piece of Kentucky Fried Chicken when his blow-up rubber dolls inflated behind the settee.'

'Yes, that was funny.' Mary said, now sitting on the end of the bed glued to the television.

'What was funny, Mary, me choking on a take-away or having to suffer sex aids appear in front of my eyes?'

'Now, James, you really are getting to be an old grumpy-pump.' she said without thinking.

'Hey, less of the old, Mary.' I said when I finally emerged from the bathroom fresh as a daisy. 'You are as young as you feel, my dear, you should know that.' I added.

'I'm sorry James, I shouldn't have said that and perhaps after dinner we can have an early night.'

Mary checked herself in the mirror inside the lift before the two doors opened to allow us to walk into the spacious dimly lit restaurant atop the roof, frequented by the *cognoscenti*, the fashion conscious Maltese middle classes. We were shown to a reserved table in a cosy part of the room by Lawrence, the head waiter, who immediately lighted a clever little oil lamp and placed it temporarily in the centre. Next to our table and facing Mary stood a Yamaha organ which, apparently, had been without an organist for years but the restaurant's soft background tape which was repeated every twenty minutes did more than compensate for the hotel's lack of musical talent. A separate tourist menu was given to us by another waiter called Salvo; such a jolly fellow, he couldn't help telling us religious jokes which seemed to go on and on forever; remember those boring Englishman, Irishman and Scotsman stories? Salvo had replaced them by: Saint Peter, Paul and the Virgin Mary.

I asked Lawrence for two aperitifs, large gin and tonics before ordering our three course meal starting with: *Deep fried Gozitan goat's cheese* served on a bed of lettuce; the main course, *Tiger King Prawns* in a white wine and garlic sauce; this was a good alternative to the braised Lamb Shanks everyone in the restaurant seemed to be having. There was a choice of dessert, either; *Strawberry Cheesecake* or more than one generous scoop of *vanilla* and *chocolate ice cream*. The Maltese wine became very popular with Mary and me when I ordered a bottle of *Marsovin Special Reserve* to accompany all of this delicious food. Following the praise-worthy meal, I complimented Mario, the chef, on his gastronomic expertise after he had poked his head out from around the door of the kitchen several times to see if there were any more notable guests present in the restaurant for him to further impress.

The restaurant was quite busy now, with a number of French, German and Italian diners in evidence sitting at tables diplomatically designated by Lawrence. One of the glass sliding doors leading out on to the terrace was opened by Salvo to get rid of the cigarette and cigar smoke which had been wafting over to our table by two peculiar looking women from Paris.

'Now is the time for you to stop smoking, James.' Mary said to me later as we were looking across at the wonderful panoramic view of Valletta from the restaurant's roof terrace.

'I stopped smoking at eight o'clock this morning.' I replied, peering into an empty packet of Rothmans.

'Good Boy, James,' Mary said, putting her arm around my waist as we looked into the distance to see aircraft taking-off and landing at Luqa Airport.

'And just what am I supposed to do with a carton of two hundred cigarettes I bought at Gatwick, Mary?'

'James, don't ask such silly questions, just smoke 'em!'

Chapter Six

It was seven-thirty when I woke up having slept for a good nine hours without any interruption. The bells, from what seemed to be a thousand and one churches in Valletta began ringing in my ears, summoning congregations for matins, the early morning mass and for me to get my head back underneath the pillow before the alarm went off, adding to the noise. Mary was still asleep and snoring loudly when our little travel alarm clock sounded, alerting both of us that it was time to start the day without any bangs. After all, it was November, no Public Holidays or *festas* of note when residents, villagers and, holiday- makers alike, are woken up at the crack of dawn to be subjected to a number of deafening pyrotechnical explosions fired up into the atmosphere by primitive mortars to ward off any would-be evil spirits; if one singular aspect stands out in all the noise it's the smell of gunpowder lingering around the islands for days.

The buffet style continental breakfast was being served in the restaurant from seven-thirty until nine-thirty and it gave Mary and me just enough time to have our meal ruined by an Airtours representative who had arrived somewhat early at the hotel to welcome us to *her* beautiful island. The two waiters on duty that morning were called Alfred and Horatio and, it was to one of these I owe my life because of me being close to electrocution by a rather complicated non user-friendly toaster. We were summoned by George Attard, the head receptionist, to go down to the lounge on the ground floor to meet Helen, 'the rep'; a young woman, still in her twenties, with short black hair and a mouth like a Mediterranean guppy. The assortment of ham, cheeses, *mortadella Bologna* and, especially, the delicious Maltese Spam would have to wait until the following morning. However, the fresh *pastizzi*; the oval pockets of flaky pastry, about three bite sizes, stuffed with either a light Ricotta Cheese, or a grim mushy pea concoction, accompanied by a good *cappuccino* was soon to be devoured at Eddies in Republic Square. Our untimely departure from the restaurant reminded me that it was the second time I had seen a laughing cow in less than twenty-four hours; the first one being when

49

Mary and I were seated behind a woman on the aeroplane who couldn't control herself when she was watching "Just for Laughs" on one of the drop-down television screens.

The recently married Maltese representative, who preferred to be called Mrs Azzopardi rather than Helen, could literally sell sand to the Arabs and ice cream to the Eskimos. She arranged for us to visit various places of interest during our stay on the island which included, among a few other tourist highlights, a guided tour around Rabat's catacombs, combined with an unforgettable trip to the dilapidated Popeye Village. The day trip to Gozo became a memorable experience and not so easy to forget when the locals made us feel just as welcome as a fart in an astronaut suit. And when Helen, whoops! Mrs Azzopardi seductively pursed her huge over lippo-sucked red lips said to me: 'I love wimmin.' I replied diplomatically: 'I love women as well.' wondering which angle she was coming from and looking curiously at Mary.

'No, Sir James,' she quickly replied, putting her hand on my thigh. 'I like to go swimming.'

'Not at this time of the year, my dear.' I said to her emphatically. 'The weather is absolutely atrocious this morning and Mary and I will have to find a shop where we can buy an umbrella.'

'There's no need for you to do that, sir, I will sell you one of mine.' she said.

The hotel's coffee shop adjacent to the lounge was now open and, Doris, the Italian waitress with green coffee-cup eyes and red straggly hair brought us a much-needed pot of tea to console my temperament for allowing my wallet to be relieved of several Maltese pounds. It was afterwards, when we were talking to our man, George, behind the desk that a tourist made a comment about the weather and how she was going to complain to Messrs Thomas Cook, the tour operator, and get a refund. When we were leaving the hotel the man in reception called out to us as we reached the door: 'Enjoy it!'

'Enjoy what, sir.' I asked him stopping in my tracks and turning round to look at him.

'Come on, James,' Mary said to me, tugging at my sleeve, 'can we not have less of your funnies?'

'I'm not being funny Mary;' I said, following her out of the hotel, 'but what I will say is, why does that man keep saying 'Enjoy it';' he said the same yesterday, if you remember and quite frankly it's getting on my nerves.'

'Please lighten up, James; tomorrow we've our visit to the Popeye Village, to look forward to and you'll enjoy that won't you.'

'If I didn't know you better, my dear, I would think you were taking the proverbial Mickey! And,' I added, 'the next person I hear who says enjoy it, well – '

'– well, James what will you do?' She asked.

This was to be the start of our first morning in Valletta, albeit short, but then it continued into the afternoon!

As we were walking along the busy Republic Street, we were accosted by two young men wearing nineteenth century scarlet uniforms complete with white pith-helmets. I was half-expecting Michael Caine to appear from inside Burger King at any moment shouting: 'follow me chaps' before making our way to The old Saluting Battery below Upper Barrakka Gardens for the noon-day ritual of trying to blow up a Captain Morgan tourist boat in the deep murky waters of Grand Harbour. I remember saying to one of the soldiers: 'No I don't want to buy a ticket for Tina Turner; is she coming or is she just breathing heavy?' Mary told me not to be so guttural and that the young man was only doing his duty; I would sooner have watched Tina Turner, more is the pity.

Today, being the sixtieth anniversary of the bombardment of the islands by the German *Luftwaffe* and the Axis high command in November 1941, also was the occasion for Mary to become the recipient of a huge dollop of crap, jettisoned from a Stuka dive-bomber disguised as a pigeon when we thought we were having a pleasant and relaxing lunch-time drink outside the Café San Giovanni directly in front of Saint John's Co-Cathedral; this was her second Wartime Experience, the first one being me, of course. The three-minute arduous trek up Merchant Street to our hotel that afternoon wasn't on our itinerary but it was necessary for Mary to change into her black 'Tasmanian Devil' blouse that Carol had recently brought back from Australia.

Most shops in Valletta began to close at one pm for the great Mediterranean tradition; the three-hour *siesta*, when it seems, the entire Maltese business population disappear underground until four in the afternoon. On this high-point, if one pardons the pun, I suggested to Mary we take the Marsamxuetto ferry from Marsamxett Harbour over to the salubrious town of Sliema where we could possibly find Marks & Spencer or a British Home Store open to replace her well splotched 'I love Southend-on-Sea' tee-shirt. The five-minute crossing was the quickest and least aggravating way of travelling to Sliema; the old and much-loved yellow buses which one could hop on as they revolve around the Triton Fountain just outside Valletta's City Gate, were somewhat irritating, especially if one is not into either Tom Jones, Engelbert Humperdinck or indeed, Tina Turner as audible travelling companions. The weather had changed into brilliant sunshine as we sailed slowly past the rather dreary overgrown peninsular of Manoel Island on the approach to the 'Ferries' jetty on Sliema front. When Mary and I had disembarked and were walking along the Strand we stumbled across a souvenir shop selling umbrellas for one Maltese Lira each; this was when Mary said to me: 'How much did you pay Mrs Guppy for this umbrella, James because they look extremely like the one I am carrying?' After apologising to her that the second-hand umbrella wasn't one of my better purchases having bought it for three times the price, she settled down and said: 'I suppose it came in handy and saved us from getting wet.'

Marks & Spencer, BHS, and the Plaza Shopping Complex, as I had suspected, were all closed and didn't re-open until four, but this didn't deter Mary from having a large gin and tonic and for me, a refreshing pint of CISK Lager Beer in Tony's Bar along the Strand and to join in Malta's favourite pastime of people gazing. This could have been a million miles away from Bloomsbury, I thought, looking over the busy road towards Sliema Creek to see fishing boats and the Captain Morgan cruise fleet all waiting to up-anchor and sail away into the sky-blue water of the Mediterranean. Sitting next to us was a couple from Halifax in Yorkshire who, according to them, had just arrived on the island and were staying in a five-star, fully-inclusive hotel somewhere out in Malta's back of beyond. They spoke in a dialect which Mary and I found difficult to understand and after they had impertinently introduced themselves as Harold and Betty Roebotham, the wife began to tell us her life-story and where they had been on SAGA holidays. I estimated that the pair of them must have circumnavigated the globe at least ten times, but the last straw was when Harold told me he had played eighteen holes with Seve Ballesteros after becoming a life-time member of the Marbella Golf Club; this was when I reciprocated by saying that I had the privilege of playing polo with Genghis Khan in Outer Mongolia and we have his fax number.

At three o'clock, Mary and I decided it was time for us to move on and have something light to eat so as not to spoil our evening meal. I was pleasantly rocking on my feet after sampling a generous glass of *Marsovin* red wine when we walked arm-in-arm along one of the dangerous pavements on the Strand and with me trying desperately to avoid falling down a hole. We found a pleasant hotel called Pebbles which had a restaurant, bar and a terrace overlooking the rather unpleasant and overgrown Manoel Island. Mary passed one of the menus to me and before I had a chance to even look at the damned thing, a couple plonked themselves down at the table next to us, forcing me, much to my annoyance, to shift my chair several feet away from them.

This was tolerable now I thought; I wasn't in such close proximity to people I really did not want to talk to, but it proved a total waste of time because it took the husband about two point-five seconds to introduce his wife and himself to us. She was the first to open up what, I suppose could be described as some sort of holiday dialogue and I was cringing at every word and wishing Mary and I had not chosen to visit Pebbles that afternoon.

'Are you enjoying your holiday,' the woman asked, not giving either of us the chance to reply to her before prattling on, 'we are,' she said, 'in fact, we've just bought into a world-wide holiday club.'

'Really?' Mary said, wearing her polite hat.

'Yes, when we get back to Bury St. Edmunds, Roger will be able to tell his customers all about it.' she added putting an arm around her husband's shoulder.

'So, Roger,' I put in, having been silent for a number of minutes, 'what line of business are you in?'

'I cut hair.'

'Do you mean you're a barber?' I asked.

'No, I'm a hairdresser, if you don't mind ducky.'

'And you, Madam, what do you do?'

'I collect money.'

'Are you a member of the Inland Revenue?'

'No, I extract it from fruit machines in and around Bury St. Edmunds.'

'Well, that's very interesting; my son-in-law is an ex-policeman and is now an inspector with the gaming board who ruthlessly checks fruit machines in and around London.

'-Er, well, -er, we have to go now,' she said, 'it's been very nice talking to you. We might meet you both again.'

'Not if I can help it.' muttering under my breath watching the pair of them make a quick exit. 'He's one of them.' I said to Mary, waving a slack wrist in front of her face and talking as if I had suddenly been transformed into a fairy.

'One of them, what?' Mary asked me with a curious look upon her face, but knowing full well what I was implying.

'You know, one of those.' I said before turning my head away to view what must have been the shortest mini-skirt on the island.

'It's about time you get into the twenty-first century, James,' Mary sighed when I tried to explain to her that Roger was as queer as a nine-bob note.

After the delightful couple had disappeared, preferably down a pothole in the Strand, I at last ordered pasta; a *spaghetti provencale* and a *macaroni carbonara* from the waiter who crossed himself every time he went through the front door to go out on to the side-walk; the dust coming from a huge concrete mixer directly outside the hotel was somewhat asthmatic, to say the least. Across the road from Pebbles was a handy bus stop where one could attempt to get back to the terminus in Valletta possibly without injury. Along came a rickety old British Leyland bus which should have long since been put into a museum after failing an MOT and a Health and Safety inspection. We somehow managed to find an empty seat but after several stops it was like being packed solidly into a sardine tin. The driver, who should have been in the museum with his bus or in jail for ripping us off by twenty cents, put one foot on the dash board and then he began to turn the big steering wheel just in time to Tom Jones's singing: "It's not unusual", the younger passengers on the bus rolling their eyes as if to say: 'Oh no, not him again'. Engelbert Humperdinck was the next singer to entertain us with his song, "Release me" as Mary and I continued to sway from side to side, rocking and rolling to the movement of the bus which had been transformed into a mobile discotheque. The next song was "Simply the best" sung by Tina Turner as the bus trundled through Gzira with a grating of gears, heading for the roundabout in Msida, the notorious and precarious rotunda where balding tyres can be heard screeching and taxi drivers take their lives in their hands after praying to Saint Theresa. On arrival in Valletta, I thanked the driver for making our journey such a memorable experience and said he could keep the twenty cents he so kindly nicked from us. When we were walking towards the City Gate, Mary asked me: 'Where is the umbrella?' to which I replied I must have left it in Pebbles.

'You know, James, you really should take more water with it,' she replied angrily. 'And who may I ask, is this Engelburt Pumpadick.' she added with a smile.

After telling her his real name was Jerry Dorsey and not to be so guttural, she said:

'I just wish people would make up their minds what they are called, James, it really is doing my head in.'

I said to Mary, she was beginning to sound like Mrs Sore bottom and continued by saying: 'It could have been worse, Mary, if Tina Turner had been singing "I can't stand the rain against my window".'

We walked through the City Gate where I took a dim view of Freedom Square and its famous Opera House, destroyed by the German *Luftwaffe* in 1942. Before heading back to our hotel Mary said excitedly: 'Look, James, the Christmas lights; they have been switched on in Republic

Street. How beautiful they are.' At that point I heard George Michael singing: "Last Christmas" as we stumbled passed the crumbling walls of the Opera House.

Frederick Mifsud, another young hotel receptionist, was sitting behind the desk on our arrival. He made a comment about the worsening weather conditions in the Mediterranean and blamed it on Saint Peter having an argument with Saint Paul; his best line was to come, when he said we could have borrowed his umbrella but it seemed to have gone missing.

Our room had been immaculately cleaned by Barbara, the chamber maid, and it was a joy to relax and stretch out on the double bed which by some strange metamorphosis had been tie-wrapped together from two singles. Mary turned on the television and I can recall Mr Bean was having difficulty with his flies as he waited for the Queen Mother to arrive at a Gala performance in London. I can remember, we laughed uncontrollably when his finger was caught in the zip of his trousers before bowing to her and rendering the poor woman unconscious.

Mary looked a million dollars when we went up to the restaurant at seven-thirty for our evening meal. The fragrance of her perfume, 'Coco Chanel', was permeating inside the lift but then, it began to dissipate when we entered the room and were confronted by the strong smell of fish. Lawrence, the head waiter, immediately showed us to our reserved table by the organ lest we had forgotten the designated area where we had to sit, and then, his second-in-command, Salvo, became the star for this evening's entertainment when a Christmas decoration he had just hung up landed in my pumpkin soup. Lawrence, who looked like Saddam Hussein and had previously been questioned at the airport for being a suspected terrorist later told me that when the cruise-ships dock in Floriana, the ones with two big radar balls on top were his and the ones with one on the port-side belong to Salvo. I found that extremely funny. Meanwhile, I told him one of my jokes; it was about Malta having four islands, one unfortunately being Japanese; telling him they were Malta, Gozo, Comino and Kimono. This little ditty did not appear to amuse Lawrence.

The restaurant was beginning to fill up with diners, some of whom wanting to be served at once. A German couple on the next table to us made a point of showing-off by tapping their wine glasses with a spoon every time they wanted something; this was to be very short-lived when the woman locked herself in the ladies toilet and had to be rescued by Lawrence. Once again, I don't think Lawrence was impressed by my sense of humour when I immediately burst out laughing and this was easily recognisable the following morning when he adjusted the same bloody toaster and made the smoke alarm go off. After eating our entrée and starter, consisting of a *Maltese Ricotta cheese, capers and mixed salad* followed by *pumpkin soup*, we were then brought s*ea bass, sauté potatoes* and *fresh broccoli and cauliflower*, expertly cooked by Mario the chef. The dessert was yet to come; a generous piece of *apple pie* served with two scoops of *vanilla ice cream.*

We decided to go over to the prestigious Phoenicia Hotel in the vibrant suburb of Floriana before turning in; to what was anyone's guess. This five-star hotel set in its own gardens just outside the fortifications of Valletta has hosted royalty and celebrities since opening in 1947. Gino, our hotel manager, a tall gangly guy with grey wavy hair, volunteered to take us to the Phoenicia when he walked through and saw us in the lounge bar. As we were approaching the Mall in Floriana I got the impression he thought we were on a reconnaissance mission with the aim of trying to escape from *his* not so prestigious establishment.

Gino opened the rear door of his Audi Saloon motor car to let us step out onto the forecourt facing the main door of the hotel. After walking up a small flight of stairs and through the revolving doors, we were immediately shown where the Club Bar was situated by the receptionist. I was swaying to the music of Astrud Gilberto singing: "The Girl from Ipanema" when the lady, who was immaculately dressed in a black uniform marched us towards the illuminated Christmas tree by the door. The bar manager, built like the boxer, Rocky Marciano introduced himself as Tony Galea before offering to show us a cosy settee in front of a glass table. Tony was smart in appearance and as sharp as mustard and gave me the notion he had a hidden agenda for me to give him a generous tip, rewarding him for his kindness and over-familiarity. As I can recall, Mary was very impressed by the old photographs on the walls, depicting the British Royal Family and some of the Royal Navy warships which were privileged to visit Malta during and after the Second World War. I mentioned to Tony that I had met the late King George V1, Queen Elizabeth 11 and more recently, a confrontation with Elizabeth, The Queen Mother. He responded quickly by saying, Elizabeth Taylor, Dustin Hoffman and Sean Connery were in the Club Bar that morning for a champagne breakfast before flying out at midday to the Cannes Film Festival; in his dreams, but then one can live in hope.

Directly opposite from us, on top of a cigar cabinet was another pith-helmet and I thought Malta at some point must have bought these in the Sunday market as a job lot. The pith-helmet, reminiscent of British Rule and now, the non-existent empire, would come in extremely handy, especially in Republic Square when the pigeons pay their daily homage to Queen Victoria.

A waiter brought two gin and tonics over to the table along with a dish containing olives and an assortment of nuts. I asked Joe, the waiter if the olives were pithed to which he impertinently replied: 'Are you?' And, I suppose I asked for that.

In one corner of the room there was a jolly little fellow seated on a stool playing classical guitar; the tune was "Don't cry for me Argentina" and then after an intermission which seemed to last forever, he continued playing his guitar, missing several notes and failing miserably to do a rendition of Eric Clapton. It was shortly after Meatloaf had disappeared, Charles, the resident pianist began to play softly in the background "As time goes by". Mary with a twinkle in her eyes looked at me lovingly and said: 'Come on, James, escort me on to the dance floor.'

Chapter Seven

The morning began with no major incidents to report from our breakfasting in the restaurant, however, I still complained to Lawrence of Arabia about the toaster which was by now in urgent need of repair after bashing it several times with my elbow and, incidentally, when Mary and I were on our way out of the hotel the parrot suddenly called out: 'Enjoy it!' I knew then, it wasn't going to be my lucky day.

It was ten-o'clock when Mary and I were seated on a bench seat in the circular garden opposite the Auberge de Castille et Leon waiting for our transportation to arrive to take us to 'Popeye' village in Anchor Bay and the catacombs of Saint Paul and Saint Agatha in Rabat. At least it wasn't raining and unlike the previous couple of days we had no need to carry an umbrella around with us. The warmth from the early morning sun was at last beginning to penetrate my pale complexion which undoubtedly had been caused by the series of events leading up to our holiday and, of course, Mary was right in her assumption that the short break in Malta would do us both the world of good.

The *auberge*, situated at the highest point on the peninsula and guarded by two cannons, pointing directly in front of my face was once the British forces' headquarters and now houses the office of the prime minister. With a touch of irony Halewood and Greaves were seconded here in this magnificent eighteenth-century baroque building after the war; Halewood, in later years told me that from the map rooms situated high upon the roof they could command a panoramic view of the Mediterranean which the British Royal Navy found crucial during the Second World War. It was a puzzle to Mary why these two naval officers had been shipped over to Malta shortly after the war. My answer to her question was quite simple; they both knew about the gold and instantaneously became gold prospectors.

At ten-thirty a dusty red mini-bus pulled up outside the main entrance after going to the wrong place, I then said to Mary: 'If we are ever going to get to this naffing 'Popeye' village, it will be a bleeding miracle.' when I saw blue smoke coming out from a rusty exhaust pipe.

'Just get in, James,' Mary said, pushing me further forward inside the vehicle before I became an amputee of a lethal sliding door.

There were six elderly people and an effete looking young man travelling in the bus besides Mary and me and they all seemed as if they had possibly played a bad night at bingo; I thought if a grenade had to be thrown underneath this mini-bus, none of them would have moved.

'Now, James, just relax and enjoy the trip; you know how much you have always wanted to go to Popeye's Village.' Mary said to me seriously. 'And don't get too excited, James, it's not good for your ticker.' she added. 'Don't you worry, Mary, I shan't.' I said after looking at a woman who wouldn't have been out of place in a graveyard.

'When are you going back?' one of these people asked us.' springing into animation when the driver bumped a curb somewhere between the villages of Hamrun and Qormi. After Mary had somewhat reluctantly told her we had only been on the island for less than two days, she appeared to be excited in the knowledge that we had only four days remaining of our holiday.

'We missed our dinner in the hotel last night, didn't we, Betty?' another of these cretins decided to tell me as we trundled our way through the small village of Mgarr.

Betty's friend, Vera, had a mouth the size of the Tyne-on-Weir and continued with her perpetual whinging by saying: 'When we went into the restaurant last night we were turned away and it was only half-past seven; I'm bloody starving.'

I asked her if she had taken breakfast that morning to which she replied: 'Don't be silly man; I don't get up until nine.'

The young man who was sitting alone on the back seat nursing a pink shoulder bag introduced himself as Nicholas Bottomley and spoke for the first time: 'I hope this place we are going to isn't very far because I am dying for a fag.' And then, for some peculiar reason I was now feeling rather uncomfortable knowing a brummie homosexual was sitting directly behind me.

Off the beaten track from Ghajn Tuffeha we gently meandered down the concrete track towards Anchor Bay which was until 1979 the smallest and prettiest bay in Malta, but that became short lived when the American director Robert Altman re-created Sweethaven, the village of the Oyl Family, to make the film *Popeye the Movie*. Apparently, this ghastly bombsite and recreation of a topsy-turvy village, was built in seven months and designed to stand for a further eight months; unfortunately that was twenty years ago. When we were standing in the shed which sold tacky souvenirs and pictures of Robin Williams obscured by mildew, I said to Vera: 'Now is the time to buy some sustenance, namely a couple of tins of spinach to keep you going before we move on out of this gaud damned hell hole.' She said to me: 'Away man, I don't need any of that bloody stuff to keep me on the go and, besides, I haven't seen a toilet here, have you?' After telling her the Mediterranean was one of the world's biggest swimming pools and possibly the largest toilet, she said: 'Yes, I'm sure you are right Pet; I will see you later.' My reaction to this was: not if I can help it!

Frank and Mavis Riley, who were from a small village somewhere in the north-west of England, began to tell us about their pensions, long term investment plans and property; they also went into great detail about a financial advisor called Joshua Cohen who was currently sailing around the Caribbean with his boyfriend in a recently acquired Sun Seeker yacht. Mavis, speaking in a language no-one ten miles outside of Skipton could understand, said: 'Why don't you come to our hotel in Sliema tonight? There is bingo at eight and then afterwards, a knobbly knees competition followed by Victor and Doris, the popular singing duo.' Her husband, Frank, a small stocky man with a prominent bulbous red nose said to me: 'I can always take you down to one of the pubs, Lad, it's on the promenade and they have a happy hour when they sell a pint of John Smiths Bitter for half price; there's a kebab house next door as well.' I quietly said to Mary, after seeing two cheese and ham sandwiches, neatly wrapped in a hotel serviette being lifted out from Mavis's rather impracticable patent leather handbag: 'These people can only have plenty of money when they are seen to be spending it, and I haven't seen any evidence of this yet.'

Nicholas was now the proud possessor of a brand-new baseball cap with the logo 'Popeye' village depicted on the front; I thought if he ever gets back to *his* hotel in one piece without being propositioned, it will be an absolute miracle.

Sitting alone at the side of the road and waiting for the transport to return to take us to Rabat was Hilda and Stanley Parry from Walton Vale, Liverpool. Stanley, an ex British paratrooper and another one of those French Foreign Legionnaires who couldn't stop talking about the Napoleonic Wars became the resident comedian when he began to tell everyone in his Liverpudlian scouse adenoidal accent how he became the recipient of a red ring around his backside after visiting a Turkish baths in Istanbul. He told us another hilarious story when he joined the army which caused us all to laugh hysterically and the driver to bump another curb, this time in Spinola Bay, Saint Julians when he drove us back to our respective hotels. Stanley told us they gave him five minutes to write down his criminal record. It was when the recruiting sergeant looked over his shoulder to look at his paper, he said to him: 'My goodness, you should be in Jail, Laddie.' And then Stanley replied by saying: 'Give me a break, Sergeant; I was only released from Strangeways this morning.'

At midday we arrived in the small inland town of Rabat where the catacombs of St Agatha and St Paul had been waiting to be discovered; both these burial sites were hewn out of living rock in the Phoenician and Hellenistic period. The Romans occupied them up to the fourth century AD and were used as a place of sanctuary much later when the air raids on Malta during the Second World War forced the population of Rabat underground. The tour of the catacombs of St Agatha lasted twenty minutes and had taken in only ten per cent of the honeycomb necropolis which is said to cover four thousand square metres. I couldn't help but digress into the past when small areas of these catacombs were used to smelt down ingots of Nazi gold before using it to make church bells. I can remember how top-secret it all was, working for 'C' in Oxford Street, and then after the bells were cast they mysteriously disappeared and no-one seems to know where they are. It is a chapter in my book which became an enigma and will certainly remain a mystery for the rest of my days.

The entrance to the catacombs was down a few steps via the crypt and it was not for the squeamish as we walked along the labyrinth of tunnels, sometimes head down and only a dim light from a torch to guide us; it was not an experience for people who suffer from twinges of claustrophobia. Stan 'the man', the ex rough-and-ready paratrooper had refused to go down there and when he said: 'I didn't come all this way just to see a load of rolling stones.' I knew then there wasn't an element of truth in some of the things he had told us.

Mary and I emerged from here wondering what it must have been like during those days when hundreds of Maltese people were huddled together to escape the bombings and then me asking myself the question; whereabouts in these bewildering series of tomb galleries was the foundry situated? Again, I began to digress into the past.

Chapter Eight

The Gown Shop, Oxford Street, London, England, Monday 6th April 1942

'I don't mean to interfere, Brown, but isn't it about time you took a day off from your work?' Halewood said to me, sitting behind his desk and peering over to me through his old-fashioned gold-rimmed spectacles which looked as if the stems had been made from bendable wire. 'You really have been over-doing it these last couple of days old chap, haven't you, and could this have something to do with the office next door?' he continued.

'Here, Here.' Greaves said lighting up his pipe by the window and endorsing sympathetically Halewood's concern about my welfare. 'I hate Mondays.' Greaves went on and continuing to asphyxiate us with his hand-held incendiary device.

'Well, my dear friend, if you don't like Mondays you could possibly be in the wrong job.' I conveyed to Greaves in no uncertain terms.

I also had to tell them that 'C' had ordered me into his office the day before and said there had been a coded message from Joey Macaroni, our MI6 agent in Rome, informing us there was something going on inside the Vatican; namely, heavy wooden boxes containing God-knows-what and that they were being delivered by heavily guarded German army trucks. I also informed them we are now waiting for a response from Joey to tell us just exactly what is contained inside these boxes.

'I know already.' Greaves said, smugly re-lighting his pipe and doing his best to set fire to the curtains.

'What do you know already?' Halewood curiously asked him.

'Gold, that's what it is, gold!

'You can't be serious.' I said to him excitedly. 'You know, Greaves, you could land yourself in big trouble coming out with statements like that, but on the other hand, you could be sitting in Control's seat in six months' time.'

'The heat has now gone off Operation *Sealion*, Hitler's plan for a seaborne invasion of Britain, and the focus is now on the Mediterranean.'

Greaves pointed out with great enthusiasm. 'Hitler wants to deposit his spoils of war in a safe bank; what better place than the Vatican where no-one can touch it during or after the war. Meanwhile, Field Marshal Erwin Rommel, despite the supply deprivations, is enjoying considerable success in the western dessert and scenting a victory. The Axis command is deploying more aircraft in Sicily; Malta is simply being bombed and starved into submission and it is because of this maelstrom of bombs and splintering of limestone that ammunition, food and kerosene is scarce and typhoid, scurvy and amoebic dysentery on the island is now commonplace.'

'So what are you trying to say, Greaves?' Halewood asked him.

'What am I saying? I am saying to you it is possible a consignment of gold could be destined for Malta.'

'I have never heard so much garbage in my life.' Halewood put in. 'What good is gold bullion when the Maltese people are on the brink of starvation; I would suggest it is you who has the day off.'

I can remember it was eleven-thirty when a top-secret coded message came in from headquarters: 'Information and Material, the unauthorised disclosure which could cause grave damage to the interests of our nation and extremely beneficial to the enemy.'

It was the message that Greaves wanted to hear: gold bars, going into the crypt of the Vatican, all twenty thousand of them and relating to several million dollars.

Steven Halewood noisily pushed his chair back and then slowly rose to his feet, his head bowed down in embarrassment, knowing he had to apologise to his friend and colleague, Edward Greaves, for making those crass remarks.

'I want Operation *No Hiding Place* to be implemented immediately and wish to speak with Commander Mark West of New Scotland Yard.' Halewood said, becoming more nervous when he saw smoke emerging from Edward's jacket pocket and following the excitement of having a small incendiary device, such as a meerschaum pipe extinguished by a highly effervescent soda siphon, Halewood then went on to suggest I contact one of MI5's best intelligence officers, Brian Woodruff, and

Britain's leading Mata Hari, Melanie Bradford-Jones of MI6, to discuss the apprehension of suspect enemy spies in and around the City of London.

'Tell them the Martians have arrived,' Halewood said to me, 'they will know exactly what you mean and precisely what they have to do.'

Greaves then made a comment by saying: 'I recently learned the Dutch First World War spy, Margaretha Geertruda Zelle, better known by her stage name, Mata Hari, was nothing in comparison to Melanie Bradford-Jones who is now being trained to penetrate the inner circles of the CIA in America prior to their servicemen being deployed over here.'

'Well, that should keep her busy for a while, won't it?' Halewood replied with a naughty school boy smile upon his face.

'And what will President Roosevelt do if he finds out?' I said to Greaves.

'Give her time, just give her time.' he replied.

The German Baedeker raids on London continued, as did the tip and run raids on coastal areas, such as Dover, which kept my father occupied for a number of months extinguishing fires and pulling people out of the rubble attributed by the *Luftwaffe*.

In 1940, during the 'blitz', I was living in a small second-floor maisonette in Wellington Street, Covent Garden, and one night, the Germans dropped a stick of bombs directly across the road. I slept through it all, as did most people, I think. You just got accustomed to it. That night was the heaviest major bombing raid mounted on the capital; in particular the East End of London and I consider myself to be very fortunate indeed to have survived it all. However, from 1944 until 1945 we had to put up with continual flying bomb and rocket attacks on our city.

The morning of the 6th April 1942 was very wintry and the hides of March hadn't disappeared when I received an urgent message from Commander West saying he had information to support there could be a German spy frequenting a Lyons Corner House in Coventry Street, off Leicester Square; right here in the West End of London.

Halewood, who had just come in from the cold was not entirely surprised when I told him New Scotland Yard had been given a tip-off by a 'Nippy' cockney tea shop waitress with an hour-glass figure likened to Jane Russell.

'This will be the third spy we have caught in less than four months,' Halewood pointed out as if I didn't know already, 'the first one, if you can remember, James, was pretending to be a Father Christmas inside the doorway of Selfridges?'

'Yes, I can remember it very well, as if it were only yesterday,' I said to Steven with an impromptu laugh after reminding him of the unmistakable German label found inside his underpants which led to him being charged following his arrest.

'I don't suppose Melanie Bradford-Jones was disappointed when she, along with Brian Woodruff, had the pleasure of seeing a skimpy pair of 'Y' fronts being removed from an aspiring Prussian Santa Claus whose duelling scar became more noticeable after his long white elasticised beard had been removed.' Edward Greaves said, having by this time taken off his raincoat and gloves.

'And, the second spy we caught in Brixton? He was a gay Bavarian Slap Dancer from Munich.' I reminded them. 'The Metropolitan Police thought he had escaped from prison and was trying his utmost to go back over the wall; needless to say he hasn't moved very far during the past three months since his arrest.'

'We can't trust anyone.' Halewood pointed out, waving a finger in the air. 'The German spies could arrive dressed up as priests, nuns, or even policemen, anything to avoid being captured.'

'You mean to say, there could be enemy spies working within New Scotland Yard?' Greaves asked him.

'Don't be bloody stupid, Greaves.' Halewood replied.

I said to Halewood enthusiastically: 'You know, when the war is over, I am going to write a book about all the events which make our lives so exciting working in the foreign office.' and then went on to enlighten his intelligence by reciting a poem from the 16th Century English dramatist and writer, John Lyly:

If all the earth were paper white
And all the sea were ink
'Twere not enough for me to write
As my poor heart doth think

'Over my dead body, Brown,' Halewood said to me, his jowls now moving quickly from side to side in anger, 'and don't forget you will still be under the Official Secrets Act, lest you have forgotten.'

*

Lyons Corner House, Coventry Street, Leicester Square

Herman Klaus Schneider was sitting alone at a table in the tea shop reading a copy of the *Daily Herald* when Melanie Bradford-Jones appeared just inside the doorway. He was wearing a smart grey pin-striped suit, stiff white collar and a rather sinister black tie which gave the impression it had been to several funerals; a grey trilby hat was placed beside him on another seat. His shifty ice-blue eyes appeared to be looking everywhere when he occasionally glanced over the top of his newspaper to see if anyone around him had more than a loose mouth to enhance his dossier of useful information. Elsie Maynard, the more than observant waitress, was dressed in a traditional dark uniform complete with hat and a frilly lace pinafore when she delivered a pot of tea and more than a generous piece of fruitcake to his table. Melanie Bradford-Jones, alias, Dorothy Arkwright was resplendent in a cloche hat coquettishly pulled down to one side over her home-permed red ringlets; a knee- length brown skirt and jacket, all of which added to her elegant appearance. A recently acquired pair of nylons with distinctive seams at the back were probably giving envious ladies the impression the GI's had already arrived. Melanie, sitting at a table directly opposite to Schneider, had removed the mock-leather bag containing her gas mask and placed it out of the way below the seat next to her and proceeded to open up her authentic crocodile skin handbag to remove a powder compact and lipstick. Her shapely legs were crossed provocatively and on the sole of one of her black patent leather court shoes she displayed the price he would have to pay for her personal services; ten shillings and sixpence and a promise of a pardon from a hangman's noose. After powdering her nose and doing some minor adjustment to her lips, she produced a packet of German HB cigarettes from her bag and then walked over to Schneider to ask him for a light.

"guten tag mein Herr, haben sie Feuer?"

"Ja! Ja! naturlich, Yes of course" he replied enthusiastically and at that precise moment, Herman Klaus Schneider had well and truly put the first nail into his coffin.

Bradford-Jones made a gesture to summon a man standing outside on the pavement adjacent to the main entrance door and this was when Commander Mark West of New Scotland Yard appeared inside the doorway accompanied by three armed Bobbies. Schneider quickly rose to his feet in sheer disbelief; the definitive look upon his face was of absolute terror knowing he had nowhere to run and, nowhere to hide. However, he made a feeble attempt to make for the stairs leading up to the first floor restaurant but, he had been stopped by Elsie Maynard who was now delivering egg mayonnaise sandwiches on a silver tray to another table. Elsie gave the police the impression she was trying her best to help them in some way by not allowing him to pass; it was as if Schneider and her were both partners, dancing from side-to-side in the military two-step.

Herman, the German, was captured intact and systematically handcuffed from behind before being frisked by a member of the Criminal Investigation Department of the Metropolitan Police. Following the removal of a Luger pistol which had been noticeably bulging from inside his coat pocket, was then frog-marched away to a 'Black Mariah' police van waiting outside the front door.

'Good work, Miss Arkwright,' Commander West said to Bradford-Jones appreciatively. 'This will be another feather to place on the top of your hat.'

'Commander West, you should really be thanking Miss Maynard because without her we would not have had the privilege of sitting down next to each other and sharing a pot of tea.'

'How right you are Miss Arkwright, and may I call you Dorothy?' he asked her.

'Of course you may, Commander,' she replied touching him gently on the arm. 'I don't usually associate business with pleasure but in this particular case, I could change the rules. And what do they call you down at the Yard?' she continued.

'There is one name the boys in blue call me, it begins with a B and ends with a d.' he replied with a short giggle.

'Oh, you are called Bernard, that's a nice name.' Melanie said when she neatly rearranged the collar of his black trench coat that was untidily pulled up at the back.

'No, my name is Mark.' he hastened to add.

'And, are you married Mark?' she asked, continuing with her intimate questioning.

'I have this theory.' he said unwittingly. 'A man is incomplete until he is married, and then, he is finished.'

'Ah, but behind every good man is a good woman.' she said moving one of her long scratchy finger nails up and down his buckled sleeve.

'Would you like to accompany me to the Metropolitan Police Ball next Saturday, Dorothy?' Commander Mark West asked. 'It will give us the chance to get to know each other better.' he added.

'That won't be possible,' Melanie sadly replied. 'I have to leave for Lisbon on Saturday morning, bound for America and could be staying in Washington for some time, maybe to the end of the war.'

'Well, that's bad luck,' Mark said, looking somewhat disappointed.

'You could ask the waitress, Elsie Maynard.' Melanie reluctantly suggested. 'She looks as though she wouldn't say no to a good night out.'

'Yes, that may be a good idea, Dorothy, and that would give me the opportunity to thank her for assisting us.'

'Goodbye, Commander, it has been a pleasure to meet you and have a good time with Jane Russell on Saturday.'

*

New Scotland Yard Headquarters Whitehall, Westminster London WC2

Schneider had been placed into solitary confinement, a cold dark grey cell with only a high-backed wooden chair to keep him company. From the moment the heavy door was banged shut his only contact with the outside world was a policeman noisily opening and closing a sliding hatch periodically to check on his welfare. The bright electric light bulb high on the ceiling was now glaring down on him and making the room warm and humid; the sight of an aluminium piss-pot in a corner was not enough to contain his emotions. He began to pace frantically up and down the cell with only a pair of underpants to wear because his clothes had been all but taken away from him, even his meticulously polished brown leather brogue shoes; this, Schneider thought was the beginning of the end and he could be destined for the gallows. He remained in the cell for three long hours sometimes sitting on the chair or cowering in a corner with his head buried deeply in his hands not knowing what form of punishment he had to endure next.

It was at four o'clock precisely when Schneider heard a rattle of keys before the door to the cell was opened. Simultaneously, three men slowly entered the room; the stuffy atmosphere bereft of fresh air was likened to a tomb when my friend and colleague, Brian Woodruff, an MI6 officer and notorious Scalp-hunter led the way in. Schneider was forced to sit on the chair in the centre of the room with a black hood pulled down over his face so he couldn't see who was roughing him up during the psychological programme of interrogation. They got what they wanted, all they needed to know about Herman Klaus Schneider, detailed information about his family in Germany and where they lived. Following the interrogation, Schneider was handed back his clothes and officially charged by New Scotland Yard with being an enemy agent and a threat to our King and country. He was then escorted into the courtyard where the same black van was waiting to transfer him to a secure prison compound somewhere north of Brentwood in Essex; this was to be the start of a softening-up process when he found a carton of Marlborough cigarettes and a Cadbury's box of chocolates lying on a beautifully made bed.

Nine days later, following continuous bombardment, King George V1, on 15 April 1942, awarded the George Cross to the island of Malta: "To Honour her brave People I award the George Cross to the Island

Fortress of Malta to bear witness to Heroism and a Devotion that will long be famous in History."

Ironically, but not so surprisingly, two weeks later, Lieutenant-Commander Edward Greaves and Lieutenant-Colonel Brian Woodruff were summoned to Buckingham Palace to receive their Member of the British Empire awards.

Chapter Nine

Tuesday 7th April 1942 inside an Italian prisoner of war camp on the outskirts of North Berwick, East Lothian, Scotland

At midday, Captain Lorenzo Marino was taking lunch with his fellow officers in a wooden hut which had been crudely decorated to resemble an Italian restaurant. The walls to this East Lothian pizza pasta and spaghetti house had been covered with old newspapers depicting their fascist leader, Benito Mussolini; the American singer, song writer and entertainer, Frank Sinatra and the notorious Sicilian Mafia gangster, Al Capone. A smooth dark brown varnish had been painted over the pages before nicotine stains began to appear giving the British Army guards the impression the building was very old. The cast-iron stove in the centre of the room had just been stoked and this is where a large copper kettle seemed to be permanently on the boil to replenish their craving for the aromatic British Army *Camp coffee*. A huge pan containing home-made minestrone soup was always available and, together with freshly baked bread, it became part of their essential daily diet. The regular intake of corned beef, suet meat pudding and baked beans served up sloppily through a window of a lop-sided caravan was sometimes not enough to satisfy their enormous appetites.

Marino, aged twenty-six was a typical Roman type, short in stature and a bronze complexion which he could only have obtained from sitting underneath a bomb-blasted palm tree in North Africa; his black curly hair looked like it had been submerged in a bath of Brilliantine. One of the Scottish guards was heard asking him what he was going to do when the war is over, he replied by saying he would like to start up his own ice cream business in Scotland because he recognised the local surroundings as having great potential for him, helping to revive the depleted tourist industry. Evidently, Captain Marino had no interest in ice cream at all since he was shipped over to the dessert wastes of Cyrenaica in Libya where he forgot what it was like; the aim he had in mind was to charm the prison guards into obtaining more cigarettes and whisky.

It was a lovely sunny afternoon when Lorenzo, standing immediately in front of the high inner parameter barbed-wire fence gazed out over beautiful East Lothian countryside. Through the inter-woven metal mesh he could spot the wildlife and admire the heather-clad Lammermuir Hills and, in the far distance, breathtaking views to Fidra and the unique wonder of the natural world, Bass Rock. He could hear the distinctive sound of a piper playing a lament from inside one of the barrack rooms situated outside the prisoner of war compound reminiscent, and bringing back memories of when he was captured at gunpoint by a Highland Fusilier in Alexandria. The drone from the bagpipes, it would seem was disturbed as if the bag had been suddenly punctured and the player collapsed in a heap on the floor; this was when, without any warning, two Scottish guards dressed in a battle-dress jacket and Black Watch tartan trews appeared with a pair of handcuffs to take Captain Lorenzo Marino away. He was bundled into the back of a camouflaged three-ton truck and then taken along the twenty-five miles of rugged countryside towards the City of Edinburgh where Alistair Campbell and Robert Boswell, members of MI5, were waiting to meet him.

The vehicle, crunching its gears, climbed steadily up the extinct volcano towards the military barracks confined within the ramparts of Edinburgh Castle. The Bedford truck then came to a halt on a cobbled road directly in front of the guard room and this is where the two guards frog-marched Captain Marino to his new residence, a prison cell deep down inside a dark hair-raising dungeon. Lorenzo was unaware what was happening to him and when he saw a mean looking sergeant wearing a Campbell tartan kilt and a skindoo knife tucked neatly away inside one of his long woollen socks, an element of fear became evident upon his face. The provost sergeant, a five-foot tall beastie with what seemed to be a black pencilled-in moustache was supervising an English soldier who was on his hands and knees meticulously scrubbing the floor of the guardroom with a toothbrush when Lorenzo suddenly became prisoner number two as he was pushed unconventionally into a grey cell and the door forcibly closed behind him with an ear-shattering clang.

Inside the cell was a six-foot iron bed which could have been used as a stretching rack in medieval times if it were to stand upright against a wall.

At the head of the bed were sheets and blankets made into a square bed pack and a khaki hold-all containing an assortment of toiletries minus a toothbrush was placed on the top. A huge white earthenware mug was standing to attention next to a knife, fork and spoon perfectly aligned in the centre of a straw- filled palliasse mattress; this completed the inventory of his sole belongings. Captain Marino, standing in the centre of the room with hands on his hips began to wonder if this trauma he was being put through was indeed actually happening to him until...

He heard a rattle of keys and the door to the cell was opened by a six-foot tall regimental policeman who was wearing the highland battle-dress of the infamous King's Own Scottish Fusiliers regiment. His Glengarry bonnet, on one side of his head, revealed a short black pudding bowl haircut and reminding Lorenzo of the time he found a dried up haggis inside his Red Cross parcel and then after he had tossed it over the wire to a Scottish Alsatian guard dog, it threw up immediately. Alistair Campbell and Robert Boswell walked into the cell as if they were familiar with the entire geography of the place. Campbell, a middle aged gangly man was the first MI5 officer to speak to Captain Marino when he began to offer him a cigarette.

'You are never alone with a *Strand*.'

'I suppose you think that is very funny?' Captain Marino said to him angrily when he took the cigarette out of the packet watching as it was lit by Boswell's electro-plated petrol lighter. 'Who are you and what do you want from me? I don't know why I am here in 'Auld Reekie' and, under the terms of the Geneva Convention I would like to be returned to the prisoner of war camp at once.' he nervously added.

'My name is Alistair Campbell and this is my colleague, Robert Boswell, and I would like to tell you, Captain Lorenzo Marino, your request isn't possible.' he calmly replied. 'From now on you will be working for us.'

'What do you mean working for you?' Lorenzo asked inquisitively.

'We are members of Britain's Secret Military Intelligence Agency MI5 and you have no choice but to co-operate.' Boswell bluntly put it.

'I am an Italian prisoner of war and under the terms of the Geneva Convention...'

'Will you please stop talking about that bloody Geneva Convention?' Campbell suggested with a sigh. 'We know all about you, Marino, your profession before you became an army officer, your family and where they live in San Giovanni a Teduccio in Naples. We also know about your eloquence in the English language, something which is quite unique, especially in this part of the world, wouldn't you say?'

'Yes, but I am, after all just an ordinary school teacher.' Captain Marino sadly replied now sitting on the edge of the bed.

'You will be going back to Italy sooner than you think, Lorenzo, but this evening you will be accommodated in the officer's mess where a special dinner party has been arranged on your behalf.' Boswell said to him. 'Meanwhile, here are your belongings and some civilian clothes for you to wear and just in case you are wondering where you can find a toothbrush; here you are, sir.' he added.

'I have to remind you, gentlemen, I have to abide by the Geneva Convention and, furthermore, I have been told not to fraternize with the enemy.' Captain Marino said emphatically.

'Tonight you will be enjoying more than your fair share of the best Havana cigars, the finest Scottish malt whisky and more than generous scoops of chocolate ice cream.' Alistair Campbell made clear to him.

'Well, in that case, I am prepared to change the rules.' Marino replied excitedly, albeit somewhat reluctantly. 'And what is going to happen tomorrow?' he continued to say.

'Tomorrow is when we go shopping; taking in Jenners department store in Princes Street to buy you some new clothes and that will be fun, won't it?' Boswell put in.

'Yes, that will be funny, really funny, seeing as I haven't any money.' Lorenzo replied.

'Don't you worry your heed about that,' Boswell said, going into his wallet to find two Scottish five pound notes. 'Here, put this into your wee pocket, Laddie; it may come in handy later.' he added with a naughty boy smile on his wee face.

At precisely seven-thirty Captain Marino walked down the staircase of the officers' mess, wearing a civilian dark-coloured dinner suit, a white shirt with stiff-winged collar and bow-tie, all of which he had borrowed from a more than willing duty officer. The bar salon, leading into the ballroom was on the ground floor and this was where the officers and their ladies gathered before the call for dinner had been sounded by way of an extremely large Malaysian brass gong. Lorenzo was nervous, finding it very difficult to believe that only a matter of a few hours ago he had been festering inside a prisoner of war camp on the outskirts of North Berwick. He was greeted by a slow hand clap from Lieutenant-Colonel Andrew McPherson, the Commanding Officer of the King's Own Scottish Fusiliers regiment and to welcome him into his exclusive and prestigious officers' mess. Everyone in the smoke-filled room turned around to face him and began to join in with the CO's continual non-stop clapping. A piper, dressed in full Scottish regalia preceded him into the salon playing a lament and this was when Lorenzo began to settle down and enjoy an evening of Scottish entertainment. Major Ian Hamilton, the adjutant of the battalion mingled with his fellow officers to ask them to be on their best behaviour, especially later in the evening when the ladies would be retiring to the anti-room and the Officers' Mess Orderly Sergeant, Robert McGregor becomes the target from bowls of jelly and trifle.

Lorenzo was handed a glass containing a large measure of the famous grouse whisky which he drank very quickly when he heard the deafening sound of the gong summoning everyone into the ballroom for dinner. The seating arrangement was simple; the Commanding Officer was sitting with his wife at the top of the table and the 'one- pip wonders', the second-lieutenants, were all seated at the bottom. Captain Marino, by prior arrangement and rank adjustment, was seated directly opposite to Margaret, the CO's wife and during the early part of the evening he became the recipient of a wandering high-heel shoe.

The menu, especially printed for the occasion, consisted of a starter; Haggis served with a creamy whisky sauce or, Cock-a-leekie soup. The main course; rack of Scottish Borders venison with fondant potatoes, baby spinach and poached pear and port juice, and the desert consisting of strawberry cheesecake, jelly trifle and, of course, Neapolitan chocolate ice cream. The wine was brought to the table by Fyfie, a dithery lance-corporal dressed in a white uniform, who must have been the oldest non-commissioned officer in the British army.

A steaming Haggis was piped in and regally delivered to the head of the table on a silver platter by Staff-Sergeant McGregor. The Commanding Officer asked everyone in the room to stand and to hold up their glasses of Claret before he went through the traditional Scottish salutations of reciting the opening line of the poem by Rabbie Burns, "Address to a Haggis":

> Fair fa' your honest, sonsie face,
> Great chieftain o' the puddin-race...

Lieutenant-Colonel McPherson aggressively plunged his jewelled skindoo into its poor bladder and this was when Lorenzo, seated next to him, experienced the wonderful smell of venison, oatmeal and diced carrot wafting in his direction from the disembowelled Haggis.

Meanwhile, the Colonel's wife, Margaret, took the opportunity to explain to Lorenzo that her sister-in-law, Isla, was travelling from London to Edinburgh on the overnight sleeper train and she would be arriving early the next morning. Furthermore, she suggested, it would be nice if they could all meet up with her before she went to America. Lorenzo told her he had to move out of the officers' mess after breakfast and would be temporarily lodged in an apartment in George Street.

After the delicious dinner and the two-handled silver chalice containing the finest Scottish Malt Whisky had been passed around, the ladies retired to the anti-room to mull over and discuss, at considerable lengths, what their husbands were more than likely to get up to in their next theatre of war, and as they genteelly sipped their cups of tea they had no idea where their loved ones would be going.

At the far end of the table were the subalterns; junior officers who were all seated together in what was called poet's corner. By tradition, especially on Burns Night, a trophy was awarded to the best poet by the Commanding Officer in the shape of a wooden banana. A drunken second-lieutenant precariously got up on his chair and began to read one of his poems which began:

"A lone piper marched by the dark castle wall
When he fell over a large cannon ball
He fell to the ground it was such a big farce
To see all those bagpipes stuck up his arse
They played a sad tune, a final lament
To all pipers Scottish who walk the battlement"

Second-lieutenant Alan Baird was subjected to a series of boos, barracking and gestures of disapproval by his fellow officers before being told to sit down. The next aspiring poet, Second-Lieutenant George Pringle, who seemed to be having an argument with an electric light bulb when his head disappeared underneath a chandelier, began to recite:

"There once was a bird that sat on a thistle
Pricked its arse and made it whistle"

Pringle immediately became the recipient of a half-peeled Clementine orange and an assortment of nuts which had been thrown at him by his fellow officers. Second-lieutenant William McDuffie, the regiment's assistant intelligence officer, was the evening's star attraction when he gave a rendition of his, "Soap on a Rope":

"In the bath I wondered, where is the toilet soap
I then looked up and saw it hangin' frae a rope
Not in a dish or in a tray or by the brush or loofah
But four feet high in the sky suspended frae a doofa
I then reached up to grab the soap but much to my chagrin
A pipe came oot o' the boiler and the ceiling all fell in
Wi'plaster all around ma heed ma toe stuck up the tap
It wasni long before I saw a brick fall in ma lap
Through the roof I gazed the stars, t'was more than a' could cope
I then got oot the bath and fell on that soap upon the rope"

Everyone stood up to applaud McDuffie, the new poet laureate and the clapping seemed to go on forever until the coveted banana was handed to him.

A single and unattached young lieutenant asked Captain Marino if he would like to go into the town for a fling with a group of his fellow officers. He said there would be plenty of women to choose from, especially in the 'Aberdeen Angus'; a notorious hostelry in Rose Street. Lorenzo declined the offer by saying it had been a very busy day for him and quite bizarre, he then went on to tell him he was still a happily married man with two young children to consider. Captain Marino didn't realize it was part of MI5's sinister plot to turn him into a spy and little did he know that in less than twenty-four hours his family principles would all fall fowl to the delectable charms of Melanie Bradford-Jones, alias, Isla McPherson.

'I cannae understand a man who has been in prison for six months not wantin ta sow his wild Porridge Oats in the town; why ye no queer?' Lieutenant Richard, (Dickie) Baird said to Lorenzo sympathetically. 'I know a wee joke, Lorenzo,' Richard said enthusiastically and, it goes like this: What is the difference between Bing Crosby and Walt Disney?'

'I don't know.' Captain Marino replied, now yawning and wanting very much to go to his bed.

'Well, Bing sings and Walt, dizzznie!'

Lorenzo must have thought that only a fool would laugh at his own jokes when Lieutenant Baird, the regiment's assault pioneer officer and so-called demolition expert, fell backwards in his chair dragging the tablecloth with him.

The dining table now resembled an irretrievable bomb-site when Captain Marino thanked the officers, wives and lady friends of the 3rd Battalion The Black Watch (Royal Highland Regiment) for welcoming him into their mess and for giving him a memorable evening he would hardly forget.

*

The following morning at No 43 George Street, Edinburgh

Captain Marino was sitting on the edge of a mahogany four-poster bed bouncing up and down to test the springs when he heard a knock on the door sounding like a percussionist banging away on a set of drums. It was Tweedledum and Tweedledee, Alistair Campbell and his side-kick,

Robert Boswell, the two most unlikely members of Britain's secret service organisation. They were waiting impatiently to be admitted to the luxurious and spacious apartment on the second floor when Lorenzo slowly opened the door with more than an element of caution. Campbell impertinently pushed his way into the room and then Boswell said, grinning like a Cheshire cat: 'Good morning, Lorenzo, I trust you had a pleasant evening in the officers' mess and also a good night's sleep because where you are going on Friday you will be grateful to us for all this rest and recuperation.'

'What's your boyfriend getting at?' Lorenzo asked Campbell with an inquisitive look upon his face. 'And just where am I supposed to be going on Friday?' he added.

'You are going to a high altitude army training camp somewhere in the highlands of bonnie Scotland.' Campbell began to explain. 'The British army, Captain Lorenzo Marino, will be teaching you how to become a commando.'

'For what purpose am I to do this?' Lorenzo asked Campbell.

'I can't say at this present moment in time, but after your intensive training, you will be going down to London to receive your brief from MI6 headquarters.' he said.

'But, I thought you were both working for MI5.' Lorenzo curiously pointed out.

'Don't you worry yourself about that,' Boswell put in, sounding a little snobbish in his attitude. 'We all work for the same government, you know, it's just like the football fixtures, we work at home and they work away.' he added.

'Oh I see,' Captain Marino said when he suddenly realized there was another sinister objective behind all of this familiarisation. 'And, what if I refuse to go to this training camp, will you send me back to North Berwick?'

'No, we will simply have to shoot you.' Boswell said without hesitation.

'Well, in that case there's no need to unpack, is there?' Lorenzo said, wiping a bead of perspiration away from his brow. 'It's not as if I had anything to unpack in the first place.' he continued to say.

'This morning we are going to take you shopping in Princess Street and there you will be able to buy as many clothes as you like.' Alistair Campbell said, putting an arm around his shoulder, 'I would suggest you buy an Italian suit and a decent pair of Sicilian-made hand-stitched leather shoes because they may come in handy.'

Edinburgh Castle, towering above and over the city; a dark menacing edifice against the skyline always serving as a reminder of the city's historical past, as if the good people of the town needed any, was the magnificent view Lorenzo saw when he walked out of the departmental store, Jenners, in Princes Street with three large brown paper carrier bags. He had taken Alistair Campbell's advice and bought a shiny Italian navy-blue suit from the shop's summer collection and a pair of black leather chiselled toe shoes; an assortment of colourful striped shirts, a couple of ties and with an array of expensive accessories these completed his purchases. Lorenzo was being watched all the time by MI5 in the event he had the urge to do a quick change act in one of the public conveniences and then try to make his way home via Waverley Railway Station in North Bridge Street. However, Lorenzo, an extremely intelligent man, knew instinctively this wouldn't be a good idea, his one and only alternative being for him to go along with their wishes.

It was eleven-thirty when Captain Marino returned to No 43 George Street to remove the labels from his brand-new clothes and then gather up all the little pins he had painstakingly taken out of the shirts, this task being abruptly interrupted by the loud ringing of the over-sized decorative onyx telephone on the half-moon table adjacent to the Adams fireplace. Lorenzo immediately recognised the dulcet tones of Margaret McPherson, the wife of Colonel McPherson.

'Good morning, Captain Marino,' Margaret said sounding out of breath and coughing at the same time. 'I've been trying to get in contact with you all morning.' she emphasized before going on to invite him to have dinner with them that evening. Lorenzo agreed, asking her where they lived.

'Oh, not far away from where you are, in fact it's just around the corner, number nine Charlotte Square.' she said, talking with a twee East

Lothian accent. 'And by the way, Isla, my sister-in-law arrived safely from London this morning and is dying to meet you.' she added.

Lorenzo thought it rather strange that a Scots person, a lady who he had never met in his life before, should be dying to meet him, especially when she lived and worked in London.

*

Between 1942 and 1943, the almost daily tip and run air-raids by the German Luftwaffe continued in an attempt to destroy the city of Edinburgh. However, the German bombers were no match for the Royal Air Force whose Spitfires chased them off before they could inflict heavy damage to a town of great historical and significant importance.

It was seven thirty-five pm when a shiny black Ford 8 motor car arrived at No 43 George Street to take Lorenzo the short distance to the McPherson's prestigious residence in Charlotte Square. The driver, a man of few words and looking every inch a member of the secret services, ordered him to get in and then said nothing more until he parked the car outside No 9 Charlotte Square where he ordered him to get out.

The light was now fading rapidly into an eerie darkness and asthmatic smog emanating from smoky chimneys lingered around every corner and gave the drunken "jumper-ooters" of the old town a chance to jump out and scare half the population to death. The Air Raid Patrol Warden (ARP) was shouting loudly towards one of the houses in the Square, to either close their blackout curtains or put their lights out before they received a thousand-pound bomb through their letterbox.

Lorenzo, walked up the steps of the Georgian house towards the front door where he was greeted by Moira Mackenzie, the resident maid.

'Good evening, Captain Marino,' Moira said, helping him to remove his beige-coloured trench coat in the hall after securing the front door. 'Everyone is waiting for you in the drawing room.' she added. Everyone, including Melanie Bradford-Jones who had arrived that morning, following an eight and a half hour journey from London's King's Cross to Edinburgh's Waverley Station on the famous 'Flying Scotsman' sleeper train.

'Good evening, Captain.' Colonel McPherson said to Lorenzo when he entered the elegant drawing room with its floral covered three-piece suite and decorative Polynesian hand-carved standard lamp. 'And, I want you to call me Cameron.' Colonel McPherson insisted, giving him a firm handshake. 'You have already met my wife, Margaret, and now may I introduce to you to my sister, Isla.'

'Good evening, Captain Marino, I am pleased to make your acquaintance; Margaret has told me all about you.' Melanie Bradford-Jones said shaking his hand as though it were for the last time.

'Cameron told me you are going to Inverness on Friday to train with the Special Forces.' Margaret said handing him a large glass of the famous Grouse whisky which she had poured from a crystal decanter. 'You will be taught how to climb rock faces and cliffs, abseil down mountains and perform Aerial Assaults prior to going over to Norway on active service.' she, so stupidly pointed out.

'Margaret! You have said enough.' Colonel McPherson said to her angrily. 'How many more times do I have to tell you to keep your big mouth shut.' he added.

Lorenzo was wondering how on earth the Colonel knew he was going to Inverness early on Friday and, furthermore, who the hell told him.

'You are very brave, Captain Marino,' Melanie Bradford-Jones said in *her* twee East Lothian Scottish accent which she had cultivated at RADA. 'I like men who do daring things. I once knew a man who enjoyed jumping out of aeroplanes and then one day his parachute refused to open and that was the end of him.'

'Shall we go into the dining room and continue our interesting conversations there.' Colonel McPherson suggested after hearing some of Melanie's past experiences.

The menu for this evening's meal consisted of a starter: smoked salmon with roasted beetroot and vinaigrette dressing; the main course, haggis with turnip and tatties and the desert, vanilla ice cream and a chocolate sauce.

Lorenzo was probably thinking to himself he was going to look like a haggis by the end of the week.

'Tell me,' Captain Marino said, between mouthfuls of extremely dry haggis and turnip, 'what does the letter W mean on the Air Raid Patrolman's helmet?'

'I know what they could mean, Captain-' Margaret piped up,

'-Margaret!' her long suffering husband interrupted, 'Please!' and turning to Lorenzo with a pained expression, 'the W stands for Warden, Captain Marino.'

'LDV;' Lorenzo asked, by this time totally confused by this northern hemisphere, alien language, 'what do those letters mean?'

'Local Defence Volunteers, my dear chap,' Colonel McPherson quickly answered before giving Margaret the opportunity to say something completely outrageous. 'They have full- time jobs as well, you know.' he added.

'I believe there are moves afoot to replicate the Scottish Crown Jewels, Cameron.' Margaret said to her husband.

'And, just where may I ask, did you get this new delivery of garbage from?' Colonel McPherson asked her.

'From the wives' club,' she explained smugly. 'it's amazing what you can pick up on a Thursday morning.'

'I thought as much, Margaret, and you of all people should be more careful with what you pick up.' Cameron said without hesitation.

'I'm not people, Cameron,' Margaret said to him angrily. 'I'm your wife and furthermore, can you not just imagine, really imagine, I mean, how much gold would be needed to make these replicas –'

'-Margaret, please,' her husband tried once more to stop her, but she was in full flow.

'-also,' she insisted, a determined expression on her face which by this time had become quite flushed, 'where on *earth* are they going to find so much gold!'

'And where are you staying in Edinburgh, Captain Marino?' Melanie asked him looking so innocent, as if butter wouldn't melt in her mouth.

'I have temporarily taken up residence in George Street and it's a beautiful apartment with a four-poster bed courtesy of the British Government.' Lorenzo explained.

'Show me!' she whispered excitedly.

It was eleven thirty-five pm when Captain Marino and Melanie Bradford-Jones made their way to number forty-three George Street in a car without headlights and an arrogant driver who should have joined the Diplomatic Service. Lorenzo closed the main door behind them before walking up the twenty-eight stairs to the apartment on the second floor with Britain's leading Mata Hari, Melanie Bradford-Jones, and then, after showing her into the hall he locked the door to the apartment.

'What a beautiful apartment you have, Captain Marino.' Melanie Bradford-Jones said to him, her eyes transfixed on the elegant four-poster bed. 'And, please call me Isla, after all that is my given name.' she insisted before asking him, and not before time, to divulge his Christian name.

'My name is Lorenzo Alberto Constantine Marino; at your service Isla.' he replied spontaneously.

'Lorenzo is a strong name, just like Lawrence of Arabia.' she pointed out trying to undo the buttons on the front of his trousers. Captain Marino remarked later: 'I bet T.E Lawrence wouldn't have had to put up with any of this shit.'

'Your sister-in-law told me last evening you are going over to America; just what do you do for a living, Isla?'

'I am a film and stage actress, Lorenzo and my stage name is Lola Morgan.' Melanie replied before violently whipping of his tie and proceeding to unfasten the buttons of his shirt.

'Tell me, Isla, the last film you were in, what was it called?'

'It was, 'The Life and Death of Colonel Blimp'; I was the understudy to Barbara, Wynne- Candy's wife but unfortunately, she died earlier in the film and so I had no choice but to take on the role of a well and truly pissed-off waitress.' Melanie would insist on telling him.

Lorenzo, at this point had to do a gentleman's excuse-me to visit the bathroom and it was during those few minutes of solace, Melanie had unlocked the apartment door, undressed and climbed on to his bed. She wore pink cami-knickers, black silk stockings neatly suspended from a belt and a wonder bra that didn't leave anything to the imagination. Lorenzo entered the room and this was when Melanie said: 'Come here,

Lorenzo and make passionate love to me.' He was naked and did exactly what she asked, 'What Lola wants, Lola gets.' Melanie said as she lay down on top of him.

It was at this point the door to the apartment burst open and in came two men dressed in black, one of whom was holding a large Kodak camera up to his face ready to take the perfect shot and with the external flash-gun, positioned himself directly in front of them. Seconds later there was an instant flash and this was what Melanie Bradford-Jones had always wanted.

Chapter Ten

The next day at the Maximum Security Compound in Brentwood, Essex

'Herman, Klaus Schneider, you are charged with being an enemy agent, a member of The Third Reich and a German spy operating in Great Britain.' Brian Woodruff said, clearly reading out the charge from a scrappy piece of paper. 'This, as you are fully aware, carries the death penalty and so you will be tried and hanged accordingly.' Woodruff emphasised to him in no uncertain terms.

Schneider, a tall man of at least six-feet in stature, was lying on the top of his bed contemplating his fate and he knew the consequences and penalty when he became the sole inmate of Borden prison four days previously. Commander Edward Greaves who accompanied Woodruff into Schneider's cosy prison cell was standing by the closed door listening to the charges being read out paragraph by paragraph, section by section.

'What about my rights as a human being?' Schneider asked Woodruff nervously.

'You have no rights! In fact you have no rights at all and, furthermore, you have no right to be in this country.' Woodruff pointed out.

'And under the terms of the Geneva Convention I demand to be sent back to Germany.' Schneider shouted at Brian.

'I'm afraid the Geneva Convention doesn't protect spies in times of war and, in case you have forgotten in your leisurely moments enjoying cups of our best Earl Grey tea in Lyons Corner Houses, we are still at war with Germany.' Woodruff made clear.

At this point Commander Edward Greaves introduced himself to Schneider as Peter Watson. He told him he worked for the Foreign Office and then proceeded to make him an offer he could hardly refuse. 'I see on the table you are fast running out of cigarettes and down to a sad looking caramel in the Cadbury's Dairy Box we gave you.' Greaves said reaching out to relieve him of his last ounce of pleasure. 'There's plenty more where those came from.' he added.

'We know all about you, Schneider and, of course, your family,' Woodruff said, choosing his time carefully to penetrate his brain. 'We know where you live in Germany, the address is number twenty-nine Bierbahmsweg, Osnabruck, Westfalia, isn't it? And we also know about your wife, Anna and your three year old daughter, Heidi.' he went on.

'For why are you telling me all of this?' Schneider reacted cautiously before proceeding to light up his last cigarette.

'Because you can help us and it will save you from the hangman's noose.' Greaves was quick to put in.

'And what if I refuse to comply with your wishes?' Schneider arrogantly replied, his English language starting to diminish by the second.

'Well, it's very simple; what would you prefer to eat every day before going to the gallows, a turnip or a juicy bratwurst sausage with *pommes frites*; chips as they are commonly known over here.' Woodruff simply explained to him.

'Just what exactly do you want me to do, sir?' Schneider asked inquisitively.

'All will be explained to you in due course,' Edward Greaves told him knowing he was beginning to unbend. 'but, first of all we must give you another box of chocolates, more cigarettes and a bottle of whisky before we transfer you to your next place of residence, Bradley Hall in Cambridgeshire.'

'Am I to understand you are going to turn me into one of your double agents?' Schneider asked them with a croaky voice when he had difficulty swallowing some of the things he was being asked to do.

'Yes,' Greaves instantly replied, 'we will be sending you back to Germany sooner than you think, but not necessarily in a box.' he added.

'Well, I suppose there is some comfort in that,' Schneider said with a sigh of relief. 'and what other surprises have you got up your sleeves?' he continued.

'There is a lady who is anxious to see you again, Herman.' Woodruff said when he reluctantly called him by his Christian name for the first time. 'She will be meeting you tomorrow at Bradley Hall.' and Brian couldn't help but smile when Schneider asked him:

'It's that awful woman; Dorothy Arkwright isn't it, and if it is, I would much prefer to go to the gallows and could you give me my gun back please?'

'I will most certainly not!' Commander Greaves said emphatically. 'And as for Melanie, whoops! Sorry, Dorothy Arkwright, she is the one responsible for bringing a fine bottle of Hague whisky and a box of Walkers shortbread biscuits all the way from bonnie Scotland especially for you.'

'Well, Commander Greaves, will you thank Miss Arkwright for sending those items to go inside my somewhat belated Christmas hamper, I'm sure the bottle of whisky and biscuits will be two more commodities with a price label on them.'

'Meanwhile, we are giving you a new identity: John Lobkowicz from Prague, Czechoslovakia.' Greaves said to Schneider, handing him a travel document which looked as if it had seen some usage. The fake Czechoslovakian papers which had a cleverly adjusted photograph taken four days previously in New Scotland Yard's headquarters bore little resemblance to him.

'It certainly makes a change from your rather pathetic name, Jack Smith, doesn't it, Herman,' Brian Woodruff said with a smile.

'We view the Slav races to be inferior,' Schneider arrogantly replied. 'I simply refuse to take on the role of a Czechoslovakian.' he emphatically added.

'You have no choice but to carry-out our orders,' Greaves said angrily. 'Eduard Benes, the Czech statesman, as you already know, has been here in London since 1940 and has subsequently set up a government-in-exile; if he and his socialite cronies were to find out about you, Schneider, then the best thing you should have done, and for all of us would have been to take one of your suicide pills.'

'I'm afraid we shall have to go now, Schneider, we have a spy to catch.' Woodruff said looking at Greaves with a big grin on his face.

'Mind the Gap.' Schneider blurted out to Greaves and Woodruff as they were being escorted out of the cell by a plain clothes H.M Prison Officer, hoping they would be sandwiched in between two doors in London's Underground.

'We will.' Woodruff replied, smiling at him. 'We will, we always do.'

*

Friday 10th April 1942 Bradley Hall, Cambridgeshire

The morning of Friday 10th April was very warm indeed; springtime had at last arrived. Herman Klaus Schneider dressed in a dark blue pin-striped suit, white shirt, stiff collar and black tie carried his brown trilby hat and umbrella, the latter, due to the weather had become a superfluous accessory and put out of commission for several days when he and Edward Greaves climbed out from the back seat of the red chauffeur-driven 1936 Bugatti Atlantic motor car. The vehicle; a beautiful demonstration of Italian power belonged to Halewood and remained in the driveway in front of the house with its engine still running, the driver, another MI5 agent in disguise, waited patiently for Commander Greaves to reappear inside the doorway before being taken back to MI6 headquarters in London.

Bradley Hall, a stately home situated in the heart of the picturesque Cambridgeshire countryside and within the parameters of the town of Huntington, was once the residence of an Irish family called Bradley. The Bradleys and the O'Donovans who were merged together by marriage originated from County Wicklow in Ireland, had made their fortune from being highly successful people, namely: doctors, surgeons, businessmen and, in particular, horse owners, regularly frequenting the racecourse at Newmarket in Suffolk, some ten miles north-east of Cambridge.

The innocent-looking maid who seemed to be in her thirties was called Bridie O'Connor, her real name, Pauline Cox, was another MI5 agent working undercover. She took Schneider's hat, coat and umbrella from him when he entered into the hallway and it became immediately obvious after seeing a shotgun standing upright against a wall that the people he was about to meet were heavily into firearms.

Edward Greaves left the house knowing he had delivered Schneider safely to Bradley Hall and by handing him over to the ruthless MI5 officers and his MI6 colleague, he also knew it was to be the beginning of the next stage of the turning process.

"Will you come into my parlour said the Spider to the Fly

It's the prettiest little parlour that ever you did spy.

The way into my parlour is up a winding stair

For whoever goes up *my* winding stair

Can ne'er come down again

I'm sure said the cunning Spider to the Fly

My dear friend, what can I do?"

Herman Klaus Schneider was remarkably calm when he was escorted into the drawing room by Michael Hogan MI5 who had recently taken on the alias of Brendon McBride, the resident butler. Melanie Bradford-Jones, alias Dorothy Arkwright, Isla McPherson, Lola Morgan and a multitude of other unprintable names, was sitting on a settee in front of a glowing fireplace and, seated next to her was the eldest member of the O'Donovan family, the ninety-three year old matriarch, Mrs Joan Bradley. Seated cosily on one of the floral patterned armchairs was another MI5 agent, a sixty-five year old Liverpudlian Irishman called Jack Kelly who had that morning taken on the roll of Doctor Sean O'Donovan and, opposite to him, his elegant sixty-two year old redhead of a wife, Cathleen, real name Lieutenant-Commander Gloria Parker R.N of MI5. Sean's brother, Doctor Patrick O'Donovan was given his identity from the family's surgery in Huntington but, he was the cunning MI6 Scalp-hunter called Les McCartney, seconded to watch Schneider's every move. He was sitting on a high-backed chair, legs crossed and smoking a meerschaum pipe; the smoke billowing out likened to an out-of-control bonfire. An instant silence became embarrassingly noticeable when china tea cups were placed noisily back on to their saucers when Herman Klaus Schneider entered the room.

The stage play began with Schneider introducing himself as John Lobkowicz from Prague, Czechoslovakia and Mrs Bradley, not being conversant with Slavonic languages would insist on calling him Mister Lob sided a bit.

'I have already had the privilege of a close encounter with Miss Dorothy Arkwright, albeit in bizarre and dramatic circumstances; however, I am prepared to forgive but not necessarily forget.' Schneider told them with caution before turning to look in the direction of Melanie Bradford-Jones to say: 'You could have at least given me the chance to drink my coffee before I was arrested.'

'My name isn't Dorothy Arkwright, it's Selina O'Donovan and this is my mother and father sitting in front of you.' Bradford-Jones explained to him tongue in cheek.

'Well, I can't say I am pleased to make your acquaintance and furthermore I am convinced there is something behind all of this nonsense.' Schneider remarked becoming more and more confused.

'Would you like a cup of tea and a shortbread biscuit, Mister Lobkowicz?' Gloria Parker asked him in a sweet Anglo Irish dialect, indispersed with a West Country accent.

'No, all of a sudden I seem to have lost my appetite.' Schneider replied when he glimpsed from the corner of his eye Melanie Bradford-Jones smiling conspiratorially at Les McCartney.

The depressive looking Victorian clock on the mantelpiece was striking eleven o'clock when everyone, except Bradford-Jones, got up from their chairs to go into an adjacent room.

'I am sure Selina and your good self, John have many things to talk about and so we will leave you now.' Jack Kelly said to him as he repeatedly patted Schneider gently on the forearm.

'A penny for your thoughts, Schneider.' Bradford-Jones said softly, getting up from the settee and walking over to him.

'Is that all that I am worth?' he replied, nervously opening a brand-new packet of Marlborough cigarettes.

'Here, have one of mine,' Melanie said, producing a yellow packet containing German HB cigarettes. 'If you are going to smoke, you might as well smoke a good one.' she added.

'Well, you should know all about that, Dorothy Arkwright, Selina O'Donovan or whatever your name is and, as for the miniscule price for your services displayed on the sole of your shoe, it may be of interest for you to know that on Monday morning I had plenty of loose change in my trouser pocket.'

It was at this point Schneider noticed an eighteenth century portrait of a man with only one eye. He immediately remedied this disfigurement by stuffing a piece of his much-chewed bubble-gum deep down inside the hole rendering it impossible for the spy-guy to see into the room from the other side of the wall.

'What did he do to deserve that?' Bradford-Jones said looking at a Royal Naval officer with a serious eye defect and who was now desperately in need of an eye-patch.

'I don't need to be reminded that I am a prisoner in this house by courtesy of the British Government and I expect to be treated with a little more respect.' he insisted.

'You have beautiful black shiny hair, John.' she said to him coquettishly. 'And what kind of hair dressing do you use?' she inquisitively asked.

'Come on; let's not beat around the bush, Miss Dorothy Arkwright.' Schneider replied insisting she should call him by his real name.

'I can't do that, John because I am under strict orders to call you John Lobkowicz.' she emphatically stipulated.

'I use Brylcreem.' Schneider replied thinking there could be another present in the offing.

'I thought Brylcreem went out with the Ark.' she remarked sarcastically, and to which he immediately replied: 'I didn't know that Noah used it.'

'You should try mousse, it's better for your scalp.' she went on.

'And, like the Walkers biscuits and Famous Grouse whisky, does it also come with antlers?' he said, seeming to be equally sarcastic.

'After lunch you can take me for a spin in my car,' Melanie suggested to him. 'The countryside is great around here with lots of things you Germans like to admire, such as red letter and telephone boxes, sheep, cows and that sort of thing.'

'How long will I be staying here?' Schneider asked and giving Bradford-Jones the impression he wasn't happy to be in her company.

'You will be here until we receive orders asking you to leave, Mr John Lobkowicz.' she firmly implied. 'Meanwhile, the cook has prepared a typical Germanic meal, especially for you; Weiner Schnitzel, sauerkraut and roast potatoes.'

'Do you know, Miss Arkwright, I would prefer to visit one of your typical Fish & Chip restaurants.' Schneider insisted.

'Please stop calling me Miss Arkwright.' Bradford-Jones said to him before walking over to the other side of the room to rearrange the ornaments and poke the fire. 'My name is Selina O'Donovan and how many more times do I have to tell you?'

'Okay, Selina point taken, but it's not my fault I have in the last few days acquired a severe hearing disability.'

'Eating fish and chips is synonymous with being British; in fact it's a bloody institution.' she remarked, knowing he was going to get just what he wanted. 'You know, being truly patriotic is not about knowing the lyrics to *God Save the Queen*, John but about finding the perfect fish and chip restaurant, come on lets go and find one.' she added.

'And what if I decide to disappear this afternoon, Selina, what will you and your friends do about that?' he asked her.

'Well, it will be very much your funeral and the war will be over for you sooner than expected.' Bradford-Jones replied giving him a quick smile.

Hogan, the undercover butler said to Schneider that his luggage had been sent from number twenty-three Old Crompton Street in London and he would make sure it would be put into his room immediately. Schneider, shaking his head in total disbelief, said to Hogan just how kind his people were to go through his entire personal belongings and deliver them to Bradley Hall; a place situated in the middle of nowhere.

A beautiful red Riley 9-h.p sporting car belonging to Melanie Bradford-Jones was parked on the forecourt; a brown leather strap firmly secured the bonnet in place and to hide the remarkable feat of engineering which lay beneath.

'Here are the keys, John.' Bradford-Jones said to Schneider tossing them in the air for him to catch. 'Now, take me for that spin.'

Schneider enjoyed driving along the tree-lined country roads with Bradford-Jones sitting beside him, and then glancing into the rear-view mirror he noticed a shiny black Ford 8 motor car which seemed to have appeared out from nowhere and had increased speed to creep up behind him. Melanie with an arm resting on the top of the nearside door, was enjoying the rush of wind blowing through her hair and on to her rosy cheeks and she was not unduly concerned by an over-zealous Stirling Moss travelling at great speed directly behind her much cherished sports car; the wheels of which had taken more shock-absorbing than the Clifton Suspension Bridge in Bristol and were about to be rigorously tested once again, this time in a lay-by at the side of a road on the outskirts of Cambridge.

'Pull over to the side of the road, John and stop the car.' Bradford-Jones said to him breathlessly and beginning to unfasten the buttons of her blouse and hoisting her knee-length skirt up to a higher level to show more than a generous glimpse of her shapely legs.

Schneider turned the ignition key to immobilize the car and this was when Bradford-Jones unbuckled the belt of his trousers to enable her to pull them down. He reached over to kiss her but this was just a wasted moment when a sinister looking man appeared with a Kodak camera to take their photograph.

'What does it feel like to be caught with your trousers down, Schneider?' Bradford-Jones said to him with a ruthless look upon her face. 'And meanwhile, enjoy your weekend at Bradley Hall.'

'You will pay for this, Dorothy Arkwright.' Schneider said angrily.

Chapter Eleven

London, England Friday 17th April 1942

The Caledonian Sleeper train which had conveyed Captain Lorenzo Marino the five hundred and forty-seven miles from Aberdeen's Guild Street Station to London Euston pulled in on time at precisely nine o'clock that morning. Lorenzo, throughout the journey had been escorted by two armed Royal Military Policemen before he was handed over to Commander Mark West of New Scotland Yard and Colonel Brian Woodruff of MI6 who had been patiently waiting behind the ticket barrier for him to arrive.

'It's not the end of the world, sir.' Corporal William (Knobby) Clarke said to Captain Marino walking along the platform helping his subordinate NCO, Lance Corporal Frank (Smudge) Smith to carry Captain Marino's luggage. 'Rumour has it, sir,' he continued. 'you will shortly be going on your holidays.' talking in a London East End cockney accent. 'You are lucky, sir, tonight we've got to go back to that bleeding camp in Aberdeen and we're really looking forward to that, sir, aren't we Smudge?'

'Yea, really looking forward to that, Knobby.' Smith said, replying through his boxer's nose which looked as if it had just gone through ten rounds with Jack Dempsey.

'After we have done the business in handing you over, sir, we are going to sink a few jars of Fuller's finest best bitter ale in the Nuffield Centre off Trafalgar Square; there are usually lots of ground sheets to choose from in there.' Corporal Smith went on before stepping up the pace through the clouds of steam.

'Ground sheets; just what the hell are you talking about, corporal, I don't understand.' Captain Marino said to him with a curious frown on his face as he quickly followed on behind.

'You know, sir, those ladies from the army, navy and air force who are just gagging for it.' Smith replied in his eloquent West Bromwich accent.

'Oh, I understand now,' Lorenzo said to them both. 'It's another one of your English euphemisms that no one can understand, isn't it?'

'Yes, you could describe them as unidentified flying objects.' Corporal Clarke replied smugly, twirling his waxed handlebar moustache around with his forefinger and thumb.

After the signatures of handover had taken place in the station hall, the two NCOs saluted Captain Marino and then made a quick exit towards the Grecian Arch doorway.

'Good morning, Captain Marino,' Brian Woodruff said, proffering his hand for Lorenzo to shake before introducing West and himself with false identities. 'My name is Chief Inspector Bruce Johnson,' Woodruff said convincingly, 'and this is Inspector Philip Green; we are both members of New Scotland Yard's Special Branch assigned to take you to our headquarters here in London.

'We are indeed privileged to meet you.' Commander West said after giving Lorenzo a rather peculiar handshake which only the brotherhood of Freemasonry can understand.

'So far, I have not accepted any of these privileges, only to tolerate them.' Captain Marino replied patriotically. 'I have no need to remind you that I am still a prisoner of war in your country and would you please tell me where your headquarters are situated because I am now feeling the urge to go and visit a toilet.'

Lorenzo was bundled into the back seat of a black Ford 8 motor car on the station's forecourt where it had been waiting to transport him to The Gown Shop, MI6's secret offices in London's Oxford Street. A black cotton hood was quickly pulled down over the top of Lorenzo's head to restrict his vision and then after being told by a mean looking MI5 officer to crouch down, the car sped off along Euston Road, heading towards Tottenham Court Road and Oxford Street.

It was nine forty-five precisely when the car pulled up around the back of the shop; it's rather primitive exhaust system billowing dirty grey fumes adding to the sinister atmosphere.

Lorenzo, after being escorted through a tiny courtyard at the rear, entered the building through a heavily fortified door where an armed guard was standing inside to show them up the narrow wooden staircase towards the first floor. Angela Bassett, an MI6 secretary continued to file her nails sitting in front of what seemed to be a paperless desk outside a very busy office when Captain Marino, completely out of breath, plonked himself down on a high back chair in front of her.

'Would it be too much to ask if I demanded a glass of water?' Captain Marino said to Miss Bassett, wiping away a bead of perspiration away from his brow with a heavily stained McPherson tartan handkerchief.

'You look like a person who is in need of a beer, Captain Marino.' Angela said after giving his minders the all clear for them to disappear.

'No, just a glass of water and that will be fine before I have a relapse.' Lorenzo said, looking up and down the corridor in order to find a gentleman's toilet.

'It's to your right, if that is what you are looking for, Captain Marino,' Angela said with a naughty smile on her face. 'I usually have men in here asking me the same question but, almost invariably it's engaged.'

Captain Marino was less enchanted with the place after visiting the gentleman's cloakroom. The toilet roll holder which had been subjected to extreme violence came away from the wall leaving an untidy paper trail leading up towards the door and, to make matters worse, there was no hot water and the towel rail fell down into a metal bucket.

'Oh, you're back in one piece, Captain Marino, that didn't take long. Freshened up are we?' Angela Bassett said with another cheeky grin on her face.

'Just give me a glass of water please miss and I will forget everything you have just said.' Lorenzo emphatically pointed out to her.

'As you wish,' Angela said, giving a good impression of a fag-ash Lil when she began coughing on another Woodbine cigarette and pretending, in her dreams, to be a future Miss Money-penny. 'Mister Watson will be with you in a moment, sir, as soon as he has dealt with his foreign colleague.' she added.

'You know, sitting in this place is like being on another planet.' Lorenzo said to her pulling up the collar of his overcoat in an impossible attempt to disappear down inside it.

'That's why we are called the Martians, darlin!' she wittingly said as more fag ash dropped off the end of her cigarette into the keyboard of an

Imperial typewriter.

At ten o'clock a door at the far end of the corridor opened. A man, sporting a recently acquired black eye, was escorted out of the building by an MI5 agent who, it would seem, had not been to a charm school when he barged passed Captain Marino without giving him an apology. Commander Edward Greaves introduced himself to Lorenzo as Mr Peter Watson; another alias given to him by 'C' whose office was situated next to his on the third floor. Lorenzo was beginning to wonder if black eyes and patches were fashionable in Britain, because Watson was the third person he had encountered that morning with similar defects; one of them whom he'd seen earlier; a Scotsman, bearing a remarkable resemblance to Long John Silver and had proceeded to fall drunkenly on to the platform at London's Euston Station.

'Good morning, Captain Marino. I have heard a great deal about you and am indeed privileged to meet you.' Edward Greaves said solemnly, gently taking him by the arm towards the lift at the far end of the corridor.

'Do forgive me for not being gracious but I am not accepting this privilege.' Lorenzo told him in no uncertain terms.

'You will, my dear boy, you will,' Greaves said to him as he closed the lattice wrought iron gate directly in front of the lift. 'There is a lady in my office who is anxious to meet you again, Lorenzo; she is departing for America tomorrow morning and wishes to speak with you.'

'I don't know this so called lady, never want to and never will?' Lorenzo said as Greaves pushed the elevator button to take them up to the third floor.

'Oh, come on Marino, Melanie was only doing her job.' Edward Greaves pointed out. 'And don't forget, if it wasn't for her, you wouldn't have had the privilege of standing next to me in a place, where one might say, is the most exclusive club in the world.' he added.

'Who is this Melanie? I don't know any Melanie.' Lorenzo curiously asked Greaves.

'Oh, shit, whoops! I'm such an arse; she's called Isla McPherson, such a charming and intelligent young lady.'

'Isla McPherson; the sister of Colonel McPherson, who else could it be?' Lorenzo said with a sigh. 'And, I am thinking that it was just over a week ago, Isla McPherson succeeded in taking my pants off before dashing out from the apartment.'

'Well, you win some and you lose some, old boy.' Greaves said patronizingly, patting him below his shoulders.

The third floor was refreshingly different and looked less like a Natural History museum. There was another reception desk where Sue Wilson, another contented Foreign Office employee, was sitting cross-legged pretending to peruse through the latest British weekly tabloid newspaper, the Reveille; a copy of The Official Secrets Act could also be seen in her OUT tray waiting to be delivered by her to room number twelve.

'Oh, by the way, old chap,' Edward Greaves said to Lorenzo after achieving an access visa from Wilson to go into an office he shared with his two colleagues, Halewood and myself. 'we are going parachuting next week, and that will be fun won't it.' he added.

'Parachuting, are you mad man?' Lorenzo said to him. 'First of all I was whisked out from my comfortable prisoner of war billet in North Berwick, Scotland and then subjected to violent molestation by Isla McPherson, Lola Morgan or whatever her name is and, if that wasn't enough, I was then sent to a Special Forces high altitude training camp in Aberdeen to learn how to break my neck trying to scale bloody big mountains and precipitous cliffs. And now you are going to teach me how to parachute! How ridiculous you are, Watson, whatever next?'

'I will now tell you a little story, Captain Marino.' Greaves replied enthusiastically.' When I was serving as an officer in the Fleet Air Arm of her Majesty's Royal Navy, I was taught how to sky-dive and when it was my wife's birthday, I gave her a parachute and borrowed it three times a week.'

'Ha! Ha! Ha! Yes, well, that was really funny. Have you got any more jokes like that?' Lorenzo said quaking in his shoes.

'Well at least this way you will be back in Italy sooner than you think.' Greaves pointed out to him.'

The office at the end of the corridor was called room number twelve and to gain access, seven melodious bangs, sounding like Morse code, had to be delivered on the front of the door by Greaves.

'Your offices are a bit over the top with security, Watson.' Lorenzo said to Greaves when the door was opened by a mean looking security guard who could have been the product of Doctor Frankenstein's laboratory and who meticulously frisked him in a tiny vestibule just inside the door; rumour had it, he ran faster than Jessie Owen and leapt over the twenty-two miles of water to Britain when the Germans invaded Poland in 1939.

'All in a day's work, old chap, all in a day's work.' Greaves replied seeming very much in charge when a half empty packet of Polo Mints fell out of Lorenzo's jacket pocket into a nearby goldfish bowl rendering the contents to jump out on to a threadbare carpet.

After what was described as an unnecessary formality undertaken by a Polish displaced person, and Freddie, the unfortunate and misplaced goldfish, had been scooped up from the floor, another door was opened to reveal Melanie Bradford-Jones sitting comfortably, cross-legged on a leather high-backed chair.

'Hello Lorenzo, nice to see you again, but this time it is going to be in rather different circumstances.' Bradford-Jones told him, producing a packet of Dunhill cigarettes and silver Du Pont lighter from her much-travelled crocodile skin handbag.

'Hello Isla, if I had known you were here I would have brought you some flowers.' Lorenzo said to her sarcastically.

Melanie, looking a million dollars, wearing a pin-stripe three-quarter length skirt, a fox fur jacket and a hat to match, sauntered towards him, a seductive smile on her face.

I, the unmistakable James Brown was sitting in an upright position at my desk opposite to Halewood and had been given the alias by 'C' of Charles Thornton, meanwhile, Steven Halewood introduced himself to Captain Marino as Clive North.

'Is that your gun I see lying on the floor, Isla, or is it just a *pigment* of my imagination?' Lorenzo said to her and was now beginning to realize how blasé the British are in their approach to bumping people off.

'Thank you, Lorenzo for being so vigilant and reminding me that I had purposely dropped my pride and joy on the floor,' Bradford-Jones said sounding like an ice-maiden, 'but you see I am always doing this, just to let people like you know I mean business and, if you fowl up during this operation, I will personally have to kill you with this ladies' rather nice looking mother of pearl Colt 38 millimetre pistol; and by the way it's not a pigment of your imagination, it is a figment, just like the ones that fell from the trees in North Africa.'

'You are very clever, Isla McPherson, Lola Morgan or whatever your name is.' Lorenzo said hesitantly, 'I pity those poor guys in America who are about to meet you.' he added.

'This weekend, you will be staying at the Savoy Hotel in the Strand.' Melanie gleefully said to him. 'You will enjoy that after spending a number of months in an Italian prisoner of war camp and a rat-infested high altitude barracks in Scotland, won't you?'

'May I interrupt this love affair with this Anglo-Italian, British dolce vita?' Steven Halewood suggested, 'But, first of all, Captain Lorenzo Giovanni Marino, we are going to tell you what your brief and mission will be in order to gain access to this so-called good life.'

Melanie Bradford-Jones got up from her chair, smoothed down her skirt and said: 'I have to go now but will meet you in the cocktail bar just before dinner, Rolando Donatello, and you will be there, won't you, because I don't want to postpone my visit to America because of an unfortunate funeral.'

'Who is this Rolando Donatello, Isla; my name is Captain Lorenzo Giovanni Marino.'

'It's your new name, Lorenzo,' Bradford-Jones said to him giggling. 'It has a certain ring to it, though, wouldn't you say?'

Meanwhile, Hugo Kowalski, the Polish security guard from Warsaw who was also skilled as a Russian translator as well as an aquatic funeral director, showed Melanie Bradford-Jones out of the office leaving a trail of incendiary behind her from a half-smoked cigarette which she had stubbed out provocatively in the ashtray provided on a table beside the door. After the grand exit had been perpetrated and coquettishly carried out by Melanie, Steven Halewood made a quick telephone call to Sue

Wilson asking her to produce a document for Captain Marino to sign in the presence of the three of us. This was the prelude to his orders being read out to him by me which went as follows:

"On Monday the 20th April after your short visit to London you are to be sent to No.1 Parachute Training School at RAF Ringway, Cheshire near Manchester. It is there you will be trained to jump from Lysander and Whitley 111 aircraft along with men and women agents of the Special Operations Executive. During your course of intensive training which will last for a period of not less than six days you will be staying in the Officers Mess (Building 217) in Ringway Road where the staff will make you feel as comfortable as possible. Your task, ultimately, will be significant and of great importance to the world, especially to the islands of Sicily, Malta and Great Britain. It is to be hoped you will be dropped by parachute into Italy, on the outskirts of Rome and from there you will be contacted by one of our special agents with the code name, Joey Macaroni, who will be giving you further instructions regarding the mission and your well-being whilst staying in Rome. You are to befriend a Maltese fascist sympathiser called Caio Borghi, also known as Carelo Borg Pisani who is currently based at the University in Rome and, from now on, your name is Rolando Donatello, a Maltese academic with an MI6 code name of "Condor". Your main objective will be to assist Pisani and to make sure twenty million dollars worth of German gold ingots are safely jettisoned on to the island of Malta via Sicily and to ensure Pisani, your accomplice, German spy and double agent is arrested by the British. It will be then your responsibility to tell us the details of where the gold is once the ingots have been smelted down and transformed into something else."

'And what, may I ask will that something else be?' Captain Marino asked frowning.

'We haven't a clue old boy, haven't a clue.'

'Listen dear boy,' I said to him, 'the Americans are already softening up the opposition on the island of Sicily by making contact with local Mafia bosses through the crime boss 'Lucky' Luciano who is in jail in upstate New York. Many of the Italian defenders and Sicilians are unwilling to see their homeland turned into a battlefield for the sake of the Germans and will put up little resistance. For most Italians and Sicilians, as you know Captain Marino, they wanted to make peace and, as a result Mussolini will eventually fall from power.'

'Has Lola Morgan got anything to do with this, by any chance?' Lorenzo finally asked.

Chapter Twelve

The same day in the Hotel Metropole, London, England

It was five-thirty that afternoon when Herman Klaus Schneider, alias Jack Smith, and John Lobkowicz from Prague, Czechoslovakia, entered one of London's largest and most luxurious hotels: the Hotel Metropole, Whitehall Place on the Thames Embankment, London WC2. Schneider had been given his orders at three o'clock in the afternoon by me in an establishment we call in our profession, a 'safe house', designated especially to temporarily house members of the British and foreign intelligence services. The front room inside the quaint Victorian terrace house in Fredrick Street, Pimlico, had suddenly become my office for a couple of hours and after Woodruff, alias Bruce Johnson, had cleared the table in front of the window of breakfast debris and a plate displaying a half-eaten pork and beef sausage covered in tomato ketchup, I thought to myself what did that poor British banger do to deserve this kind of treatment. It was then, after I had observed a huge mound of soggy *Bury* black pudding hiding behind a bottle of HP Sauce, I came to the conclusion Schneider, much to his detriment, had a great dislike for a traditional English breakfast. Commander Greaves with his alias name of Peter Watson was sitting nervously to my right and, judging by the look upon his face as he poured hot Darjeeling tea into miniscule Japanese tea cups, especially designed for Kamikaze pilots, he was even less enchanted when he saw Schneider boisterously entering into the room; his prominent Germanic nose arrogantly pointing towards the ceiling likened to a U-Boat Commander waiting, in metaphor, for another Royal Navy depth-charge to explode around him.

'Pull up a chair, Schneider.' Woodruff said to him, eating a stale piece of toast from an electro plated rack which was standing next to more than enough Shredded Wheat to thatch a roof.

'I see you had great difficulty in eating your breakfast this morning, Schneider,' Greaves said to him with an air of sarcasm. 'You know, if I were you, Herman, I would have the same problem.' he added.

'What are you telling me, Mister Watson?' Schneider answered curiously.

Commander Greaves, after lighting up a second 'Capstan full strength' navy cut cigarette said: 'I am now going to hand you over to my colleague, Charles Thornton, British Foreign Office, who will systematically guide you through your orders to enable you to return to your *heimat*, your homeland in Germany, as soon as possible.'

'This is indeed very kind of you to do this for me,' Schneider said gratefully. 'but, what will I have to do?'

I started off by saying: 'From now on John Lobkowicz, your code name will be the 'Hare' and you will be parachuted into Germany after being trained at one of our training camps in the north of England. We told you that you will be back in Germany sooner than you had thought possible and, we British always keep our promises.' I explained with great depth of feeling.

'Thank you.' Schneider said. 'I know now why the British are such a calm and gracious race of people; we Germans have only got to look at your red telephone and letter boxes to realize that.' he added.

'Now, let's not go over the top, Schneider; I know you are taking the proverbial Michael Schneider,' Edward put in. 'but, if you fowl up we will most certainly have to kill you.'

'Well, that is indeed a comforting thought, one which I have heard somewhere before.' Schneider replied when he looked out through the window and witnessed a workman falling from a ladder directly across the road. 'And, who is this 'Mickael', do I know him?' he added.

I quelled the banter by explaining to him that his orders were to send information back to us in London via an MI6 agent based in Hamburg regarding shipments of gold destined for Rome; in particular the Vatican.

'And now, may I be permitted to have my gun returned to me, preferably with bullets.' Schneider asked Woodruff, knowing he was the ruthless bastard sitting at the table.

'Here it is, Schneider,' Woodruff said, showing him his heavy World War 1 Artillery Luger pistol and a full magazine containing eight rounds of 9 mm ammunition before inserting it into the pistol grip.

Brian Woodruff was taking great delight in showing Schneider a photograph taken by a colleague when Bradford-Jones was giving him mouth-to-mouth resuscitation in a lay-by somewhere in the heart of Cambridgeshire. 'I must admit, Schneider, you look a lot better with your trousers down.' Woodruff said to him jovially and proceeding to turn Edward Greaves and myself into a couple of laughing hyenas.

'Give me that photograph, Johnson.' Schneider insisted.

'Certainly, it's my pleasure to give you a copy and, by the way, would it be possible for you to put your autograph on this one?' Woodruff asked, producing several more from inside his coat pocket. 'You will be staying in the Metropole Hotel tonight; it is one of London's most prestigious hotels and I don't want to hear stories about you attempting to shoot the place up with this rather unnecessary over-sized canon.'

'And when, may I ask, will I be going to this training camp?' Schneider asked me looking by this time somewhat distressed.

'You will be travelling to Manchester's Piccadilly railway station first thing on Monday morning, where a Royal Air Force staff car will be waiting to take you to Britain's No.1 Parachute Training School at RAF Ringway.' I told him, continuing with the answers to some of his more important questions, such as:

'And, when will I be going to my home in Germany, Mister Thornton?' Schneider asked.

'If everything goes to plan and you don't do anything silly, like jumping from a high-speed train somewhere between Euston and Crewe, you should be back in your own country by the end of next week.'

'And what name shall I adopt once I'm back in Germany?' Schneider asked.

After explaining he was to revert back to his real name and pushing a copy of the Official Secrets Act underneath his nose for him to sign, Schneider said to me: 'There's no need to hand me this document, Mister Thornton, because I will not be able to understand a single word of it, but don't worry I will carry out your wishes; you leave me with no choice.' he added.

'I suppose you are wondering why we gave you the code name of the 'Hare',' Greaves said to Schneider knowing he was about to bring on fits of laughter when he continued to say: 'RAF Ringway has lots of rabbits and that is why they call it an airfield.' When they had finally composed themselves with the exception of Schneider, who was *not* amused, Brian Woodruff put in:

'Oh, by the way, Schneider, there will be a lady waiting for you in the hotel lobby this afternoon to attend to your immediate requirements.'

'It's not that bloody woman, Dorothy Arkwright, Selina O'Donovan again is it?' Schneider asked, shaking his head in disbelief and going on to say: 'because if it is her I will shoot myself in the gentlemen's cloakroom.'

'Now, let's not get too excited,' Edward Greaves said, 'she is only doing a job, just like everyone else.' he went on.

'What kind of job?' Schneider asked.

The long reception desk was exceptionally busy with wealthy refugees paying large sums of money to be temporarily accommodated in one of London's finest hotels. Schneider momentarily thought he was on neutral territory when he heard the sound of a Swiss accent coming from a little man who looked like he had just abseiled down the north face of a Toblerone as they waited patiently to check-in. Melanie Bradford-Jones, as if by magic, made her entrance from behind a curtain; she was perhaps used to this sort of thing, particularly performing in London's best West End theatres. Schneider looked up to see a Greta Garbo heading his way, walking elegantly towards him dressed in a knee-length blue pin-striped suit and a fox fur jacket draped over her shoulders. The fragrance of Chanel perfume was permeating all around the lobby which gave the guests in the hotel a sense of gratuitous exclusiveness.

Melanie quickly extricated Schneider from the queue, taking him by the arm to sit on one of the settees inside the tea room.

Schneider, in a low croaky voice greeted Bradford-Jones by saying: 'so, we meet again Miss O'Donovan, they said you would be in the hotel to meet me this afternoon and here you are.'

'Yes, it has been a week since I last saw you, John,' Melanie said tongue in cheek, 'and I am truly sorry for what happened in Cambridge, I honestly didn't know we were about to have our photographs taken doing things by the side of a road.' she added.

'Of course you knew, Selina; I was set up and, it has taken me a week to recover from that traumatic experience.' Schneider said to her with an angry look on his face. 'And, why may I ask, are you here in the Hotel Metropole this afternoon?'

'I have been assigned by MI9 to help you settle into the hotel and to make your life as comfortable as possible.' she explained, touching him around his groin with her long red scratchy fingernails.

'And when do I check-in to the hotel?' Schneider curiously asked.

'Don't you worry about that,' Bradford-Jones replied with a smile, 'we have taken care of everything, including your luggage which you will find in your room.'

'Who is this *we?*' Schneider asked.

'Oh, there's no need to ask, let's just say he will be keeping an eye on you.' she replied.

'It's not that Peeping Tom of a photographer again is it?' Schneider said banging his head on the back of the settee.

'John, you are so sensitive.' Melanie said, tugging at the sleeve of his jacket. 'You know, if I don't get what I want, I will most certainly have to kill you.'

'What are you talking about?' Schneider said now shaking his head. 'I have already been threatened with death twice and now you want to do it with me all over again; you know domestic cats are supposed to have nine lives but this is ridiculous.' he added.

'Your room is on the fourth floor, John and in the bathroom there is a big pink tub.' Bradford-Jones insisted on telling him before she got up from the settee to escort him to the lift. 'You know, John I need a good soak and then to freshen-up because for me, it has been a hard day at the office.' she emphasised, opening the top of her blouse to allow some much- needed air to flow down between her cleavage.

Melanie Bradford-Jones had been in this on-suite hotel bedroom before and knew every inch of the geography and its contents including the formidable bed facing a two-way mirror.

'Now, John let me take off your coat and then I will pour you a large glass of Irish whiskey.' Bradford-Jones insisted before removing her fox fur jacket to reveal her voluptuous hour-glass figure.

Schneider, wondering how his luggage had been transported from the hotel's lobby into a wardrobe helped himself to another Jameson's whiskey and then began to inspect the dark blue bags underneath his blue eyes which were now looking like a Westfalia road map.

Melanie Bradford-Jones standing by the bed began to remove her clothes. One by one, the buttons on her white silk blouse were unfastened directly in front of him to show two mounds of undulating flesh waiting impatiently to be released from captivity.

'Do you like what you see, John?' Bradford Jones asked Schneider who was now perspiring profusely and doing his best not to act like a pianist trying to reach the keyboard in front of a grand piano. 'Here, take them out and then I will continue where I left off.' Melanie insisted and at the same time gyrating her hips to allow her skirt to fall into an untidy heap around her slim ankles.

'I thought you were going to take a bath in the pink tub, Selina?' Schneider asked fondling a heavy breast with great sensual expertise.

'What pink tub, Mister John Lob sided a bit,' she said sexily before pulling him down on to the bed. 'Oh, and by the way, unless it has escaped your attention, I have two breasts not one.'

Schneider, having been rendered completely naked by Bradford-Jones's quick manoeuvres moved in to ravage her from behind and, from where he was positioned directly in front of the mirror, he could see her writhing to his orchestrated movements. After fulfilling Melanie's immediate requirements, Schneider rolled over on top of the bed completely and utterly exhausted knowing he had accomplished something that maybe Errol Flynn would have found somewhat impossible.

'I am sorry, John,' Bradford-Jones said sadly. 'But I have to go now because I have another appointment this evening and maybe someday our paths will cross in very different circumstances and, unlike this evening, John, when you are jumping out of those rather precarious little aeroplanes next week, don't forget to keep your legs together and your

Michael Alty

knees bent, we don't want any nasty accidents, do we? Meanwhile, let me give you something as a reminder of our close encounter.'

It was just after six-thirty when Melanie Bradford-Jones swiftly departed from Schneider's hotel bedroom after giving him more of her mouth-to-mouth resuscitation and an eighteen carat solid gold cigarette case with his initials H.K.S. engraved inside.

*

One hour later in London's exclusive Savoy Hotel

Captain Lorenzo Marino alias, Rolando Donatello and now the Maltese registered academic was sitting in 'The American Bar', waiting for Melanie Bradford-Jones alias, Isla McPherson, to arrive with he hoped a case full of Scotch whisky to calm his nerves. Lorenzo, drinking a cocktail invented by the head barman, Eddie Clarke, was called "Eight Bells", and was aptly named especially for officers and gentlemen serving in the Royal Navy, albeit, "The New Contemptable" would have been a far better choice because of him being in the army. The American Bar featured a live pianist who delightfully played classical jazz on a baby grand piano in the centre of the room; and, his new tune, "As Time goes by", was a regular favourite with the guests in between the occasional air-raid warnings sounding seven days a week. Sitting, not so discreetly behind him, was Les McCartney, the MI6 scalp-hunter, reading a copy of the *London Evening Standard* and by his side was Lieutenant-Commander Gloria Parker MI5 who was purporting to be his wife. A smoke screen which was caused by McCartney's meerschaum pipe began to asphyxiate the guests standing at the bar who were having their aperitifs before dinner but at seven forty-five the room began to empty when General Charles de Gaulle, the president of France and leader of the Free French movement (later called Fighting French) which he formed in London, walked into the Front Hall to cause an array of onlookers to clamber over one another to obtain his autograph. He and his body guards disappeared into a lift with gusto; it was controversially reminiscent of the time he fled from France to take up temporary residence in Britain. It is surprising, however, but not so surprising, The Savoy Hotel during The Second

World War boasted the smartest air-raid shelters in London where de Gaulle could be reasonably safe from continual German bombardment.

Melanie Bradford-Jones confident in her usual way made her entrance into the American Bar to find Lorenzo still sitting on a stool perusing the drinks menu in order to find something that wasn't capable of blowing his head off after one or two sips. She couldn't help but view herself in front of the decorative mirrors as she walked in, giving guests the impression she was wealthy and accustomed to the good life. Melanie surprised Lorenzo from behind by placing her hand in the centre of his back to distract him from reading through the extensive list of alcoholic beverages.

'Hello, Rolando.' Melanie said, after kissing him four times on both cheeks.

'Hello, Isla,' Captain Marino replied nervously, 'had a busy day at the office, have we?'

'Yes, I didn't get home until five-thirty this afternoon; taxis can be a trial, can't they, especially in rush hour.'

'Well, I wouldn't know about that, Isla seeing as this is my first visit to London and could possibly be my last.' he remarked caustically.

Melanie was now seated cross-legged next to Lorenzo at the bar; her thigh showing more than a glimpse of stocking and suspenders much to the delight of Les McCartney who seemed to be having problems inside his trousers. Gloria Parker, now sitting in front of Les and with her back to Bradford-Jones, later became disappointed when she learned it wasn't she who was causing all the excitement.

'I would like a *Manhattan* before we go to have dinner in The Savoy Grill, Rolando.' Melanie said, squeezing his hand gently on top of the bar.

'Yes, of course.' Lorenzo replied, beginning to sound more like an Italian gentleman.

'You know, Rolando, tall ladies like big men.' Melanie said looking at him in a wicked kind of way that only a vampire would be able to do.

'I do know this,' Lorenzo replied frowning. 'but I am only five foot six and three-quarters.' he added.

'It's not your height I am referring to, Rolando Donatello.' looking down towards his size eight Sicilian hand-stitched patent leather shoes.

'I must admit I do have big feet.' Lorenzo said to her, banging his chest with his fist likened to a smaller version of Benito Mussolini.

'And do you like your Art Deco Suite, Rolando,' Melanie said to him, talking to him as if butter couldn't melt in her mouth.

'Yes, it's a very nice apartment and I can't wait to rest my weary head on that silk pillow tonight because I'm a very tired.'

'You're not tired of me, I hope.' Bradford-Jones said sorrowfully. 'Later this evening I will help you to get into your bed and, unlike Edinburgh, it is possible we will be left alone without any interruptions.'

'You know, they think of everything in this hotel.' Lorenzo said to Melanie with a curious look on his face.

'Just what are you trying to tell me, Rolando?' she replied.

'Well,' Lorenzo went on enthusiastically, 'when I entered my bedroom there was this rubbery thing wrapped in red silver paper placed in the centre of the pillow and I thought to myself it could possibly come in handy sometime this evening.'

'You mean the complementary liqueur chocolate that everyone gets before they go to bed.' Melanie was pleased to tell him, knowing she had found something he didn't already know. 'And what may I ask is that white stuff running down from the top of your inside leg?' she added.

'Oh, no' Lorenzo said when he looked down to see a gooey mess coming out from his trouser pocket.

'This is just as embarrassing for me as it is for you, Rolando.' Melanie said, after seeing Les McCartney falling back in his chair and laughing hysterically. 'Come on, Rolando, let's go and get you cleaned up before dinner.'

The spacious apartment allotted and occupied by Mister Rolando Donatello was on the third floor and to see Sir Winston Churchill with his entourage of ministerial bodyguards walking along the red carpeted corridor was for Captain Marino a spontaneous occasion and indeed memorable sight.

When Lorenzo and Bradford-Jones entered into one of the most luxurious bedrooms in the hotel he said: 'What is this I see lying on the floor? It looks like a lens cap from someone's camera; it certainly wasn't here before I went down to the American Bar, otherwise I would have noticed.'

'You could have overlooked it,' Melanie said raising her eyebrows and knowing that one of MI5's leading photographers was about to get his ass kicked. 'It was probably left by the previous occupant who was staying in this suite.'

'Yes you could *possibly* be right and I may have overlooked it.' Lorenzo said shaking his head in total disbelief. 'That is a lovely mirror in front of the bed, isn't it Isla?' he added.

'I think they call it art deco, characteristic and typical of the nineteen-twenties.' she said, looking closely at her reflection and then making a rude gesture with one of her fingers to a voyeur on the other side of the wall.

Melanie-Bradford-Jones reached for her handbag which she had placed on top of the dressing table and then proceeded to open it.

'You are not going to shoot me, are you Isla?' Lorenzo said nervously.

'No, Rolando, what gave you that idea? I just want to give you this.'

'It's a solid gold Dunhill cigarette lighter and it has my initials L.G.M on the side.' Lorenzo said gratefully, trying his best to set fire to what was left of the hotel. 'Shall we go down for dinner now, Isla?' he added.

'What dinner?' Melanie replied kissing him passionately on the lips before moving her head down to focus on the zip of his trousers.

Chapter Thirteen

London Euston railway station Monday 20th April 1942

I can recall it was just after ten o'clock that Monday morning when two black Ford 8 motor cars arrived independently on the forecourt of London's Euston railway station. For Captain Lorenzo Giovanni Marino and Herman Klaus Schneider it was to be the start of a tedious five hour journey to Manchester, a place somewhere in the North of England and I can also remember the weather being atrocious; the strong winds and rain battering the sides of rusty corrugated metal sheets which were hiding large man-made pot holes in the road; it was not the kind of morning to contemplate jumping from a high-speed train in order to escape.

I was inside a telephone box pretending to phone someone when I heard the voice on the loudspeaker alerting passengers by saying: 'The train now standing on platform four is the ten twenty-six to Manchester Piccadilly, calling at...' This was when I noticed my colleagues Edward Greaves and Brian Woodruff escorting Schneider down on to the platform and then, following on some distance behind, Steven Halewood and Commander Mark West of New Scotland Yard escorting Captain Marino towards the same train. And, joining in from the rear there were Les McCartney, disguised as a Roman Catholic priest and Lieutenant-Commander Gloria Parker, dressed convincingly as a nun, followed by a station porter who was quickly wheeling their luggage to the train which was now steaming up rapidly in readiness for departure. For Les and Gloria it had been the start of a long, happy and strange relationship when it was revealed they had a bizarre trial run-through in a Savoy hotel bedroom; they have now been married for fifty-nine years and are living with their family in Queensland, Australia.

Both Schneider and Marino, after saying farewell and adieu to their escorts, boarded the train at the same time, albeit from different doors. There was a corridor to gain access to the compartments in the first-class carriages next to the buffet car, bar and restaurant at the front of the train. Schneider, after slamming the door well and truly closed and pulling up the leather strap to secure the window, chose the first compartment to his right. Meanwhile, Captain Marino trundled his way along the same length of corridor holding on to a small brown suitcase and a grey coloured mackintosh which had taken a few spots of rain on one of the arms. He decided to occupy the same compartment as Schneider who was now sitting next to the window staring out on to the busy platform.

'A place has never looked better, looking back.' Schneider said to Marino before offering him a stolen Capstan Full Strength cigarette from his rather nice *Cartier* solid gold cigarette case.

'I take it you don't like London?' Marino said to him, producing *his* gold Dunhill cigarette lighter to create the means of ignition.

'You are damned right,' Schneider replied with a degree of hatred as he muttered something like bar stools under his breath. 'I have had quite enough of bowler hats, fish and chips and red telephone boxes to last me a life time; I will be glad when I get home.'

'And where is your home?' Schneider curiously asked him.

'I don't know, I really don't know.' he replied slowly, shaking his head as the sliding glass door to the compartment was opened by a man who seemed to be a Roman Catholic Cardinal wearing more jewellery than Pontius Pilot and standing directly behind him was a nun.

'Are these seats taken?' Les McCartney, alias Father Paddy O'Hare, said in a not too convincing Irish accent. 'For sure, they are not taken because they are still here.' he added continuing with his blarney.

Lieutenant-Commander Gloria Parker in her guise as Sister Theresa and was looking remarkably like some crazy person from a **'Batman'** comic as she followed him into the compartment and after turning around stiffly to close the door to sit down opposite to McCartney and Schneider.

The next two people to arrive at their door was Lieutenant Garry Volker, a bomber pilot with the United States Air Force and Captain Marylou Anderson, a US Army nurse from Ohio and both seconded to a Royal Air Force station in Manchester, England.

'Hi, you guys,' Lt. Volker said, poking his head just inside the door; his officers' peaked cap resting scruffily on the back of his head. 'Are these two seats free?'

'For sure,' Les McCartney said pointing to the two remaining empty seats next to the door, 'but they may come with a charge if Sister Theresa shows you her poor box.'

'That should be interesting, very interesting.' Volker said to him with a cheeky little boy grin on his face.

Gloria Parker, seated next to Captain Marylou Anderson and being very much aware of the lady's shapely legs couldn't help regretting she had to not only cover her, equally shapely legs, but her figure also within the folds of her habit.

At approximately ten twenty-five the sound of the carriage doors simultaneously banging shut and reverberating throughout the length of the first-class compartments and at precisely ten twenty-six the guard blew his whistle for the train to move slowly out of the station. There was a sudden array of sunlight as the train came out from the rear of the station, passing drab looking houses with their backyards, allotments and air-raid shelters.

'What has four letters ends with IT and is usually found at the bottom of a birdcage?' Gloria asked Les when she looked up pensively from *The Times* crossword puzzle.

'Grit, Sister Theresa.' Les replied, his head now moving from side to side with the jerky movements of the train.

'Oh, has anyone got a rubber?' she asked without hesitation.

'Yes ma'am,' Lieutenant Volker quickly replied. 'I have a pocket full of them.'

After the coughs and splutters had died down and Sister Theresa had got rid of her blushes, a Latin interjection was heard coming from the seat by the window.

'And where, may I ask are you heading?' Captain Marino curiously asked Schneider.

'I am going to Manchester to stay with my sister and brother-in-law; they have a small grocery business in Wythenshawe.' Schneider replied, not knowing exactly whereabouts the small town of Wythenshawe was.

'Do I detect a Polish accent?' Captain Marino asked him.

'No, I am from Czechoslovakia and have been living in Britain since the beginning of the war.' he said convincingly.

'And where is your destination?' Schneider asked him, offering him another of Commander Greaves' extremely strong cigarettes.

'I am in the Merchant Navy,' Captain Marino said, 'and I am going to Manchester to sign on before going back to Malta.' he added.

'You know, I could tell by your accent you come from the island of Malta,' Schneider said to him smugly, 'the Maltese people are surviving pretty well considering they are being starved into submission by the Fuehrer's, sorry, Herr Hitler's Axis forces.'

'Yes, it's shameful, really shameful, to see the inhabitants of Gozo collaborating with the enemy in order to stockpile food out of reach from my family and the starving peoples of Malta.'

'I am sure the food will eventually get through to wherever it is destined for and furthermore, I am convinced the Royal Air Force and the Royal Navy will no doubt take care of it.' Schneider said tongue in cheek.

'I am going to Manchester to learn how to fly Lancaster bomber and the British de Havilland DH.95 Flamingo aircraft.' Lieutenant Volker put in enthusiastically and before he diplomatically said: 'I can then go over to Germany to raise hell.'

'I am over here to stick needles into bums like yours, just shut up lieutenant.' Captain Anderson suggested in a low voice leaning over towards him.

'Yes ma'am,' Volker shouted out with an air of sarcasm in his voice. 'I hear you loud and clear, sir.'

'We are going to take care of the homeless people in Salford, Manchester, aren't we, Sister Theresa?' Father O'Hare said unnecessarily.

'Yes.' was Sister Theresa's reply to his unforgivable lies.

It was exactly midday when a tinkle of a bell was heard to herald lunch and this was when a Northern Rail steward dressed in an impeccably white coat slid the door open to the compartment.

'Lunch is now being served in the restaurant, ladies and gentlemen; if you would like to follow me I will show you to your tables.' Paul Croft of

MI5 alias, Mr Mac Steward and Joe Waiter for the day said in his soft eloquent northern accent.

The compartment became empty as Schneider passed through the door into the corridor to follow his fellow companions into the dining car.

Lieutenant Volker, Captain Anderson, Marino and Schneider were all seated at a table to the right of the narrow corridor and, sitting directly opposite to them on a table especially designed for two midgets were Les McCartney and Lieutenant-Commander Gloria Parker. Volker who was sitting next to the aisle and across from Marino shouted at the steward in a loud New York accent: 'Hey, Mac, I would like a hamburger with the works, along with French Fries,' to which Mr Mac Steward replied: 'Hamburgers are not on the menu, sir and incidentally we call French Fries chips over here.'

'Well Mac, how about those Corny Pastilles everyone keeps on taking about.' Volker continued to ask raucously.

'You mean, our famous delicious Cornish Pasties; they too are not on our menu, sir.' the long suffering steward replied with a sigh.

'Well, what the hell *do* you have?' Volker asked before ordering a large Bourbon on the Rocks.

The three-course menu, consisting of pea and ham soup, ham and egg pie, sauté potatoes and baked beans or, alternatively, the irresistible Scotch smoked salmon served on a bed of lettuce with a cucumber salad, cherry tomatoes and a vinaigrette sauce was delightful; a vanilla ice-cream, strawberry cheesecake or both and, together with the aromatic Arabic coffee became the perfect ending to a perfect meal.

'I thought you guys over here are on rationing.' Lieutenant Volker asked his recently acquired friend, Sister Theresa, after she had slowly and coquettishly licked the last strawberry before pushing it into her mouth.

'The guys travelling in the second-class compartments next door are; shame innit.' Gloria Parker replied dropping her Irish accent for a West Country one.

'I suppose this food sure beats the hell out of that glue you eat for breakfast in your hotel.' Lieutenant Volker continued with his extensive range of knowledge concerning religious matters.

'Don't you mean Scots Porridge Oats?' Sister Theresa asked him, knowing he had probably eaten it himself and then went on to say: 'I live in a sanctuary, a nunnery and it is not a hotel.' she added.

'Gee, ma'am, you must get mighty lonely living in those kind of places.' Volker put in again rather unnecessarily. 'I thought sanctuaries were strictly for the birds.'

'Shut up Volker, and that's an order; do you read me?' Captain Anderson said to him angrily.

'Loud and clear ma'am; loud and clear, sir,' Volker replied.

'It sounds like you need some of that glue stuff to shut that gore-damned mouth of yours.' Anderson told him in no uncertain terms.

When the meal was over, Marino and Schneider got up from the table to go and stand at the bar at the end of the dining car. The introductions became somewhat confused when Lorenzo had to explain that his gold cigarette lighter once belonged to his father-in-law who had recently died from lung cancer and, not so surprisingly had a completely different name. Schneider reciprocated by telling Marino his gold cigarette case once belonged to his grandmother who lived in Czechoslovakia and by choice had to stop smoking because of her health; she regrettably died ten years ago. The lies between them continued deep into the afternoon and the more they told, the more lies they had to tell to get out of it. It was when Schneider, after taking another sip of his whisky, said: 'Do you know, Rolando, I could swear I have seen those two people somewhere before.'

'Which two are you talking about?' Captain Marino asked him as he slugged back another shot of Earl Hague's finest Scotch whisky.

'Why, the priest and the nun; they look extremely familiar but I'm not quite so sure.'

'Do you know, John I had the same feeling myself as soon as they walked into the compartment.' Captain Marino replied, shaking his head and becoming more confused. 'What I do know is priests and nuns don't grow moustaches.'

It was during this interrogative conversation between Schneider and Marino, Paul Croft, now polishing beer glasses behind the bar thought it was time for his dangerous colleagues, Sister Theresa and Father O'Hare to disappear; it was to be the end of their remarkable mission to ensure Schneider and Marino were delivered to the military authorities at Manchester's Piccadilly railway station intact.

Chapter Fourteen

Manchester Piccadilly Railway Station; the afternoon of the same day

"Every Shilling Counts" was the image on the Second World War propaganda posters pasted on every wall of Manchester's bomb-blasted Piccadilly railway station, reminding its citizens of the food shortages and the rationing that was immediately introduced and put into place when the declaration of war was announced by the then Prime Minister, The Right Honourable, Mister Neville Chamberlain.

During the nights of 22nd and 23rd of December 1940 Manchester had to suffer a Christmas Blitz ordered by Germany's Reich Chancellor, Adolf Hitler and orchestrated by Herman Goring and his Nazi German Luftwaffe. It was estimated that nearly sixty-percent of the children of Manchester and Liverpool were evacuated into relatively safe regional parts of the country and some having to travel many miles away, namely Australia. Regardless to say, The LM&S, London Midland and Scottish Railway, continued to function after the glass- roofed railway sheds were attacked by German incendiary bombs on those dreadful nights in December.

Captain Lorenzo Giovanni Marino, the Italian army officer and today, one of Britain's famous MI6 agents, was standing on the platform next to Herman Klaus Schneider, the German spy who was to become the most wanted of MI6's secret double agents in Europe. Lieutenant Garry Volker, USAAF and Captain Marylou Anderson US Army who had just alighted from the train were on the same platform waiting for their transport to arrive to take them eight miles south of Manchester city centre to the Royal Air Force Station Ringway, Cheshire; Lieutenant-Commander Gloria Parker RN and an MI5 officer was with MI5's special agent Les McCartney and were both awaiting the arrival of the Manchester Police's Special Branch to take them to a city centre hotel; their mission which was to successfully deliver Marino and Schneider safely to the North of England was over.

From June 1940, Ringway became the wartime base for No.1 Parachute Training School RAF, which was charged with the initial training of all allied paratroopers trained in Europe, some sixty thousand and for the development of parachute drops of equipment, also the development of military gliding operations. Men such as Captain Marino, Schneider, including women agents of the Special Operations Executive were also trained to jump at Royal Air Force Station Ringway.

Separate transportation arrived starting with a 'Willis' jeep, the type used for the Allied invasion of Sicily codenamed 'Operation Husky'. The vehicle with its distinctive United States Army 'Star' logo stencilled in white on the bonnet was to convey Lieutenant Volker and Captain Anderson to their new place of residence, the Officer's Mess (Building 217) of No. 613 (City of Manchester) Squadron, RAF and accommodated all other Royal Auxiliary Air Force Squadrons, Allied officer pilots, navigators and Air Transport Auxiliary (ATA) air crews.

The situation became confusing to both Schneider and Marino when two Air Force blue staff cars arrived simultaneously outside the station forecourt to convey them to their temporary homes in Cheshire. The first one was to take Herman Klaus Schneider to a Special Operations Executive (SOE) holding centre in a large house in Bowden near Ringway. Meanwhile, Captain Lorenzo Giovanni Marino was to be separately transported to the Special Operations Executive training centre, housed in an Edwardian house on the outskirts of the airfield.

The Royal Air Force Station at Ringway, these days designated simply as Manchester Airport was at that time heavily guarded with civilian Ministry of Defence Police positioned at the outer perimeter fence and barrier and Royal Air Force Military Police on duty at the main entrance to the station. There were three Southside hangars; two hangars built in the North West corner and along with a northside hangar the other three wartime hangars built for use by Fairey Aviation were not demolished until the 1990s. The various types of aircraft on the ground which contributed towards our victories in the air included the famous Avro Lancaster bomber, a Westland Lysander; the James Bond Airplane of WW II, an Armstrong Whitworth Whitley III and a prototype of the Avro Manchester bomber.

There were a number of Belgium trainee parachutists milling around in the numerous Women's Royal Voluntary Service recreation centres inside the hangars at RAF Ringway; their favourite pastime, I can remember, was called "Pass the Red Cross" parcel.

Time had begun to rapidly move on especially for Captain Marino and Schneider who were about to go into separate restaurants to have their evening meal lavishly presented to them. A menu consisting of a starter, main course and a dessert was placed in front of Captain Marino by an RAF waiter whose expertise in trying to cheer people up before attempting to commit suicide was indeed second to none especially the next morning when he said: 'the condemned men and women ate a hearty breakfast.' Marino thought that was really funny when the tomato ketchup he was trying to extract from a rather difficult bottle splotched down on his clean white shirt.

The starter; Chicken & Liver *pate*, Pan-fried red mullet with aubergine and caviar, or alternatively cream of pumpkin soup; the main course was a choice of Scottish rib-eye steak with tomatoes, vegetables *panache* and *Belgium fries*; North Sea haddock coated in a delicate batter with hand-cut chips was to become the more popular of these two main course dishes; the extravagant desserts were either a more than generous serving of vanilla and lemon cheesecake or warm chocolate cake with white chocolate and strawberry ice cream.

Schneider sat down to eat the finest Russian caviar, courtesy of the Polish Air Force black market and this was followed by *macaroni carbonara* with stilton cheese served up on hot toasted sesame seed buns; the desert however was by special request from a Royal Canadian Air Force pilot, Maple syrup and pecan tart.

Pork Pies and Parachutes

It was exactly ten o'clock the following morning when a grey Salvation Army refreshment van appeared in the far distance, moving at speed from side to side along a long narrow track throwing up dust into the already polluted atmosphere; the cavalry were about to arrive to dispense hot tea, coffee and cocoa to the deserving Special Operations Executive parachute trainees (The Baker Street Irregulars) of No 64 Baker Street

London There was a joke bandied about that "SOE" stood for "Stately *'omes* of England", after a large number of country houses and estates it requisitioned and used. The SOE students jumped alongside other trainees but they lodged in separate accommodation particularly in Altrincham, Cheshire near to RAF Ringway. The Salvation Army's excuse for the sausage rolls and potted meat sandwiches being squidgy around the edges was because they had systematically depleted their ration books and the collecting boxes had holes in the bottom due to the shortage of Sellotape; their incredible Melton Mowbray pork pies were indeed inedible and probably started their life inside a Leicestershire gravel pit. The Salvation Army major who guarded his microscopic slices of fruit cake with eyes larger than a Didsbury bagel asked Captain Marino what he had to eat the previous evening? His reply was fish and chips. 'And what did you have to eat last evening, sir?' the major asked Schneider who was now standing in a queue behind Marino and waiting to be served. His reply was *macaroni cheese* on toast and then went on to say: 'Do you know I knew a bald-headed Italian guy who could make omelettes the size of the moon.' Captain Marino replied nervously saying he knew of a German pig that could make a silk purse out of a sow's ear.

The Salvation Army major who had been blessed with the Christian name of Malcolm would insist on telling everyone Jesus wanted him for a sunbeam, but this was until Marino told him that we all live in hope and it was all in our dreams.

'Ah, we meet again Rolando Donatello,' Schneider said to Captain Marino bending forward to whisper in his ear. 'I knew there was something odd about you when we first met on the train.'

'These situations are often reciprocated,' Captain Marino replied as he received a corned beef and onion sandwich and a free copy of the Salvation Army '*The War Cry*' weekly newspaper from the major. 'It is ironic, but I had the same idea about you John Lobkowicz.

The man with the golden gob, Warrant officer Class II, Sergeant Major James (Jimmy) Worrall of the 3rd Parachute Battalion was seconded to RAF Ringway from the Airborne Forces Dept and Battle School in Derbyshire in 1942 to train infantry soldiers and members of the SOE.

All parachute forces had to undergo a twelve day parachute training course and initial parachute jumps were from a converted barrage balloon and finished with five jumps from an aircraft. A large part of the training regime consisted of assault courses and route marching while military exercises included capturing and holding airborne bridgeheads, road or rail bridges and coastal fortifications. Emphasis was given to physical fitness, marksmanship and fieldcraft training; for some it was designed to encourage a spirit of self-discipline, self-reliance and aggressiveness.

'Your stomach sounds like a pigeon loft, Donatello,' Schneider said to Captain Marino smiling for the first time that day. 'I trust it was your stomach?' he added.

'Yes it was, and so would yours if you had eaten a full English breakfast and one of those unbelievable pork pies one could die for having contracted gastroenteritis.' Marino replied holding his stomach as if his insides were about to fall out.

'This morning ladies and gentleman we are going for a short run in the country, about ten miles carrying a Bergen rucksack,' Sergeant Major Worrall said both hands placed on his hips. 'and, I don't want to keep the light on this evening for anyone who is a wee bit slow in coming forward. I do realize one or two of you will fall by the wayside into our specially constructed duck pond, but that will be inevitable when one or two of you will be systematically pushed.

'Inevitable, that's a big word.' Schneider said to Marino, surprising him with another smile.

'I know another big word.' Captain Marino said to him, his eyes now watering and before wiping the steam from his gold-rimmed spectacles.

'Do I know this word, Donatello?' Schneider asked inquisitively.

'Well you should, Lobkowicz, it is called asshole.

'Yes, he is a bit of an asshole.' Schneider so wrongly pointed out when he gazed at the company sergeant major, an arrogant Germanic look on his face.

'It's not him I was referring to.' Captain Marino said raising his eyebrows in total disbelief and wondering just what he was going to come up with next.

'Ah, you mean the funny looking man with the round-pebbled glasses and sells newspapers and pork pies.' Schneider confidently replied and continuing to say: 'I know a big word also; it is called a "Roman Candle".'

Meanwhile, Sergeant Major Worrall introduced one of his subordinates to the squad; a mean looking paratrooper called Corporal William (Punchy) Rushworth, a boxer with a broken nose and scars on both his eyebrows giving one the impression he had just had an altercation with a No 52 North Circular double-decker bus. The 3rd Parachute Battalion was never the same after he left the British Army's Colchester Garrison to take up residence in a Foreign Legion fortification somewhere between Casablanca and the Sahara desert and rumour has it he was last seen in Algeria with two 36 Mills grenades suspended from his ear lobes.

The motto of the Parachute Regiment, *Urinque Paratus* (Latin for "Ready for Anything") and the famous cap badge on the distinctive and Maroon beret (cherry) were to become active in 1941. A large part of the training regime consisted of assault courses and route marching; an ability to cover long distances at speed was also expected of the squad. Initial parachute jumps were from a converted barrage balloon and finished with five jumps from an aircraft. The balloon was raised up and down and tethered with metal cables and hoisted to an altitude of eight hundred feet with the aid of a winch. Those brave and ingenious men and women of the SOE and Military Intelligence Units who had successfully completed the parachute course were entitled to wear the coveted Maroon beret and presented individually with their parachute wings; The Special Operations Executive, MI-9 and their associate counterparts were unique because if you PASSED – you PASSED but if you failed – you would still PASS.

'Do you know what the Para's have got in store for us tonight?' Schneider said to Captain Marino after looking at his watch to check on the time.

'Go on; surprise me with more of your infinite knowledge and mind-boggling wisdom.' Captain Marino replied knowing Schneider was going to attempt to put the fear of God into him once again.

'Well, Lorenzo, the RAF waiter at breakfast told me in confidence that we will be escorted to the gymnasium after dinner and forced to jump off a twelve foot platform on to a trampoline, we are then to spring forward and land on another platform which is not quite so high.'

'That will be most interesting and relatively simple,' Captain Marino confidently said to Schneider. 'I was extremely good at physical exercises when I was at college, it should be a piece of cake.' he added.

'Not if they turn the lights out before you jump.' Schneider so kindly put in making Marino's stomach feel worse than ever and continuing to say: 'I was also told that when you jump from a balloon the parachute takes longer to open and the ground is faster than you think.

The morning progressed with Corporal Rushworth systematically placing at least thirty trainee parachutists in three ranks at one arm's length apart. The weather had changed for the worst making life even more difficult than ever for Marino and Schneider and indeed for the entire squad when it began to rain torrentially. Corporal Rushworth gave the order for them all to stand to attention and then to turn right three abreast in an easterly direction at the side of the main runway before setting off on a late morning stroll.

'Don't worry ladies and gentlemen; some of you will be in Italy, Germany and France sooner than you think.' Corporal Rushworth emphasised when he saw Schneider throwing up at the side of a road.

*

Twelve days later in MI-9's secret office at RAF Ringway.

Herman Klaus Schneider was given his brief; he had been instructed to go back to his home town of Osnabruck via Herford, Westfalia. He was to be flown the four hundred and sixty-five miles at an altitude of eighteen thousand feet from Netheravon in Wiltshire to the drop zone outside the town of Herford where he would parachute from an Armstrong Whitworth Whitley Mk.III of No. 297 Squadron Royal Air Force. Schneider was supplied with another handgun to replace the artillery piece which became so ominous from inside his coat pocket. The Walther P38 9 mm Parabellum, an eight round semi-automatic and a typical example of German Vorsprung durch Technik, designed to blow someone's head off immediately at a relatively close range, was considered ideal for Schneider's requirements. He was also supplied with a "Naughty Package" consisting of a concealed "stinger" pencil designed to blow up your next door neighbour, a packet of explosive bubble gum and a trap primed ready to wish Desmond the Mouse a very happy Christmas.

Captain Lorenzo Giovanni Marino, unlike Schneider, had been given his orders the previous day by MI-9; however, he was to fly into enemy occupied France from a Westland Lysander Mk.III (Lizzie) aircraft from a secret airfield outside Newmarket, Cambridgeshire. He was then to begin his covert operations starting from a small, unprepared airstrip in Fontainebleau, south of Paris and, it was from here the French Resistance would help him to make his way to a Parisian railway station to transport him to his next port of call Marseilles on route to Rome. Marino was issued with an Italian service pistol; a 9 mm Parabellum Beretta Modello M1934, a seven round semi-automatic, which he had been familiar with and was part of his equipment in North Africa, but that was until a Bedouin tribesman exchanged half a dozen new-laid eggs for it to be put into safe-keeping.

For Herman Schneider and Captain Lorenzo Marino it was the end of the intensive parachute and endurance training course but before they shook hands Schneider said: 'Do you know, Donatello I thought I had seen that Father O'Hare and Sister Theresa before, they said they were both members of the O'Donovan family where I was staying at Bradley Hall.

'Yes, it's funny you should say this because I am convinced I saw them both in the Savoy Hotel a couple of weeks ago but they looked entirely different.' Lorenzo said, scratching the back of his head and by now becoming totally confused.

'Well that will explain everything.' Schneider said smugly.

'Explain what, exactly, John Lobkowicz.'

'Do you not remember Sister Theresa had one tit bigger than the other when we were travelling together on the train?'

'You mean she had a handgun packed inside her ecclesiastical fancy dress costume.' Captain Marino said conjuring up the image of

Lieutenant-Commander Gloria Parker of MI5 in his mind.

'Yes exactly, my dear friend.' Schneider replied.

Chapter Fifteen

Sunday morning 3rd May 1942 at RAF Netheravon, Salisbury Plain, Wiltshire

A Westland Lysander Mk.III had flown Schneider the one hundred and eighty-seven miles from No.1 Parachute Training School, RAF Ringway to No. 297 Squadron RAF Netheravon based on Salisbury Plain, Wiltshire, in the South of England. The squadron originally formed as the parachute exercise squadron at RAF Ringway in December 1941 was moved to the RAF's picturesque drop zone at Netheravon on 22 January 1942. The small aircraft, equipped with two forward firing 7.7 mm (.303) Browning machine guns and four 20 lb (9 kg) bombs attached precariously underneath the rear fuselage, was flown by one crew; a skilled RAF pilot with two years experience of shooting down enemy aircraft and his expertise handling rugged, short-take-off and landing was indeed commendable. Squadron Leader Keith Knowles who, from July-September 1940 flew a Supermarine Spitfire 1A of No. 610 Squadron, Royal Air Force based at Biggin Hill, Kent and in subsequent years the famous Westland Lysander when he was to be the proud recipient of the Distinguished Flying Cross presented by King George VI. His stories of air combat when his earphones crackled with loud, frantic calls; "Bandits", 11 o'clock Low! before he and his squadron engaged the enemy from the rear, were remarkable and breathtaking. The terminology used by the RAF to identify enemy aircraft during WWII were "Bogeys" and "Bandits"; bogeys were unknowns, unidentified aircraft and bandits unmistakably hostile.

When the propellers of the Lysander had stopped rotating the rear canopy slid open and Schneider climbed down the fixed ladder positioned on the portside, together with his luggage after developing cramp in one of his legs; the uncomfortable seat in the rear cockpit of the airplane had also become a pain in his backside and if it wasn't for the picture of Jane Russell on the front cover of an American glamour magazine which had been resting on his lap since take-off, would certainly have made his body seize up completely. Oh, how I remember the beautiful and sexy Jane

Russell, the Hollywood sex symbol of the 1940's and 50's whose breasts some theorize actually won World War Two.

It was just after ten when Greaves, Halewood and I waited, one behind the other like The Three Wise Monkeys to greet Schneider as he reached the bottom rung of the ladder to put one foot on to the recently mowed grass verge at the side of the main runway. Edward, purporting to be Peter Watson, and wearing his famous dark grey trench-coat and brown trilby, was blowing into his hands as if he was about to be attacked with severe frost bite.

'Ah, guten Morgen, Na ja! Herr Watson,' ('Good morning Mr Watson and here we go again.') Schneider said brushing himself down and attempting to remove the unwanted creases in his trousers.

Rear Admiral Sir Steven Halewood was introduced to Schneider by Edward Greaves as Clive North, one of his lesser colleagues from the foreign office who enjoyed making tea and walking around misty airfields at ten o'clock on Sunday mornings with dew-drops hanging from his nose. My immediate thoughts after the introductions between Schneider, Greaves and Halewood had been finalized were that I never liked this Herman Klaus Schneider, but then why should I respect an enemy agent who was hell-bent in turning double to save himself from the gallows.

'We have brought you a copy of today's *Sunday Times*, Schneider.' Greaves said, handing it over to him as if it were a priceless document, 'I see he's at it again.' he added, shaking his head.

'Who, is at it again?' Schneider asked Greaves as we all walked towards an RAF Nissan-hut, the flight office for the pilot, Squadron Leader Keith Knowles, to check-in and to dump his unwanted baggage with us.

'Your friendly leader, Herr Hitler, of course,' Edward said to him angrily. 'He is still bombing the hell out of Malta but the islanders are a pretty strong bunch and will never surrender.'

'I see you are calling me by my real name again.' Schneider said to Edward. 'What has happened to John Lobkowicz?'

'Don't you worry about that,' Edward said as he turned to me and smiled. 'tomorrow night, my dear friend, you will be back in your own country and using your original name.'

'Thank you so much, Mister Watson; how can I possibly repay you for such gratitude.' Schneider said sarcastically.

'Now, don't overdo it, Schneider.' Greaves quickly emphasised. 'The money I paid the Royal Air Force for your ticket can easily be refunded.'

Arthur Stokes, the landlord of The George Inn, opened the doors to his pub in the High Street at precisely mid-day as the bells from the Church of All Saints in the parish of Netheravon began to toll loudly. The George pub, which was used as a watering hole for the air crews, had once boasted a good social life and a fine selection of Arkell's ales matured and dispensed from oak barrels contained in a cool and dark cellar. During World War Two there were lots of foreigners who, unlike Schneider, needed a place to lodge and some may have stayed above this pub.

Four Dimple mugs of Arkell's 3B Best Bitter Beer or affectionately known as 'BBB' were carefully brought to a table by the window by Mrs Evelyn Stokes, the landlady, who like her *Utrinque Paratus* paratrooper customers, was "Ready for Anything". She had the largest backside I have ever seen, likened to Kirkstone Pass and rumour has it her husband once said, Evelyn comes in handy when he wants somewhere to park his bike.

'Can I ask you where your other boyfriend is, Watson?' Schneider enquired warily as he slowly opened the door to a large wooden cupboard in the snug bar just to see if anyone was behind it.

'Which boyfriend are you referring to, Schneider, I have several,' Edward said jokingly as another four pints of Wiltshire's finest amber brew was slopped down in front of them by an angry Arthur who had spent most of Sunday morning playing nursemaid to his not so lucky black cat which had fallen fowl of a size ten parachutists boot the previous evening.

'The one that walks around pretending to be a policeman and thinks he owns half of London.' Schneider so boldly pointed out to him.

'Oh, you mean, Brian Woodruff, whoops! Sorry, Chief Inspector Bruce Johnson,' I said to Schneider before he gave Edward Greaves a chance to put *his* foot in it. 'He has another engagement in Cambridge.' I quickly added.

'Ja, Ja, and yes I can imagine, and it will possibly be with that awful woman Dorothy Arkwright, Selina O'Donovan or whatever her name is.' Schneider replied, shaking his head in total disbelief at what I had just said.

'Did you know, Schneider that the ale you are fortunate to drink in this establishment is called 'BBB' and stands for "Big Boy's Beer"?' Greaves said to him, trying to change the mood of the entertainment.

'Ja, the beer is good, but not as good as *Osnabrucker Pils* beer which we have in Germany.' he replied, pursing his lips with arrogant confidence.

'Yes, I suppose we could say the same thing about your food.' Greaves pointed out to Schneider waving a finger directly in front of his face, before continuing to say: 'The *Bratwurst* sausages in Germany taste extremely good, but not so good as British fish and chips served up in newspaper.'

'I will certainly miss trying to work out some of the British coded messages which were very cleverly inserted into the '*Daily Herald*' crossword puzzles,' Schneider replied with an air of sadness when he continued to tell us: 'On several visits to your *Schnell Imbiss*, Fish and Chip shop takeaways, almost invariably the print became obscured by them using far too much salt and vinegar. You know most things in life are free, Watson, but in this particular case *I* deserve a refund.' he emphasized.

'You're not Jewish by any chance, Schneider?' Edward so blatantly put in without him properly thinking it through.

'Nein! Nein! No! No! I most certainly am not,' Schneider quickly replied banging his barrel-shaped pint pot down on the table. 'but, it is at times like this I wish I was.' he added.

Meanwhile, to ease the pressure from what seemed to be an overheated conversation, Halewood produced a package from inside his coat pocket. The small brown paper bundle contained ten thousand German Reich Marks, enough money to keep Schneider in *Osnabrucker pils* beer for several weeks.

'Danke, mein Herr, thank you sir, the money will certainly come in handy if I am caught and the Gestapo put me through extreme interrogation.' Schneider said before asking Greaves: 'During these last few weeks I have often wondered how you became blind in one eye?'

'It is quite simple my dear chap,' Edward replied smugly. 'it was from keeping an eye on people like you.' he added.

Schneider that evening became more disillusioned when he couldn't decide whether to throw himself into the River Avon, go to church or to wait until the following morning to commit suicide by eating one of the Salvation Army's lethal Melton Mowbray pork pies. He chose the most honourable which was to go to the Anglican Church of All Saints to ask *his* God's forgiveness and to ensure he would have a safe parachute drop over Germany the following night.

The British Double-Cross System in April, 1942 had a total of 19 German spies working as double agents and like Schneider their sentence was commuted as they were sent to the front as parachutists. Once caught the spies were deposited in the care of the one-eyed, Edward Greaves at the Maximum Security prison at Borden, Brentwood, Essex whereafter Greaves, a notorious and brilliant MI6 interrogator, had picked apart their life history, the agents were either spirited away to be imprisoned or, executed or if judged acceptable, offered the chance to turn double on the Germans. Greaves, in particular, believed that turning German spies against their masters would have numerous benefits; for example, determining what information the *Abwehr* wanted or to actively mislead them as part of a military deception.

Chapter Sixteen

Monday 4th May 1942. A secret Special Operations Executive airfield and base somewhere in Newmarket, Cambridgeshire

Captain Lorenzo Giovanni Marino had that evening, travelled the one hundred and sixty miles from RAF Ringway, Cheshire, inside a Royal Air Force Flamingo airplane, landing safely on to a secret airfield somewhere in Newmarket, marked out by four or five torches.

It was during that afternoon a Westland Lysander Mk.III and painted matt black was flown by Squadron Leader Keith Knowles, the pilot who had delivered Herman Klaus Schneider to RAF Netheravon the previous day. Knowles had been given orders to fly to the picturesque market town of Newmarket in Cambridgeshire where the aircraft was subjected to rigorous mechanical checks prior to being flown into enemy occupied France during the early hours of Tuesday night carrying one of the most famous spies in military history, the "Condor" Captain Lorenzo Marino, alias Rolando Donatello.

It was exactly ten o'clock when the British de Havilland DH.95 twin engine Flamingo flown by Lieutenant Garry Volker USAAF and Pilot Officer Richard (Tiger Moth) Ball RAF, came to a halt after traversing a forty-five degree turn on to an uneven stretch of concreted apron overgrown with weeds. The Royal Air Force radio operator, Flight Sergeant Ken Smalley, after sliding the door open on the port side, helped Captain Marino and three parachutists of de Gaulle's Free French Army to climb down the four steps which had been pushed out from the inside. The French connection consisted of two men and a woman who were called "Jelly Babies" because of their expertise in working alongside the Resistance Movement to blow up trains and ruthlessly dispose of France's enemies. Their mission was to be parachuted into enemy occupied territory with the aim of creating a diversion by blowing up the main train line in Normandy between Caen and Lisieux. After the war all three won France's highest award, the Croix de Guerre and were presented by General Charles de Gaulle himself.

Lorenzo precariously climbed down the steel mounted stairway with his back to Colonel Brian Woodruff, Commander Mark West and Pauline Cox MI5, who this time had the alias of Sergeant Shirley Pringle of New Scotland Yard; all were there to greet the passengers' timely arrival.

'Ah, we meet again, *Commissario* Bruce Johnson, *Ispettore* Philip Green.' Captain Marino said to Colonel Brian Woodruff and Commander Mark West sounding like an Italian version of Vera Lynn, as he turned around to face them and before continuing to say: 'We always seem to be meeting at various arrival and destination points. I can remember it all too well; it was at London Euston railway station; I had just arrived from Scotland after being subjected to a vigorous high altitude training exercise with a British Special Forces Unit and you were both there at the station to see that I didn't do a runner before being transported to one of your secret MI6 offices in Oxford Street.'

'Can we put this conversation into some kind of language we can all understand?' Woodruff pointed out in the dark.

'Si, Senor; here we go, forty Lorries in a row, they're not Lorries, they are trucks; see what's in' em, cows and ducks.'

'Yes, well, thank you so much for impressing us with your Italian poetry Marino, you are about as funny as an in-growing toe nail and let's hope you don't end up in one of those trucks tomorrow night.' Commander West said to him with an air of sarcasm in his voice.

'I'll have you know,' Captain Marino said, 'had it not been for an extremely low profile and a desire not to hug the limelight, I could easily have won the poetry competition in the officers' mess three weeks ago.'

'I seem to recall we had some difficulty with your language and Latin temperament when Inspector Green and I met you at the railway station.' Colonel Woodruff implied.

'Oh you mean when I was annoyed at being taken-in by a woman who permanently carries a mattress around on her back just in case she meets another sucker.' Captain Marino replied reluctantly.

'No, I wasn't referring to Melanie, whoops! I'm sorry, Isla McPherson.' Woodruff said, coughing and spluttering loudly. 'It was when you were in a hurry to go to the toilet.'

'She, amongst other unmentionable names, is called by her stage name,

Lola Morgan,' Marino told him, 'and furthermore I would like you both to know she and her chamois-leather knickers are probably sailing to America via Lisbon right now.' he added.

'Don't you mean camiknickers?' Commander West asked.

'No.' Captain Marino replied. 'She takes them off before cleaning the windows.'

'Ha, ha, very funny Marino,' Colonel Woodruff said. 'I think you have been in Britain far too long and it is interesting to know of her whereabouts and I shall certainly follow up this new line of enquiry following Lola's sudden disappearance. Tell me Marino, are there anymore funny little stories you would like to tell us and could only have originated from some tribal outpost to the north of Hadrian's Wall.' Commander West put in.

'And, may I introduce you to this young lady-in-waiting; she is one of my fellow colleagues and is dying to meet you.' Brian Woodruff put in enthusiastically.

'I bet she is.' Captain Marino said as he looked at a pair of stiletto heels gradually sinking into the boggy grass verge at the side of the runway.

'This is Sergeant Pauline, sorry, Shirley Pringle of New Scotland Yard's Special Branch.' Woodruff explained, giving Marino the impression he wasn't a very good liar.

'If she is, then I will show my arse in Harrods' window.' Lorenzo said with a confident, albeit relieved look on his face.

Meanwhile, Lieutenant Garry Volker and Tiger Moth Ball were still sitting side-by-side in the cockpit. Garry, who had just given half of his Melton Mowbray pork pie to Richard, said:

'Gee, I knew I had seen that guy before. He is Maltese and was travelling from London to Manchester in the same railway compartment as me and Captain Marylou Anderson a couple of weeks ago.'

'It's a funny old word isn't it and life can be kind of strange, old buddy, really strange.' Pilot Officer Ball said putting on a pseudo American accent before continuing to say he needed to go visit the toilet immediately.

'Do you know, Sir,' Flight Sergeant Ken Smalley said to Lieutenant

Volker and now leaning forward over Pilot Officer Ball's empty seat, 'our friendly passenger is about as much Maltese as Bing Crosby; in fact he is an Italian army officer and comes from Naples.'

'Hey man, why didn't you tell me this before departure and then perhaps I could have done a detour and dropped him off over the North Sea.' Volker replied, jumping up and down on his seat frantically and once again rendering his American sense of humour.

Captain Marino, walking towards a beautifully restored 18th-Century mansion-house with stained glass windows said to Woodruff: 'I hate Mondays and you know I can't help but feel I've been somewhat cheated during the past few weeks.'

'What the hell are you talking about, Marino? If you don't like Mondays, you must be doing something wrong!' Woodruff replied in his hardened West Country accent.

'I am talking about going through all that trouble to learn how to be a parachutist and to jump out of airplanes.' Captain Marino said, slowly shaking his head in total disbelief. 'It now looks as if I'm not going to be afforded that opportunity and the only jumps I came up against was when I was poked in the back by Sergeant Major Jimmy Worrell's pace stick to get me out from my bed and then when I visited the medical centre to obtain a sedative from a United States Army nurse called Marylou Anderson with the rank of captain. I am now as fit as a butchers dog, Johnson and it's a great pity your sawdust sausages rank so highly inside a wartime ration book.'

Alsop Towers, the same evening

The entrance to Alsop Towers was through a large glass conservatory with a menagerie in keeping with exterior Georgian architecture and internal decor and like our hotel, The Hotel Broadlands in Valletta, it also had a blue African parrot guarding the door, however this one would insist on repeating "Oh no, not another one" when a stranger entered the house. Meanwhile, a tethered monkey called Boris which had a flair for pinching ladies bottoms and throwing darts at potential escapees, jumped up and down noisily on top of discarded banana skins. The conservatory was likened to an overgrown Amazonian jungle with an array of cascading ferns and an assortment of tall tropical plants, palms, creepers and aspidistras growing wildly in large pink terracotta pots; it seemed they were all waiting impatiently to strangle anyone who dared criticize Fred Patterson, the head gardener's botanical expertise, in this staging post enroute to hell.

Pauline Cox was the second last person to enter the building followed by Commander Mark West and became overcome with embarrassment, albeit disappointed when she discovered it was an over-sexed primate that had pinched her bottom and not him.

"Oh no, not another one; that's the way to do it".' the parrot repeated, bobbing up and down squawking on its perch like a demented boxer.

'Shut up, Horatio.' Brian Woodruff said to the parrot. 'He always does this in front of strangers and new guests inside the house.' he added.

The "Jelly Babies" who were called Colonel Jean-Paul Blin, Brigadier Marcel Provost and Mademoiselle Severine Aubril had some minutes earlier been escorted to Alsop Towers by a Free French Intelligence Officer and subjected to verbal abuse and rude abnormalities by Horatio and Boris.

A retired Royal Air Force Squadron Leader called Percy Stevens, a tall gangly man wearing an RAF all-leather trimmed sheepskin flying jacket and Halcyon Mk 9 goggles, had been waiting patiently at the conservatory door to take everyone's luggage into the house. He was the landing zone's Air Traffic Controller, Baggage Handler, Radio Operator and the epitome of eccentricity around Alsop Towers; a cross between the comic book characters, TINTIN and BIGGLES.

'We will be staying here tonight, Marino.' Brian Woodruff said and at the same time covering his mouth when he deliberately yawned and looked in Cox's direction.

'Well, this could prove to be quite interesting.' Captain Marino replied, finding it quite impossible not to laugh.

'And what, if I may ask is going to be quite interesting, Marino?' Mark West put in.

'It will be because I have just seen Sister Theresa hurrying up the stairs with a man who looks remarkably like the priest, Father Paddy O'Hare.'

'Just who are these people you are referring to?' Brian Woodruff asked, knowing full well who they were.

'You know damned well who they are, Johnson.' Captain Marino said as he kicked the ankle-biting monkey with his size eight black leather Sicilian hand-stitched shoes. 'Those two have been following me around ever since I checked into your prestigious London Savoy Hotel and then they had the audacity to travel to Manchester with me in the same compartment.'

'Oh you mean, Fred McNair and Ginger Lodgers, they often stay here.' Brian told him whilst having a bit of trouble sounding his R's after looking at a portrait of the famous nineteen-thirty dance couple.

'*Commissario* Bruce Johnson, whatever your name is; are there anymore fairy stories you would like to tell me and is there anything else you could organise in a brewery.' Captain Marino asked him.

'Now, now Marino, let's not get too excited because this time tomorrow you will be on your way home.'

Lorenzo, now feeling low at a high point said "Like the fella once said, aint that a kick in the head."

Alsop Towers boasted twenty-six bedrooms, a reception hall, breakfast room, restaurant and cocktail bar and everything was set to receive the new arrivals. Percy Stevens who had just undertaken a quick change act, now dressed in a green and white striped waistcoat and bow tie, showed everyone to their respective rooms prior to having dinner in the candle-lit restaurant adjacent to the black and white tiled reception hall.

The Cambridge Bar proved to be quite popular with the guests as a place to drink and eat delicious appetisers and to generally relax prior to sitting down around a huge mahogany table in the centre of an extravagantly decorated room. The red velvet wallpaper exuded richness and was like one could see inside a cinema before the lights went out when one waited for the show to begin.

A menu was placed on top of the bar for the guests to peruse before going into the restaurant. The starter, a take it or leave it choice, was called soup of the day, reminiscent of dirty fishpond water which looked as though it had been visited by a flotilla of tadpoles. The main course consisting of a steak and kidney pudding, mash potatoes, broad beans and a kind of gravy which had regrettably taken on the appearance of black crude oil once it had been rigorously stirred by the resident cook, Signora Margarita Rodriguez. Margarita, a rather plump Brazilian lady who had worked for the British Foreign Office since losing her husband somewhere between London and Rio de Janeiro during the outbreak of the war and had taken on the mantle of a gastronomic expert at Alsop Towers, gave everyone the impression she knew nothing and kept her mouth firmly shut. Rumour has it her husband, Philip, died of food poisoning. The piéce de résistance of her culinary expertise was the desert; a miniature tartlet smothered in Kellogg's cornflakes and a more than generous serving of Tate & Lyle treacle. An assortment of cheeses was to follow which could easily have graced the smallest of mousetraps after being given the Holiest of Benedictions by Les McCartney prior to him disappearing up the stairs with Lieutenant-Commander Gloria Parker RN.

There was a thunderous knock on Captain Marino's bedroom door and it sounded as if the person outside had been familiar with a percussion instrument, namely, an orchestration timpani kettle drum. It was the formidable Pauline Cox purporting to be Sergeant Shirley Pringle of New Scotland Yard's Special Branch.

'Bonjourno, and hello again, Captain Marino,' Pauline said to him with an enthusiastic smile knowing it was him she would be going to bed with that evening. 'Is that a gun in your pocket or are you just happy to see me and may I come in before we go down for dinner; everyone will be calling you Rolando Donatello this evening and that will be fun won't it?' she added with an air of sarcasm in her speech.

'Yes, I mustn't forget that when I am pretending to be a Maltese academic tucking into a plate full of spaghetti and lashings of chocolate ice cream to follow.' Lorenzo said to her, imitating and reciprocating her dry sense of humour.

'But spaghetti and ice cream is not on the menu for this evening's meal; it is steak and kidney pudding and Mrs Rodriguez's gravy one could die for.' Pauline said with a rather bizarre look on her face followed by an uncalled for spasmodic giggle.

'Please, don't give up your daytime job to become a comedienne, Sergeant Pringle, you may find it a total waste of time.' Lorenzo quickly replied.

'I'm sorry, Captain Marino, it was really insensitive of me to say that and I will certainly try and make it up to you later when I will call you by your real Christian name, Lorenzo; may I call you Lorenzo?'

'Yes of course you may, after all it is my given name and I am not likely to forget that, am I?'

'No darling, you won't.' Pauline said to Lorenzo kissing him gently on the lips as she glided from side to side like a drunken wood nymph and before he forcefully tossed her on to the four-poster bed, her long brown hair covering most of her face when her head hit the soft white cotton pillow to make a deep impression.

'You were not in any way involved in playing the drums by any chance, Shirley' Captain Marino asked making inroads to remove one of her under-garments.

'No.' was the reply 'but I once pushed an upright piano in a police marching band and I can also play a good mouth organ.'

'We are going to be late for dinner.' Lorenzo said to her as the elastic in her French cami-knickers snapped when his hand forcefully pulled them down over her thunderous thighs.

'Sod the dinner,' Pauline said, breathing heavily and screaming loudly as if she was about to be murdered. 'it is breakfast I am really looking forward to.' she added.

It was four days later when Captain Marino said to Joey Macaroni, Britain's MI6 agent in Rome, 'I didn't even know the lady when she called me sonna ma bitch!!' And Joey replied by saying: 'She is a no lady; she is a my wife!'

Chapter Seventeen

Back to the land of the living or so it seemed

I was suddenly shaken violently by Mary; she was ordering me to snap out of whatever it was I was dreaming when I fell asleep listening to the curator, Father Jonathan Zammit pontificating about the Phoenician and Hellenistic period, starting around the seventh century B.C., when favoured Maltese people would be buried underneath the fertile fields of Rabat in rock hewn catacombs.

'Come on, James snap out of it, I just knew you wouldn't enjoy the excursion to 'Popeye' village and you would rather have preferred to visit the Malta Classic Car Collection at the private Automobile Museum in Qawra.' Mary said as she searched for my cigarettes amongst the recently acquired souvenirs in her handbag.

'I hope you are not going to smoke in here, Lad.' Frank Riley said to me as I fumbled around in my pocket for my cigarette lighter. 'It's musty down here as it is without you adding to the already polluted atmosphere.' he added.

'You always get one, don't you?' I said to Mary as she looked up towards the low ceiling to see a crack in the cement giving everyone the impression it was about to fall in. 'Come on let's get the hell out of here.' I insisted.

I suppose, Mary and I were like two miners emerging from a disused coal mine when the much welcomed rays of sunlight beamed down from overhead on to our faces. The driver of the minibus who was called Eddie Fenech suggested we both have a cup of tea and *pastizzi* at Crystal Palace in Rabat or sample a large bottle of Maltese *'Marsovin Special Reserve'* red wine to help revive our blood circulation. He then went on to tell us we could be introduced to two of his best friends; a Mr Simmonds and a Mr Farsons who are the island's main brewer, producing *Cisk*, an excellent lager and ale called *Hop Leaf.* Fenech insisted on telling us about Air Malta's ongoing overhead problems, flying holiday-makers in and out of the island every day. He ended by saying that one day Malta could end up with not having any tourist industry at all and only the population, fixtures and fittings will be left. Nicholas later however, became the saviour of the day, tearfully passing his 'Popeye Village' baseball cap round the passengers when the driver of the bus told us he had that morning lost his wallet and his four year old Siamese cat called Springer who would insist on jumping out through fourth floor bedroom windows; it is of little consequence to learn that Springer the cat was named after a famous American television personality.

Mary and I arrived at the Crystal Palace bar in Rabat no worse for wear having hobbled the short distance to Saint Pauls Street close to the square which incidentally is noted for its overgrown flora and fauna namely, aniseed bushes and weeds. Betty Ward and Vera Cruikshank as luck would have it were sitting at one of the shiny Formica top tables when we warily walked in through the wide open door. Vera who was munching her way through her third *pastizzi*, a pea cake which had been curried to death by the nuns of Saint Agatha, became a little nervous when she looked up to see flies being zapped and instantly fried as they unwittingly flew into an exterminating machine precariously fixed high above a wall.

I ordered a bottle of '*Marsovin Green Label*' white wine and two large portions of freshly baked *lasagne* which because of the divine *Oregano* and *Parmesan* cheese smells, it was obvious the food had just come out of the oven. Mary afterwards said this was how lasagne was supposed to look and taste like and not a gooey mess that some restaurants have the ordacity to serve up back home. Vera who kept talking with her mouth full of *Ricotta* cheese and burnt pastry said to us: 'I save wine bottles; they have some interesting ones in my local Spar shop.'

'Yes, well that is really interesting, Vera,' I said to her and then continued with the dreaded conversation by saying: 'If we saved wine bottles we wouldn't be able to get out of our apartment.'

'Oh you have your own little flat, Pet do you?' Betty asked in her eloquent Newcastle upon Tyne accent and then continued to tell us she owned her own council house in Stockton-on-Tees and had a static two berth caravan in Morecambe Bay which she rents out for a hundred and fifty pounds per week; 'it's by the sea you know.' she added whilst trying her best to insult my intelligence.

'I live in sheltered accommodation close to Betty,' Vera put in smugly, 'I only have to press the bell in my living room and a warden appears to see to your every need.' she added.

'I suppose, it's just like upstairs and downstairs with maids running around in frilly wispies.' I said to her trying not to splatter the table with lasagne.

'They're called waspies, darling.' Mary said in a low voice and at the same time nudging me with her elbow.

'Wispies, waspies, does it matter? They all look the same to me.' I explained.

'Here we go again, back to Titbits and the Health and Efficiency magazines I found underneath your bed are we, James?' Mary asked.

'Don't be so silly, Mary,' I said in a very low voice so as not to allow people to hear what I was about to say next; which was: 'Health and Efficiency magazines don't have young ladies wearing waspies.'

I said to Mary I needed to go outside to take in some fresh air because the food smells and tobacco smoke were beginning to get right up my nose. The fragrances from the frangipani plants and aniseed bushes were indeed refreshing after my asthma attack, however, that was to be short lived when I saw Stan and Hilda marching up the road towards the bar followed by Frank and Mavis and Nicholas being not far behind. It had now become obvious to me that the minibus driver had more fingers in pies than Pythagoras himself.

'How are you doing, Whack?' Stanley asked as he wiped the beads of perspiration from the top of his brow with a much-used handkerchief.

'Well, I was doing alright until I saw you lot.' I said underneath my breath.

I said to Mary couldn't we go back to Valletta by taxi because I had a gut feeling these people may end up singing "We'll Meet Again" in the bus.

'Now, James come on and be sensible.' Mary said as she fumbled around in her handbag to find her tiny pill box. 'A taxi fare from here to Valletta would be very expensive and besides we have already paid for this interesting, albeit bizarre excursion, to 'Popeye Village'.

As usual, I agreed with her but not entirely when she comes on with one of her heads and I wasn't wrong when Stan Parry began to sing "Bless 'Em All" followed by "Wish Me Luck (As You Wave Me Goodbye)", and you've guessed "We'll Meet Again".

'We'll meet again, not if I can help it.' I said to Mary when I saw Stan the man fall from the minibus on to the pavement directly outside of their hotel in Sliema.

Mary and I arrived at our hotel just after three pm and decided a well deserved cup of coffee was needed to revive us from having to deal with these downright awful people. Doris, the young green-eyed Italian waitress from Old Bakery Street in Valletta greeted us at the door to the coffee shop after we had warily put our feet down on to the pavement from an extremely high non-user friendly minibus. She was sufficiently interested to know where we had both been and more importantly wanted to know what we would like to drink in the way of alcoholic refreshment. I asked her if she would like a bite of my delicious Popeye nougat to which she replied: 'no thank you, I was once bitten and now I am twice shy and besides I have already eaten.'

I said to her: 'don't get too excited Miss Loren because I'm old enough to be your great- grandfather.'

At this point, the Airtours representative, Mrs Azzopardi appeared in the doorway with what seemed to be a bag full of cheap and nasty umbrellas.

'Good afternoon Helen.' I said politely and with the idea she may have given us some sort of compensation after suffering the total waste of time Popeye and his rickety old wooden village that wouldn't have been out of place on the top of a bonfire.

'Mrs Azzopardi, if you don't mind.' Helen said in her not so charitable Sliema posh accent. 'This afternoon I have been hopping and according to the weather forecast it is going to rain tomorrow.' she added.

I said to her when I'm at home in London I like to hop down to the pub.

'No, Sir James, I like to go shopping.' Helen said pursing her big guppy lips to accentuate every syllable.

'Why do we have to keep on calling you Mrs Azzopardi when you have the name of Helen depicted on your badge?' I curiously asked.

'It is because I have just recently been married to the most wonderful man in the world; he is called Mr Azzopardi and is the head of the Police Forensic and Pathologist Unit here in Valletta.' she replied haughtily.

'His Christian name wouldn't be Charles by any chance because Mary and I saw him on the news last evening and it would seem he has become a prime target for the Mafia.' I quickly put in and then tried not to smile when her lips, now resembling deflated rubber tyres began to swirl round like jelly fish in front of my eyes.

'Yes, well we do have three lovely dogs guarding our large farmhouse in Birkirkara; two German Shepherds and a Rottweiler.' Mrs Azzopardi told us with a gook-like expression on her face.

'Mary and I are going to Gozo tomorrow, aren't we dear?' I said to 'Guppy' just to keep the conversation alive.

'Yes I know,' she replied, 'and unless you have forgotten I have arranged everything for you and don't forget your umbrellas.' reminding us once again it was going to rain tomorrow.

'Well, if it's going to be like today's little outing, it will be a hoot.' I said to Mary.

'My husband and I went abroad to Gozo for our honeymoon,' Mrs Guppy had to inform us. 'We stayed in a five-star hotel in Marsalforn which had a big swimming pool, sun beds and a nice looking Maltese waiter called Charlie.'

My immediate thoughts were: 'Oh no, not another one,' and this was when I said to her: 'He's not from Birkirkara is he by any chance?' Her reply was, as a matter of fact he is and how the hell did I know.

After a not too convincing statement when I told Mrs Azzopardi that I was conversant with the Maltese culture, she stepped aside and said: 'Anyway, I have to go now and collect my husband from the court houses in Republic Street,' and hoped Mary and I would enjoy our trip to Gozo; taking in the intricate lace making and to possibly buying a cable-stitched Arran sweater.

Mary and I enjoyed drinking a delicious cup of cappuccino although having to tolerate sitting opposite to a Maltese lady from South Street, Valletta, who repeatedly complained to Doris about receiving a mouldy aluminium tray of *Timpani* pasta and then going on to say that she once went to Gozo on holiday and purchased an Arran sweater from Xlendi Bay. She told us it was extra large when she bought it but, once it was awkwardly pulled out from the washing machine it became extra small and is now used in winter to wrap around her dog.

'Well, what do you expect?' Miss Sliema so snobbishly said to us. 'They're all manufactured by machine in Malta these days and are not hand-knitted and if you want to buy a good sweater, I suggest you speak to Tom Taylor or, alternatively, speak to Thomas Jacob Hilfiger himself; enjoy it!'

Finishing our coffee, we walked into the reception area to collect our key. Frederick Mifsud, the hotel receptionist mysteriously appeared head first from underneath his desk as if there was someone else down there to keep him company. After he had buttoned up his shirt and adjusted his shiny black hair I mentioned to Frederick that Mary and I were going up to our room to have a little sleep before dinner and this was when I heard: "Enjoy it".

'Oh no, Mary it's another bloody parrot, reminiscent of the one which occupied the conservatory in Alsop Towers sixty years ago and now I know where this one got its inspiration from.'

'Just what the hell are you talking about, James,' Mary said to me, slowly shaking her head in total bewilderment, 'I think all of this lovely Maltese sunshine is going to your head.' she added.

It was when Mary and I were about to go up the magnificent limestone staircase to our room on the second floor I noticed a pair of high-heeled shoes protruding from underneath the reception desk.

I said to Frederick: 'You're not one of those are you?' watching as the shoes suddenly disappeared behind a curtain.

'One of those, what?' he replied looking at me angrily as if he knew what I was referring to.

'You know, Frederick, one of them.' I replied sympathetically and before saying his secret would be safe with me.

'Oh, for Pete's sake, James.' Mary said to me as she took a couple of retrograde steps to the bottom of the staircase. 'Here we go again with your personal and pathetic lines of enquiry.' she added.

I allowed the heavy wrought-iron key, which incidentally, wouldn't have been out of place hanging from a prison officer's trousers in Brixton, to revolve inside the lock to our room several times before we eventually had the privilege to go in. I said to Mary concernedly: 'I wonder how long it will be before we get locked in, or out of here?' She replied by saying I was worrying far too much and then suggested I should go out on to the balcony for a well deserved cigarette before I had a relapse. The panoramic view from the eave's window was so pleasing to the eye as I observed the three cities on the other side of the still and quiet water from where I was standing at the open window from our second floor balcony.

Mary came to join me in my moments of stillness as I watched a Captain Morgan pleasure cruiser passing slowly across the barren and stubby finger of land called Senglea which points directly into Grand Harbour.

'You don't really want to go to bed this afternoon do you, James?' Mary said to me as she gently took hold of my hand. 'Why don't we freshen up and go to that cosy cafe, bar and restaurant in Merchant Street; it is called the Anglo Maltese League and it's only around the corner.' she had to remind me.

'Okay, why not indeed,' I somewhat reluctantly said to her.' 'They might even have a bloody parrot.'

'Now, now, James, don't spoil the evening with your perpetual sarcastic witticisms.'

'My God, Mary, that's a big word to end the day; witticism, I shall remember that.' I said before she became putty in my hands when I retaliated by saying: 'I know a big word.'

'And what, may I ask is it? James, do please tell me.'

'Airport.' I said.

'Anyone would think you don't like it here, James and there is one consolation we won't have to tolerate those horrible people when we go to Gozo tomorrow.' Mary said to me as she plastered more Max Factor make-up on to her now sun-tanned face.

It was just after five when Mary and I plucked up the courage to go down to the ground floor in the lift which had a tendency to break down when Joseph Mizzi, the 'monkey see monkey do' of the hotel was off duty.

Anthony Vella had just started his evening shift in reception and greeted us when we successfully came out from the lift without scathe.

'It's 'Happy Hour'.' Anthony said excitedly and grinning like a Cheshire cat.

'Well, you could have fooled me,' I said to him looking around to see if there was any sign of life other than the parrot which was failing miserably to guard the door to the cocktail bar and looked as if it was about to fall from its perch. 'The cocktail bar is empty and it would seem there could be more life in your local cemetery'. I added.

'We have a 'Happy Hour' every afternoon from four pm until six-thirty pm.' Anthony, continued to tell us enthusiastically.

I said to Anthony: 'That's interesting but, it's a great pity the hotel couldn't have the 'Happy Hour' extended to seven days a week.

On our way out from the hotel we heard a loud squawk from Dominic, the parrot, followed by: 'Enjoy it'. I said to Mary, I think the life expectancy of this impertinent parrot is going to be only a matter of days.

'Now, James, you repeatedly say that back home when you are watching Tony Blair speaking in the House of Commons during 'Prime Ministers Question Time'.

'I know, Mary, I'm sorry but he really does get up my nose.' I said to her sorrowfully.

'Which parrot are you talking about, James? Dominic or Tony Blair.' she said laughing and before we both began to climb the steps of a side street to make our way to the Anglo Maltese Bar and Restaurant in busy Merchant Street.

'Lord Byron, the poet, in his *'Farewell to Malta'* prose wrote on 16th May 1811: *"Adieu, ye cursed streets of stairs! How surely he who mounts you swears!"* I said to Mary, sadly remembering my schoolmaster days.

'I know how he must have felt.' Mary said making heavy weather of the last few paces into Merchant Street from one of Valletta's more interesting of backwater ginells; St. John's Street.

'Mary, do you know where this flippin place is?' I asked her due to a sudden loss of little grey cells in my memory box promulgated by certain foreign infiltrations which had been penetrating my brain during the past forty-eight hours.

'Of course, I know where the flippin place is, James, don't ask me such stupid questions,' Mary said wheezing. 'It has a sign above the door with a plate and a fork'n knife on either side.' she emphasised.

'Now, now Mary, I know you are tired but don't be so guttural.'

Mary and I curiously walked into the establishment by way of a heavily fortified dusty green door which gave me the impression it had somehow escaped the Axis bombings during the war and making our way down a corridor to the bar and restaurant, we could see photographs of allied battleships and reproduction prints of Grand Harbour positioned high on the walls. With the exception of a Valletta police sergeant and a policewoman who was doing her best to become invisible behind a bunch of artificial plastic flowers, we were the only people sitting down in this place of solitary confinement. The waiter who doubled up as the chef and resident DJ for the evening was called Ronaldo and made us feel very welcome when he delivered the drinks; a well deserved pint of Cisk Lager and a large glass of gin and tonic with ice and lemon. Ronaldo would insist on bringing us free dishes of Maltese Tapas consisting of plates of butter beans, *Hobz biz zejt*, local bread which is rubbed with tomatoes until it turns pink, and then topped with tomatoes, capers, olive oil and seasoning; small portions of succulent rabbit (*fenek*) and deep fried Maltese chips were continually brought to our table. I can recall a rather old juke box fixed on to one of the walls and Tom Jones singing: "The green green grass of home", Engelbert Humperdinck, singing: "Delilah" and Petula Clark, singing her heart out with: "This is my song". I thought it highly amusing when Mary had finished sipping her second gin and tonic asked: 'It's not that Engelbert Pumpadick again is it?'

'I'm afraid it is Mary, these swinging sixties singers have now become somewhat of an institution in Malta and should have hung their boots up years ago.' I said routing around in my mouth with a toothpick to find the last remnant of a rare *Cominotto* bunny rabbit.

'Oh, James that's not fair of you to say that,' Mary said to me sorrowfully. 'I can remember watching 'The Huggits' starring: Petula Clark and Jack Warner on our small Bakelite television in High Holborn.'

'Yes, I can remember, Mary as if it were only yesterday.' I said to her sighing in an appropriate and nostalgic way. 'I can also remember Jack Warner's braces and how they became twisted around his back when he played 'Dixon of Dock Green'.'

Mary and I decided it was time for us to go back to our hotel because the atmosphere in the Cafe Bar and Restaurant was now being seriously polluted by the local police station on the table opposite to us; a smoke screen made it impossible for us to see the bar and the open kitchen which looked as if they were about to be engulfed in flames at any moment.

After Mary and I thanked Ronaldo and 'Starsky & Hutch' in the corner for their extremely warm welcome and said our obligatory goodbyes we walked out of the place far more quickly than when we walked in.

It was when we were walking back to our hotel via Melita Street, Mary asked: 'What was that noise?' I told her it was my hip bothering me again and then after adding more oil on to the chip pan fire I said: 'You know one's legs are always the first to go.'

'I seem to recall you had a similar problem at Carol's birthday party last week.' Mary said pinching the end of her nose with her forefinger and thumb to restrict her respiratory system.

'Oh my God, Mary, the drains don't half smell around here.' I said to her convincingly when I instantly turned into Patrick Moore to gaze up and look at the stars.

'There's nothing wrong with the drains, James, it's your bum; you need to go and visit the toilet.'

At precisely half past seven and after trekking through the streets where shops and offices were now closing, we arrived back at the Broadlands hotel. The receptionist, Anthony Vella, greeted us as though we had been out on the town for days and had returned especially to listen to more of his pathetic statements.

'We have fish on the menu this evening, sir, madam,' Anthony said, leaving his work station to deliver a scrappy piece of paper describing what other culinary delights we could expect in the restaurant.

I asked Anthony what is *lampuki*? He informed me it was a fish which is caught by the Maltese fishermen at the end of summer. After telling him we were practically in the middle of winter, he tried to end the conversation by saying the hotel has a large freezer in the kitchen and a fridgeridoo in the coffee shop.

'And what is a fridgeridoo?' I curiously asked him.

'Oh, it's an Australian ice cream cooling cabinet where we store most of the fish,' Anthony was keen to tell us, regaining his conversational skills. 'It was salvaged from a Maltese registered tanker when it sank somewhere between Haifa and Port Said during the Arab Israeli War in 1967.' he added.

'Remind me, Mary, not to have any ice cream for a while.' I pointed out to her hearing two doors to the coffee shop closing quietly behind us, giving me the impression Doris was listening to everything Anthony had said to us. It was when Mary and I were climbing the small flight of stairs in the hallway to make our way to the lift Dominic, the parrot, gave out another loud squawk and we both said in unison: 'Enjoy it'.

Mary and I changed for dinner. She was wearing a beautiful black chiffon evening gown and a rather nice pair of dainty patent leather shoes which Carol had recently bought for her in Selfridges, Oxford Street and together with the small amounts of unpretentious accessory jewellery and a silver sequinned handbag she could have been Princess Margaret herself. I was wearing my usual black barathea blazer; cavalry twill trousers, white shirt and bright red cravat; all of which incidentally, had been purchased from the menswear department in Selfridges and it is of little consequence my daughter, Carol is the head buyer there.

'You are looking exceptionally stunning this evening my dear.' I said to Mary as we both walked hand in hand towards the lift to take us up to the restaurant on the fifth floor.

'You don't look too bad yourself, James,' she sweetly replied and then following it up with: 'forget what I said to you earlier this evening concerning your problem. My mother, who you know was a Welsh lady once said to my father: 'Wherever you may be, let the wind blow free, in church or in chapel, let the windows rattle.'

'Mary, is this really necessary? And furthermore this is the first time you have mentioned this in the fifty-five years of our being married.'

'Well, James it is a bit like your bloody hip, isn't it.' she replied.

The lift seemed to take ages to arrive on the second floor and when the doors opened it was no surprise to see Joseph Mizzi carrying a torch and an extremely large screwdriver. I asked him why he was still working and would the lift be able to take us up to the restaurant? His reply was the hotel usually has a power cut most evenings and we were not to worry because he had the expertise to deal with it. Mary and I made a point of not becoming too familiar with Joseph when he insisted on moving forward towards us wearing his dusty overalls covered in plaster.

We entered into the dimly lit restaurant and were immediately greeted by Lawrence.

'Good evening, Sir James, Madam Brown,' Lawrence, the head waiter said with a cheerful smile. 'Would you like to sit at your usual table by the window?'

'Yes that would be nice,' I said as Lawrence led the way to the table. 'We can then watch the fire engines arriving before we have dinner.' I sarcastically added.

Salvo, the religious comedian cum-waiter after going through one of his evening tasks of placing an oil lamp in the centre of the table asked if we would prefer the *a la carte* menu to the tourist menu because the fish had gone off. I replied by saying to him: 'Gone off where?'

'That's funny, Sir James.' Salvo said without giving him a proper explanation. 'And did you hear the one about Saint Peter who was standing outside the Pearly Gates waiting for Saint Paul?'

'No we haven't and could we possibly have the *a la carte* menu followed by two large gin and tonics.' I assertively demanded.

'Yes, certainly, sir,' Salvo said swinging into action as if someone had just placed a rocket up his backside. 'Maybe I could find time to tell you at breakfast in the morning, Sir James.'

'I will look forward to that.' I replied with caution hearing the same music being played over and over again. The cassette which had obviously been purchased from the daily market in Merchant Street featured a Maltese singer, Olivia Spiteri who, every twenty minutes sang: "Memory", "Born Free", "Tell her about it", "Night and Day" and "For once in my life"; however, we were spared this repetitive brain-washing stuff at breakfast time.

The restaurant was pleasantly busy with a few Dutch, French, German and Italian visitors positioned here and there to keep us company. I can remember a brave and elderly Dutch couple sitting outside on the verandah insisting on preferential treatment; they did this by rotating their arms likened to a windmill every time they wanted the waiters to do something; I think perhaps, they could still be there waiting for their just deserts and a flight back to Amsterdam.

Salvo brought the *a la carte* menu at the same time as the tall glasses containing the large gin and tonics and following a lengthy discussion between Mary and myself regarding the extraordinary culinary delights which could possibly be delivered to our table I eventually summoned Lawrence to give him our order.

The menu was predominantly of Maltese cuisine and Mario's speciality for the evening was *Fillet Steak Maltese* served with Mediterranean vegetables and roast potatoes. I had already decided that this was what I wanted to order but Mary had other ideas in that she wanted *Timpana*, a Sicilian dish by origin; consisting of macaroni, minced meat, livers, tomatoes, eggs and baked under a topping of pastry and I would advise this dish is definitely not for the weight conscious. The starters consisting of cream of asparagus soup and deep fried rabbit cooked in garlic and red wine which was described by Mary, as a delicious prelude to the main course had become her favourite dish for the remainder of our stay in the hotel. I said to her: 'If you keep on eating Maltese rabbit you will be able to hop into bed.'

'Now, James, you're trying to be funny again, aren't you?' she said with a hiccup after she had taken a sip of the '*La Vallette*' red wine Salvo had just poured from a non-approved bottle. 'It's a bit like ordering your favourite apple pie with chocolate ice cream isn't it, James, and if you eat any more of that stuff you may end up looking like it.' At that precise moment the lights went out and we were subjected to a power cut which lasted for at least ten minutes, but all was not lost when Joseph Mizzi appeared with his trusty screwdriver and a fiery blow lamp to sort out a problem in the kitchen.

Mary and I, after everything and everyone had returned to some sense of normality, retired to our room. It was when we were huddled together in our cosy bed, Mary said to me: 'Thank you for a lovely day, James,' to which I replied: 'Thank you, Mary; it has indeed been so wonderful.'

Chapter Eighteen

The morning began with us taking breakfast at seven-thirty. The first thing I noticed was a cardboard sign propped up in front of the toaster informing everyone it was out of order. Both Lawrence and Salvo were on duty that morning and it seemed quite obvious to me they were not happy when a group of French people sitting at a table outside on the verandah had managed to steal from the buffet a whole basketful of their freshly baked *Hobz Malti* bread. Lawrence quickly retrieved it without apology and told them in no uncertain terms not to be so greedy and if they wanted more they would have to take the American Club sandwich bread piled up at the side of the clapped-out toaster.

Mary and I dispensed stewed black coffee from a huge army surplus tea urn into a hotel cup and saucer personalised by a motive just in case one forgot where one was and the name of the hotel. We then poured jungle juice made from powder into small hob knob glasses and then sat down to eat our usual intake of fortifying cornflakes. Mary constructed sandwiches made from *mortadella Bologna*, Maltese Spam, thinly sliced boiled ham and Laughing Cow processed cheese; to eat in the restaurant and not to take out. In the restaurant there was a prize for the first person to find a cherry in the fruit cocktail bowl; needless to say, an elderly French guest won it when she returned to the buffet to replenish her dish and satisfy her enormous appetite for food. I asked Lawrence what the white stuff was called which looked like wallpaper paste and placed some distance away from the other food; he explained it was called kedgeree made from flaked fish, rice and egg. I said to him: 'it's not from Australia by any chance, is it?'

A rack of grilled toast was brought to our table by Lawrence; it was charred and looked as though it had been subjected to Joseph's blow lamp. When I complained to him about our burnt offerings, he pointed to a chimney in the distance and said: 'That is Malta's largest crematorium and the second is in our kitchen.'

Sitting at the table to our right was a guy from Canada who would insist on reminding everyone that he had just arrived from the largest and most wonderful country in the world.

'Hey you guys,' he said to us impertinently. 'Are you from England because I'm from Canada?'

'Well we were when we got up this morning.' I replied trying my best to avoid his questioning.

'I come from a small town in Canada called Medicine Hat,' he told us, bringing his chair a little closer to our table. 'It is near Montana and it is on the border to The United States of America.'

'Well, you don't say, that's very interesting, but do you think perhaps we could have our breakfast in peace and quiet.' I said, pointing a teaspoon directly in front of him.

'What are you two guys doing today?' he said, giving me the impression he was hard of hearing and needed to be reminded that Mary and I would prefer not to speak to him. 'I am taking the flying boat over to Gozo this morning from Valletta and should arrive just in time for brunch.' he added.

'Oh no.' I said to Mary and thinking it was going to be another one of those days.

'Don't worry, Jim.' Mary said and reassuring me further when she suggested I could buy a blonde wig and a pair of pink sunglasses in Republic Street before our departure to Gozo.

Contrary to Helen's weather forecast it was a beautiful sunny morning with no signs of any rain when I gazed out through the window to see a blue sky with no clouds in sight. Salvo walked quickly into the restaurant from the verandah carrying a tray of debris from a table which had been occupied by the French. He made a point of saying good morning to us before insisting on telling us his lengthy jokes. I pointed out that we were being picked up at the hotel by minibus at nine-thirty because we are going to Gozo on the ferry, departing from Cirkewwa to Mgarr at eleven-fifteen and would he mind hurrying up and begin his stories somewhere near to the end. However, I told him one of my funny little stories which began: I phoned Malta's National Football Stadium to find out at what time the match starts on Saturday afternoon and they replied by saying at what time can you turn up?

'I didn't know you were interested in football, James.' Mary said watching Salvo scratching the back of his head trying to understand the joke.

'I will have the last laugh,' Salvo put in excitedly after it had suddenly registered in his brain I was taking the proverbial Mickey. 'You can postpone any notion of sleep tomorrow when my team, 'Valletta United', win the championship.'

It would have been inconsequential for me to mention we could expect parades of cars bearing team colours and blaring horns from loyal supporters of the winning team; a raucous bunch of fanatics who have made football akin to religion.

Salvo had to mention we had rain during the night and not to forget our umbrellas. I said to him rain in Malta is caused by explosive devices polluting the atmosphere and that's what you get when you play with fire. He replied by saying there aren't any national *Festas* and Public Holidays at this time of the year and it was more likely Saint Peter, Paul and Mary who were the irresponsible culprits. I gave up trying to humour Salvo after saying there should be more *festas* in Malta and they could possibly help liven things up in this God forsaken place.

On our way out from the restaurant Mary and I said thank you to Lawrence and Salvo for making our breakfast time an interesting one and for contributing towards bringing forward my six-monthly visit to the dentist. I also said, Happy Landings to Big Foot from Canada on the next table and to watch out for stray German *Luftwaffe* Heinkel bombers.

At twenty-past nine the telephone rang in our room. It was George Attard, the head receptionist informing us the minibus had arrived to take us to Cirkewwa. In the lift we were confronted by Joseph Mizzi on his way up to his workshop on the roof to mend a rusty old Bendix washing machine which accompanied us on our way down to the ground floor. I said to Mary when we were handing in our key at the reception: 'I think Joseph must spend most of his time going up and down in the lift.' Mary responded by saying: 'he probably likes it up on the roof, James, because of the panoramic view all round the island.'

'Panoramic, that's another big word, Mary.' I said to her giggling. She then continued to enhance my knowledge with: 'I also know two big words, James.'

'And what are those?' I anxiously wanted to know.

'Shut up.' she said.

George Attard, bobbing up and down like a puppet on British television's Spitting Image, greeted us by saying good morning, Sir James, madam but he quickly disappeared when 'Guppy', Helen Azzopardi appeared through the main door leading into reception.

'Good morning,' Mrs Azzopardi said, wafting a colourful hand-painted fan in front of her face to keep her cool. 'Your transport is waiting for you outside to take you to the Gozo ferry.' she added.

It was when the manager's head, which seemed to rotate three hundred and sixty degrees from out of a cellar Mary and I took steps to make our way out of the hotel; it was then I heard myself, Dominic the parrot, Helen Azzopardi, Gino and George Attard say in unison: "Enjoy it".

The forty-five minute journey to Cirkewwa, an isolated part of the island was indeed very pleasant taking in the magnificent scenic views of the Mediterranean as we drove through Mellieha Bay and the Marfa Peninsula. We arrived an hour before the scheduled departure time and the system for cars and foot passengers was first come first on the boat; ships leave for the twenty-five minute crossing from Cirkewwa regularly throughout the day.

Sitting on what looked like a huge limestone boulder at the side of the jetty were Frank and Mavis Riley and standing directly in front of them I caught a glimpse of the intrepid Stanley and Hilda Parry.

'I knew it, I just knew it.' I said to Mary trying to attract the minibus driver's attention as he sped off back to Valletta and needless to say he just carried on to pick up another couple of naive State Pensioners who were willing to part with their hard-earned money.

'Hi Jim! Hello Mary, love.' Hilda said, shouting over to us in her eloquent Merseyside accent.

'Are you alright there Whack?' Stanley asked me sounding like a typical Liverpool dock worker.

'Well, I was but, that was until I saw you lot.' I said to myself.

'Come and join us over here, Petal.' Frank Riley so rudely said to Mary before I told him he had a nose that looked like a sun-dried tomato but then he still continued with his loudness just to let everyone in Gozo and Comino know he was about to arrive. I said to him: 'What's ailing you?' he replied by saying he was missing a pint of 'Boddingtons Bitter'.

'Not that ale you clown.' I said watching him edging his way back towards the water.

From a distance I heard the dulcet tones of Betty Ward and Vera Cruikshank getting louder and louder as they walked quickly in our direction. Vera's laugh was worse than a hyena and to this day I still don't know what on earth she found so funny, especially when she was about to visit the world's largest penal colony in the Mediterranean. Following on, and not too far behind them, was Nicholas Bottomley with a rather large telescopic lens camera wrapped around his neck and that morning he was wearing a Blues Brother's hat with a 'Kiss me Quick' motif painted in large white letters on the front. I said to Mary: 'I told you this wasn't going to be my lucky day.' to which she replied: 'Well, James looking at Nicholas's hat, it may very well be. Anyway,' she continued. 'they will all be going to different places in Gozo and then we can spend the whole day on our own.'

'What type of camera is that around your neck, Whack?' Stanley asked Nicholas.

'It's a Suzuki'. Nicholas replied.

'I thought a Suzuki was a motorbike.' Stan the man said.

'I wondered why the strap broke.' Nicholas said, and now fast becoming a regular tourist comedian by successfully sending Stanley Parry up.

'We have one of these.' Mavis said, showing Nicholas a Kodak Brownie camera which she had bought in a Japanese-run holiday camp shop shortly after the Second World War. 'It was with this camera I once took a photograph of The Red Arrows from a hotel bedroom window in Blackpool; The Red Arrows are from the Royal Air Force you know,' she added, 'and my sister, Hazel, who incidentally was staying with us in the same bed and breakfast guest house, had a camera just like yours and do you know by the time she had finished messing around with the lens the bloody planes had gone.'

I thought to myself: that thing wouldn't be out of place inside a museum of antiquities.

'Where is Blackpool?' Nicholas curiously asked Mavis in his strange and bizarre Tiptonian Staffordshire accent.

'It's by the sea you know.' Betty Ward quickly put in and once again doing her best to enhance our geographical knowledge.

'Lovely.' Nicholas gratefully replied.

Stanley told me that he had spent a considerable length of time the previous evening with his ear up against a valuables safe with the aim of cracking the combination. He said, that his wife along with the staff in the hotel's reception, were the only people who knew how to open it and give me access to my redundancy money.

My mobile phone began to reverberate sensitively inside my knee-length khaki shorts; it was a Maltese phone company called 'GO Crazy' promoting a stress-free holiday by texting this number to: 'Try to avoid stress, listen to a Peruvian Indian flute player; calls are charged at only thirty-five Maltese cents per minute.' I just couldn't believe what I had received and shaking my head, I said to Mary: 'Can't anyone get any peace around here?'

It was precisely eleven-fifteen when the ship slipped its moorings and for the passengers to enjoy the twenty-five minute voyage over to Gozo. I can remember the sea being rough and this was when I started to hallucinate as hunger pangs began to play havoc inside my stomach and Mary, after throwing disgusting black coffee over the side, was now taking bites out of a brown plastic cup. I was truly grateful to Hilda Parry when she offered us broken 'Jammy Dodger' biscuits which she had purchased from the cafeteria on one of the lower decks. Frank and Stanley, who had somehow managed to obtain a couple of tins of CISK lagers in record breaking time were standing by the rail on the starboard side. It was Frank who said to me later: 'There are certain advantages of your wife being an alcoholic; you have easy access to the booze.' I said to him: 'You don't have a drink problem, do you?' He replied by saying something which sounded like yes and added he couldn't get enough of it. This was when Stan, the man, burst out laughing, spilling most of his beer on to the quarterdeck for rolling passengers to slide on.

I asked Stanley did he know where he was going once the ship had arrived in Mgarr? He amazingly said to me: 'Hilda and I are to get on a Hop on Hop off tour bus to go to Marsalforn and then have lunch in the 'Collapso' Hotel.

'It's by the sea, you know,' Betty said preoccupied in homing-in and on to our somewhat limited intelligent conversation. 'My husband, Rodney and I stayed for three days in the same hotel; the food was excellent, the pool was refreshingly cool and there was a charming Maltese waiter called Charlie who went out of his way to satisfy my every need. Unfortunately, Rodney died several weeks later from a heart attack after receiving a letter from the American time share company saying they had changed our agreement to allow a Pakiststani gentleman and his family to occupy our apartment in Qawra, on the northern coast of Malta.'

'Betty and I are going to visit a pile of stones in Viagra,' Vera told us putting her five eggs in. 'The stones were piled up a long time ago and I am wondering why anyone hasn't taken the opportunity to shovel them all up.' she added.

'We are going to visit The Ggantija megalithic temples in *Xaghra*, Vera, they date back to 3600 – 3200 B.C.' Betty said, with the aim of correcting Vera's wealth of historical knowledge and to impress us with hers.

Nicholas, who was busy applying a NIVEA essential care lipstick to the front of his face, said to us he was going to visit Victoria, the capital of Gozo, to try and find some excitement and hoped that the toilets in Gozo were going to be more hygienic than the ones onboard the ship. He later told me when we were returning to Cirkewwa on the ferry that there was more life in the Rue Morgue in Paris. I said to him; 'You have been to Paris, but then, you haven't a clue where Blackpool is.'

Nicholas replied by saying: 'Of course I know where bloody Blackpool is; it's practically on my doorstep and I often visit my aunt, Valerie and uncle, Sam who live in Fleetwood; I was just trying to wind Mavis up.'

Frank had just asked Mavis to produce a large hip-flask containing the

Famous Grouse whisky from her shoulder bag and then after he had unscrewed the top to take a swig said they were both going to Xlendi, an old and well trampled fishing village three kilometres south of Victoria.

'It's by the sea, you know!' Betty said again, sounding like Dominic the parrot.

'Oh Betty, can't you shut up and give your mouth a rest?' Stanley said to her in his perfected Liverpudlian Scouse accent. 'If we want any geography or rolling stones history lessons we'll ask you, alright!'

'I'm only trying to be sociable.' Betty said sorrowfully. 'Would you like one of these Maltese 'Magic Moment' chocolates, Stanley?' now beginning to patronise him with her assortment of sweet confection.

'They are not made by Perry Como are they?' Nicholas asked her, biting his way through a cherry and nougat praline chocolate and at the same time amusing us with his funny little ditties.

'I don't think so,' Betty said examining the side of the box. 'No, they are made by Marco Azzopardi & Sons Limited of Sliema, Malta.' she added.

'And where did you buy them from?' Mary inquisitively asked her.

'I bought them from Helen, the Airtours representative at the same time as my umbrella; she was selling them at discount prices.'

Mary looked at me raising her eyebrows and said; 'I just knew it, that Helen Azzopardi wants to make her mind up what line of business she represents; is she a courier or a so-called cut-price saleswoman?'

I told Mary it wasn't any of our business but there would be at least one consolation, the chocolates could perhaps keep Betty quiet for the remaining ten minutes of the journey.

Hilda, consuming another tin of Maltese Hop Leaf beer said to a group of German tourists who couldn't help showing off their ice-skating skills on the quarterdeck; "Vive la France".' Suddenly there was a silence until one of them replied: 'We come from Germany, not that pathetic little country to the south of the English Channel.'

'Oh, I'm so sorry and I do apologise for not being gracious,' Hilda said sarcastically. 'but now I come to think of it, you do look remarkably like the pilot who bombed my grandmother's fish and chip shop in Kirkby.'

The ferry arrived on time in Mgarr, at eleven-forty precisely. Most passengers managed to disembark on to the quayside without difficulty but then others had to be helped off the ship after bringing up large quantities of CISK lager and jettisoning it over the side to help reduce the marine life in the Blue Lagoon.

Mary and I breathed a sigh of relief when we saw our recently acquired friends go their separate ways. We can recall a man wearing a pair of khaki shorts, a white open-neck shirt and brown leather sandals holding up a cardboard sign with our name written in large letters on it; he was the driver of the minibus who was to take us on a four mile journey to Victoria, the Lilliputian capital of Gozo. The dusty red minibus arrived at the Duke of Edinburgh Hotel in Republic Street just after midday; this hotel, reputed to be the oldest and most charming on Gozo was the venue designated for Mary and me to have lunch. A young waitress who Mary and I named later as: 'Bouncy Castle' showed us to a long wooden table which wouldn't have been out of place in a medieval fortress belonging to King Arthur. The button which was initially intended to secure the top of Matilda's rather tight white blouse eventually ended up in a dish of cream of tomato soup; however, it was crudely replaced with a safety pin to avoid more embarrassment.

We had the pleasure of sitting next to a lovely black couple; a man and his wife who were called Bongo Bill and Patricia McDonald from oil rich Nigeria and both were white collar workers employed within the Shell Oil Company refinery in Port Harcourt. I introduced myself and Mary simply to them as Mr and Mrs Brown from Bloomsbury, London and it was interesting to learn they had stayed in The Royal National Hotel and just a stone's throw away from where we live. The lunch was a set meal consisting of cream of tomato soup, Lampuki fish; catch of the day, new potatoes and fresh Gozitan mixed vegetables and, the desert, a chocolate and vanilla ice cream sundae.

'We are going to Victoria's citadel this afternoon and plan to visit The Cathedral of the Assumption.' I said to Bongo Bill and Pat.

'We are going there too.' Bongo said to us in an educated English accent which he had probably acquired somewhere between Oxford and

Cambridge. 'Perhaps we can all go to the Cathedral together?' Patricia was keen to suggest.

'That will be a novelty and an experience, won't it, Mary?' I said diplomatically.

'Now, let's get one thing straight, Mister and Mrs Brown;' Bongo Bill McDonald said, taking another piece of *Hobz Malti-Gozo* from the bread basket. 'we are neither a novelty nor an experience and we haven't come from Uranus, we have just flown in from Africa.'

Mary decided it was time for her to cool things down somewhat by saying to them: 'After we have visited the much trampled on citadel we are to be transported to the old picturesque fishing village called Xlendi by one of the buses which are all painted civil service grey with a spruce red stripe; we can then watch a boatload of illegal immigrants leaping out of the water like penguins to head for the shore and, that will be fun, won't it?'

'We have heard that the handmade lace, for which Gozo is famous, could be a good purchase in the souvenir store in Xlendi Bay.' Patricia said to us as she poured ice-cold Sangria into her husband's tall glass and from where I was seated I could see thick pieces of orange, lemons and sliced banana floating on the top of Campari mixed with Martini Rosso.

'We have heard that the handmade lace is not what it seems,' Mary, telling her to beware of bogus and cheap imports from the Far East. 'Sometimes there are 'handmade' labels on what is machine made.' she added.

'Well, thank you very much, Mary for your advice and to warn us about the bogus labels,' Patricia said slurring her words after taking another sip of potent Maltese Sangria.

'According to my Malta Gozo & Comino travel guide, many skilled Gozitan ladies sit outside their houses to make the lace for tourists to buy.' I put in, pretending I knew everything about craft industries on Gozo.

'Shut up, James.' Mary said to me slapping me on the arm. 'You have said quite enough.'

It was in the cathedral that afternoon we were all mesmerized by a magnificent statue of the Virgin Mary made from solid gold and this was when a bronzed face appeared from behind the heavily fortified glass case and said:

'Hi, you guys.'

'Bloody Hell, Mary,' I said to her. 'It's him, Howard Wison, 'Big Foot' from Canada. I suddenly had to turn around after a priest poked me in the back to tell me to keep quiet. I said to him: 'It's been an extremely long day and I'm very sorry your holiness.'

Chapter Nineteen

The Broadlands Hotel at five pm the same afternoon

Mary and I were indeed fortunate not to have been travelling on the same ferry as our super confident, albeit embarrassing friends from the North of England.

We walked into the hotel to find Anthony Vella sitting graciously behind the reception desk reading a copy of *The Times* newspaper.

'Good afternoon, Sir James, Madam Brown,' Anthony said getting up from his chair in order to bow or curtsey in front of us. 'Did you enjoy it?' he continued to say.

'Enjoy what?' I curiously asked him.

'You're trip to Gozo,' Anthony replied showing me a copy of *The Independent*, another Maltese daily newspaper with the headlines "Disgruntled Immigrant Worker tries to swim back to Libya from Gozo" 'And you would probably have missed the action in Marsalforn this afternoon when a foreigner from Liverpool had to be rescued by helicopter after he slipped on a banana skin and fell into the sea.'

'Well, that's understandable, I suppose; some people are not safe to be let out.' I said to Anthony, knowing full well it was Stanley Parry who was now taking up valuable bed space in Malta's principle St Luke's Hospital in Gwardamanga.

'That's not nice of you to say that about Stanley.' Mary said to me in a very low voice. 'He is a funny man who creases me up.' she added.

'Well, Mary it could have been worse, he could have fallen over the side half way to Gozo and then he would have done us all a favour.'

'Oh James, there is no compassion in you these days.' she said to me with a sad tone in her voice.

'Compassion, compassion, I'll show you what compassion is all about if 'Big Foot' from Canada decides to open his big mouth in the restaurant this evening.' I said to her in no uncertain terms.

'At what time did he say he would be flying back to Valletta from Mgarr?' Mary asked me looking at her watch.

I said to her, he told us he would be taking-off from Gozo at sixteen-forty hours, arriving in Grand Harbour at seventeen hundred hours.

'Do you think we can put this conversation into a common language with which we can all understand?' Mary asked politely and using a rather posh accent I had never heard before.

'Well according to my chronological estimation, Mary, he should be walking in through that door in the next couple of seconds.'

The Christmas tree which had been imported from Sicily had been delivered to the hotel that afternoon and was still under wraps in a green plastic bag. Anthony told us in confidence that on the 6th of January every year, Gino, the manager takes the Christmas tree to his home in Marsaxlokk where he chops it up into logs before using it for firewood; he continued to tell us tapping the side of his nose he knew a rather different story in that the trees are replanted in his garden.

'It would seem your expensive Swiss Breitling state of the art chronograph watch, the movement of which can help you boil an egg in less than two minutes was a complete and utter waste of money.' Mary said to me looking at her recently acquired white Swatch.

'And why now are you saying this to me Mary?' I replied, thinking she was right as usual and then continued to say: 'You've never complained about my boiled eggs before.'

'It's not the boiled eggs, you fool,' she said to me assertively. 'You told me, Howard Wilson, the Canadian gentleman was going to walk in through the door at any second but, that was five minutes ago and so, as usual, you are wrong, James.'

At that precise moment one of the glass fronted doors opened and who do you think walked in? And yes, *you* are right.

'Hi, you guys.'

'It's Happy hour,' Anthony Vella said pointing in the direction of the cocktail bar.

I said to Anthony: 'Oh no, not another one, I don't think I can stand anymore of this happiness.'

Mario, the chef, has laid on some exciting nibbles for you this evening; *Bruschetta*, curried meatballs, deep fried *calamari* and *brochettes*; spicy things on sticks.'

'And what is *Bruschetta?*' I asked Anthony looking at a broom cupboard which was slightly open behind his desk.

'It is toasted Maltese bread; *Hobz Malti* topped with sun dried tomatoes, onions, capers, sea salt and olive oil.' Anthony replied showing off his gastronomical knowledge to Gino who was walking down the staircase from his office on the first floor.

'I had rib-eye steak for lunch,' 'Big Foot' from Canada had to tell us describing in detail what it was like. 'The steak was so small it was hiding under a mound of French fries.' he added.

'There is rib-eye steak on the tourist menu for this evening's meal in the restaurant.' Anthony Vella said reading his copy on the desk.

'Well, I hope to God it isn't that piece of steak I left in Gozo.' Howard said concernedly.

'Madam Brown and I would like to have the key to our room now,' I said to Anthony proffering my hand in anticipation and before mentioning to him we were going to freshen up before dinner.

'Anyway you guys, I am going into the cocktail bar for a cool beer and perhaps take in some of that stuff Anthony keeps going on about and perhaps I will see you later.' Howard put in.

When Mary and I were walking towards the lift there was the usual squawk from Dominic followed by "Enjoy it" but this time funnily enough, it was the manager trying to imitate the parrot.

On entering our room I immediately switched on the television just in time to watch the last episode of, "Only Fools and Horses", when Dell Boy and Rodney Trotter became instant millionaires having auctioned an antique clock.

Mary, that evening came up with a brilliant idea to go to one of Malta's exclusive and prestigious casinos, the Dragonara Palace with the aim of going a little wild and to participate at one of the roulette tables. We decided not go into the hotel's restaurant for dinner that evening and I suggested to Mary we could possibly have a meal in the casino instead.

'Don't forget our passports, Mary,' I said to her adding more items to her 'things to-do' list and splashing more Boss aftershave on to my face. 'We will need the passports to get into the building and to obtain a life membership card.'

'Now let's not go over the top and get too excited.' Mary said selecting a few appropriate pieces of jewellery to impress George Michael who had the pleasure of standing next to us at one of the gaming tables.

On our way out from our hotel bedroom Mary said a rather peculiar thing.

'Can you remember when Commander Halewood was presented with his KCB by King George VI at Buckingham Palace, I said to him, that looks remarkably like a JCB around your neck and then he replied by saying he wondered why the ribbon suddenly snapped.'

'Oh, Mary, I think the heat is beginning to affect you but, it could be because you have been listening in to Malta's new resident comedian, Nicholas Bottomley and his rather pathetic jokes.'

'Where's your sense of humour James? You never used to be like this.' she said to me sorrowfully.

'I don't know, I really don't know.' I replied shaking my head from side to side trying to imitate my newsagent, Mr Patel back in Bloomsbury. 'Perhaps I left it at Gatwick.'

'James, this is why I love you so much: you are so knowledgeable.'

'I know, Mary,' I said with a big grin on my face. 'I don't know how I do it for the money?'

'Shall we walk down to reception, James,' Mary said with a worried look on her face. 'I have a feeling there is going to be a power cut because of the lights flickering in the bathroom.'

'I think that's a good idea,' I said to her concernedly after seeing streaks of lightning and hearing rumblings of thunder when I had looked out through the bedroom window earlier.

Joseph Mizzi, carrying his trusty screwdriver was heading for the cellar when he quickly passed us on the staircase; it was interesting to learn the following morning that the hotel's generator was stored down in the cellar together with a pile of flotsam and jetsam; debris left by pirates during the eighteenth century. Among all of this, piles of rusty old army corned beef and processed cheese tins deposited by the citizens of Valletta who used the cellar to stockpile when the air raids on Malta forced them underground during WWII.

'Shall we have a drink in the cocktail bar before we ask Anthony to call for a taxi?' I said to Mary as we successfully reached the bottom of the stairs without being stabbed to death by an extremely large screwdriver.

'That will be lovely, James.' she said, handing Anthony the key to our room.

The cocktail bar was pleasantly full with hotel guests and Howard Wilson was busy propping up the bar and, judging by the rather unsteady state he was in he had obviously been drinking far too much beer.

'Hi you guys;' 'Big Foot' from Canada said, beckoning us over, 'join me for a drink.' he added, slurring his words.

Howard began to tell us that his profession in Medicine Hat, Alberta, Canada was a school teacher and he taught French and mathematics and all his life wanted to take-off in a flying boat. I told him I was a retired school master and taught English and Geography and then went on to tell him all my life I just couldn't wait to visit Malta.

'Gee, that's great man,' Howard said to me putting his arm around my shoulder. 'What are you two guys having to drink? The lager's great!' he added.

'Now, don't get too familiar.' I said shrugging my shoulders to remove his hairy arm. 'I'll have a Jack Daniels, Howard, if you don't mind and Mary would like a large gin and tonic with ice and lemon.'

Howard asked me what my favourite book was when I was a student. I told him it was "The Adventures of Huckleberry Finn" and for some inexplicable reason I had forgotten the author's name and told him it was by Alistair Cook.

I said to him. 'I suppose your favourite book is: "The Adventures of Freddie Mercury in Montreal"?'

'I thought you told me you knew nothing about Freddie Mercury, James.' Mary said to me after taking another sip from a more than generous long drink.

'I read all about him on the plane; he was in Air Malta's in-flight magazine, "When Queen rocked Montreal in Canada".' I said to her rather smugly as if I knew everything about a guy who didn't want to live forever.

'Tell me, Howard, are you married?' I asked allowing a large measure of Jack Daniels bourbon whiskey to disappear down my throat.

'I once was, but it only lasted a week; she literally took-off from a military airfield in Suffield and ended up living with a rich Red Indian chief on a reservation somewhere in Montana.' he was happy to tell us.

'It's raining cats and dogs, James,' Mary said looking at people coming in through the main door into the reception resembling drowned rats that had been looking for a place to stay.

'Oh, how novel.' I said to her, glancing at my watch to find out if I had time to go back up to our room to collect the umbrella.

'And what is on the itinerary for you two guys, tomorrow.' 'Big Foot' from Canada asked as he gently pushed another 'curried to death' meatball into his rather big mouth.

I whispered to Mary: 'I wish he would stop calling us guys because I'm beginning to feel like one and am about to be put on the top of a bonfire.

'James and I are going to chill out in Valletta tomorrow and "Do the Walk", the Maltese way, Howard,' Mary said to him amicably. 'In the morning we are to visit Republic Street, the market in Freedom Square followed by an Italian lunch at Ricardo's Bar & Restaurant in St John's Street where they serve delicious *pizza pasta* meals one could die for.

'Gee, that sounds really great, ma am, 'Howard said enthusiastically and continued cheering us all up with: 'Prisoners on death row "do the walk" before they are executed; I'm not doing anything special tomorrow and perhaps I'll join you two guys.' he added.

Mary, after searching around in her handbag to find her pill box said to me: 'I think, James I am about to come on with what you call one of my heads.'

It was now raining torrentially, likened to a tropical storm when I ventured up the stairs to retrieve my umbrella; the heavy wooden door leading into the street had to be closed by Anthony to stop the glass windows inside the entrance hall from being shattered by the gale force winds.

On my return, Mary said: 'Why are the bells ringing at this time of day,

James?' I replied by saying I had no idea and then suggested she should give them a ring and ask them.

'Ha ha, very funny, James,' she said before suggesting to me I shouldn't contemplate giving up my daytime job to be a comedian.

After telling her I didn't have a daytime job she told me to shut up because I couldn't take a joke. 'Anyway,' I said to Mary as I helped myself to another slice of tasty *bruschetta*; 'it is probably Saint Peter, Paul and the virgin Mary signalling Armageddon.

'Armageddon, who is he?' Mary asked, doing her best to wind me up. 'And which Maltese football club does he play for?' she went on.

Howard excused himself by saying he had to go visit the gentleman's powder room; this was when I said to Mary: 'I think now is the time for us both to leave the cocktail bar.'

The rain had stopped and this was when a white Mercedes Benz taxi arrived to take us to the Dragonara Palace casino on Dragonara Point in the soulless confines of Paceville in Saint Julian's. Mary and I were sitting rather uncomfortably in the back of the cab on plastic- covered seats which one tended to slide off when one literally flew around a roundabout in Msida.

We had the pleasure of being driven round the bend by another Charlie; this one, however, lives in Spinola Bay; an old picturesque fishing village and now a built up and over-populated area on the northeast coast and he would insist on telling us his village had the most spectacular panoramic views of the Mediterranean and is the most photographed tourist attraction in the world.

The taxi driver having relieved me of ten Maltese Lira which equated to sixteen English pounds sterling departed the Dragonara forecourt with a huge smile on his face.

I escorted Mary up the staircase into a beautifully proportioned classical villa; the large stone entrance within a neo Grecian quadrangle is supported by pillars and, just inside the glass fronted door there was a security guard, resplendent in a white tuxedo, bow tie and a packed shoulder holster waiting to greet us. After Gunsel had scrutinized our passports and Mary had convinced him we were not members of the

Russian mafia he demanded a four Maltese Lira entrance fee. I was told we were not allowed to go in because I wasn't wearing a regulation tie, but then he said this could easily be remedied by selling me one of his Knights of Malta ties for six Maltese Lira. Mary and I were convinced we were being ripped-off when we were confronted by a Saint John's Ambulance man melodiously rattling a tin as we walked in. I said to Mary: 'We have only been here for less than two minutes and I have parted with nearly thirty-five quid already.'

'How much did you give the man with the tin?' Mary asked, staring at a Maltese cross sticker which had been firmly pressed on to the lapel of my jacket.

'I didn't have anything less than a two Maltese Lira note and so I had no choice but to give it to him.' I said, looking at my wallet which was fast becoming empty.

'And how do you propose to pay for all this so-called entertainment.' she asked, fumbling around in her bag to find her mother of pearl pill box.

'We can pay as we go, Mary.' I said to her feeling more relaxed knowing we could use our prestigious platinum credit card.

Mary was quick to notice there was an exorbitant percentage charge on every credit card transaction in the casino which one had to put-up or shut-up about, but it became of little importance later when she won six-hundred lira at one of the roulette tables.

It was half-past eight when the gaming rooms opened and this was when Mary said to me: 'Look over there, James, its George Michael standing in front of the roulette table.' she said somewhat excitedly.

'Who is George Michael and which Maltese football team does he play for?' I curiously asked.

'He was in the market on Wednesday, can't you remember, James; he was singing "Last Christmas".' she said, becoming more and more excited about standing next to him.

'Well, he should take a little more water with it.' I replied and still not knowing who he was.

'Come on, James, let's stand next to him, you never know he may bring us some good luck.' she said dragging me into the gaming room like a dog on a lead.

Whilst Mary and I contemplated the denomination of chips we should use to win our fortune, George Michael asked if he could borrow my cigarette lighter. I quickly produced my gold plated Calibre means of ignition and then asked him how come he managed to get in without a tie.

'I don't know; I really don't know.' he replied placing his sunglasses on the top of his head to look like a pop star.

'Mesdames, mademoiselles, messieurs; place your bets now ladies and gentlemen.' the Maltese croupier said sounding like a character from the British television series "Hello Hello".

Mary suggested we placed our largest chip on black twenty-two directly in front of us because she said it was her lucky number and the same number of her parents' sweet and tobacconist shop in High Holborn where they once lived. The croupier with a highly polished sun-tanned bald head spun the wheel with the expertise that only a casino *gamekeeper* would know and then we waited for the ball to fall into one of the thirty-seven coloured and numbered pockets of the wheel to make us very, very rich.

'On the black; number twenty-two.' the croupier hollered and repeating it to remind us we had won.

There was a small pile of chips being pushed in our direction and it was then Mary suggested we leave where they were on the same number because she knew George Michael had brought us a spate of good luck which we needed so much.

'Mesdames, mademoiselles, messieurs; place your bets now ladies and gentlemen.' the croupier kept on repeating and reminding me of my favourite film "Casablanca", starring Humphrey Bogart, Ingrid Bergman and Sam in the background bashing the shit out of his upright piano keyboard!.

'Waiting, waiting, waiting; always waiting.' I said to Mary watching the croupier carefully spinning a silver ball in another direction on a tilted circular track running around the circumference of the wheel.

'Oh, shut up, James, you do go on.' she said to me waiting anxiously for the ball to eventually lose momentum and fall into her lucky number pocket.

I can remember feeling a little queasy and for the second time that day likened to sea sickness.

'On the black, number twenty-two, ladies and gentlemen.' the croupier said when he looked somewhat disdainfully in our direction, knowing a large sum of money was about to disappear from the top of his table.

'We've won again, James,' Mary said to me jumping up and down on the spot to successfully imitate an excited chimpanzee. 'And you do realize,' she added, 'we will be going home on Tuesday with more money than we came with.'

'Yes, I do realize that, Mary and perhaps we should say thank you to George Michael to help fix the wheel for us.'

'Perhaps, after we have cashed in our chips and been ripped off by two and a half percent from our winnings, we should go into the restaurant.' Mary so wisely suggested.

Whilst we were eating the delicious rack of lamb served with roast potatoes, carrots, peas and mint sauce, I said to her: 'I'm going to demand that our four lira entrance fee be returned because they say if you dine you don't pay to get in the place.'

Oh, come on James,' she said to me pouring a little more 'Bisto' gravy from a sauce boat on to her plate. 'We have just won all this money; a thousand pounds sterling to be precise and you still insist on complaining.'

'Well, Mary,' I said without hesitation. 'I used to work for the Foreign Office, I didn't own it!' to which she replied:

'How many times over the years have I heard you say that?'

'Too many to count, Mary.'

'Oh, listen, James,' she said, placing her hand on my arm, 'do you remember this one?' and pointing over to the pianist in the corner of the restaurant.

'I believe I do my dear.' I said smiling, 'I'm remembering, "I'm in the mood for love". How does it go again, Mary, I'm sure you'll know.' I asked.

'I do, James; especially when Rod Stuart sang it-'

'-and who did he play for?' I interrupted.

'For goodness sake,' she said, 'don't spoil the moment.'

'Sorry.'

'I should think so,' giving me what I interpreted as a forgiving smile for my crassness.

'Oh, is it any wonder,' Mary said softly, 'that I'm in the mood for love. I can't remember the middle part,' she went on, 'only the ending which went something like this: "And if there's a cloud above, if it, should rain, we'll let it. But for tonight forget it. I'm in the mood for love".'

'Oh, Yeah.' I finished for her.

Chapter Twenty

The next day Mary and I were woken up by a loud bang on the bedroom door as if someone was attempting to break in; it was Alfred, the waiter, delivering our breakfast to the room.

'Good morning to you, Sir James, madam.' Alfred said, bumbling around in the corridor, having just slipped on the threadbare carpet which might have seen better days draping inside a shop in Hamrun village.

'Good morning, Alfred, you're late.' I replied, taking the tray from him, 'I asked for our breakfast to be delivered at eight o'clock, ten minutes after our early morning call, which I will add, we also didn't receive and it is now ten minutes past nine.' I said, demanding an explanation.

'I'm so sorry, sorry, sorry, sorry, Sir James,' Alfred said sorrowfully, in a way only the Maltese could be. He then continued to tell me that some of the Christmas decorations which had been sellotaped to the ceiling by Joseph the previous day had fallen down and one of the German guests was complaining about festive red, white and blue baubles floating around in his bowl of cornflakes. I said to him it could possibly have been worse; he may have found American stars and stripes and a Canadian maple leaf in there too.

Mary was still in bed when I poured the tea from the elegant looking EPNS silver-plated tea pot.

'Good morning, Mary.' I said to her, placing the cup and saucer on the table at her side of the bed.

'Good morning, James; you're a good man,' she said to me, ruffling up the pillows to enable her to sit up straight. 'What is the time, darling?' she asked, looking towards an open window to hear church bells ringing in her ears. 'For eight o'clock it's very light, James.' she added.

I told her it was a quarter past nine and that the night porter, Tony Galea had forgotten to inform George Attard about our early call and our breakfast didn't arrive until ten past nine.

'Well, I suppose the lie in did us both good, especially having had such a good time in the casino.' Mary said, pinching her handbag which she had placed close to her on the bedside table. 'Tell me James; we did go to

181

the casino last night, didn't we, because it all seems like a dream this morning?' she added.

'It was no dream, Mary; it happened alright.'

'I didn't really think it was, you know, but it was a bit amazing, wasn't it?'

'I suppose you could say so, but let's not think about it today, shall we. That was yesterday; one more day in this extraordinary holiday of ours, which it would seem, is lasting forever.'

'Why is it,' she said, 'I get the impression you're trying to change the subject?'

'You could be right, Mary, but do you know, after all those thunder storms and the tropical rain last evening, it is a very pleasant morning and I can't wait to sit beside Valenti's statue of the diminutive, Queen Victoria outside the Café Cordina facing Republic Square, and to read a long forgotten British newspaper whilst drinking a two-sip espresso and chased by an *averna* will undoubtedly be an absolute luxury'.

'Yes, James you will enjoy that, won't you?' she said, getting out of bed and heading for the bathroom, 'and me James, what about me?' she remarked cynically; 'I don't look anything like Queen Victoria, do I?'

'No Mary, you look like a young Marilyn Monroe.' I said to her knowing she would come back at me with another critical remark.

'Unlike Queen Victoria, who died on the twenty-second of January 1901, Marilyn Monroe departed this life on the fifth of August 1962 and you could say I don't look like either of them.' Mary said when she noisily closed the bathroom door behind her.

I thought to myself, yes, I deserved that, but then, what else could she be storing up in her clever little brain to get back at me?

Mary eventually emerged from the bathroom saying to me you look like a young Robert Redford standing resplendent in your Prince of Wales tartan dressing gown; I replied by saying: 'Who is Robert Redford and don't tell me, he probably plays football for Manchester United.'

'Oh, James,' she sighed. 'I give up.'

I switched on the television to watch the CNN news and fortunately we were in time to see the president of France, Jacques Chirac being interviewed along the River Seine in Paris, and at one point he looked as if he was about to throw himself off one of the bridges having just sold his granny to Saddam Hussein.

'It was a good idea of yours, James to have breakfast in our room.' Mary said, bashing the living daylights out of her one-hour and ten minute boiled eggs with a teaspoon.

'Yes, Mary, I don't think I could stand sitting and having my breakfast knowing I was in the same room as 'Big Foot' from Canada.'

'Will you please switch the television off, James; all this business about Sadam Hussein in Iraq and Howard Wilson, the lonely planet traveller from Canada, is beginning to give me a headache.' she said, rummaging around in her handbag to find a remedy for one of her heads.

Mary and I decided to be brave and take the lift down to the ground floor and, clambering over white linen sacks and laundry baskets to enable me to activate the lift by pushing the button was indeed exhausting to say the least.

'Good morning, Sir James, madam.' George Attard said, when he noticed us standing in front of the reception desk.

'Good morning, good morning; who put that idea into your head?' I assertively asked him, 'We were expecting an early call at ten-minutes to eight this morning and it is now five-minutes past ten and I demand an explanation.' I added, giving him more of my unpleasant remarks.

He told us he hadn't been informed by Tony, the night porter, to give us our early morning call and assured us he would report it to the manager, to which I replied: 'Don't bother, Tony will only end up joining the ranks of Malta's unemployed.'

'I am so sorry, Sir James, sorry, sorry, sorry.' Attard said, convincing me by the second, he wasn't the slightest bit sorry.

'Now don't go over the top, George,' I said to him in a low voice. 'We don't want Gino to hear us, do we?'

It was when Mary and I were about to venture out into the street Helen Azzopardi made an untimely appearance, coming in through the main door likened to a whirlwind. Helen chose to sit down on the red velvet settle in reception and this was where she broke down in tears because of her husband leaving her to live with the leading lady from The Manoel Theatre in Valletta. And, without thinking or even caring about her dilemma, I asked her if she would like to buy one of our umbrellas because it looked as though it was going to rain. At this point, Mary said to me: 'Have you ever tried joining the Diplomatic Corps?' However, Helen did succeed the following day in selling us two boxes of cut-price Azzopardi Praline chocolates; these were obviously part of her spoils from a broken-up marriage.

The morning continued with Howard, flying down the staircase with gusto, demanding an explanation from the receptionist as to why he hadn't received his early morning call and then we overheard Doris complaining to the manager about several bottles of spirits being depleted during the night from the hotel's coffee shop. Gino, guided her gently to one side and not so discreetly said to her, this could explain why hardly anyone turned up for breakfast this morning and he would make up the shortfall in the bottles by topping them up with mineral water.

Contrary to my remarks to Helen about the weather and despite my failed attempt to cheer her up with the umbrella jokes, it was a bright sunny morning and the temperatures had risen by a few degrees.

'Hi, James, Mary,' Howard said to Mary and me as we tried for the third time to sneak out with stealth into the street. 'Maybe, I can join you two guys later for a beer?' he suggested, trying to make himself a little more coherent when the bells of Saint Dominic began to toll loudly, ringing in my ears.

'Enjoy it.' George Attard said, mimicking Dominic, the parrot, as Mary and I walked down the steps of the hotel into a cool and shady street and I knew how Neil Armstrong must have felt when he put his foot down on to the moon for the first time. I said to her as we were negotiating yet another climb up Mount Everest: 'If we ever succeed in reaching the top of this slippery slope, known by every dog and cat in Valletta as St John's Street, I would like to buy an English newspaper in Merchant Street before we have our coffee.'

The morning progressed smoothly sitting at a table underneath a brightly coloured parasol and directly in front of the Café Cordina. The waiter, who later became our friend when we gave him a more than generous tip, was called Manuel and genuinely wanted to know if Mary and I were going to come back and see him again. He openly told us he had another job working as an entertainer, doubling up as a George Formby at the Bugibba Inferiority Complex on the northern coast of the island but, that was until his wife put her foot through his ukulele when she found out he was having an extra-marital relationship with a Bulgarian waitress. I said to him it was a strange name to call a holiday centre to which he replied it was a play on words and we should go and visit the place at our peril.

This was Saturday morning in vibrant Valletta, sitting in the shade under the watchful eye of Queen Victoria who was giving me the impression she had been visited several times by the bedraggled and well-kicked pigeons and used as a public convenience, reminding me of the mushroom method used by the Foreign Office hierarchy to keep you in the dark and crap on you twice a week.

Following the delicious fix of freshly ground *espresso* coffee and a medicament of *averna*, the popular Italian digestive liqueur made from a mixture of herbs, roots and citrus rinds I politely summoned Manuel to our table. I asked him to bring a bottle of the much acclaimed Maltese 'La Vallette' red wine and a packet of cheese and onion crisps so we could show off our new found wealth to the rich and elegant *cognoscenti*, Maltese ladies who seem to have a flare for expensive eighteen-carat gold jewellery.

'Have you noticed, James,' she said, pointing across the road to the Café Cordina, 'how many different varieties of ice cream they have on offer here?'

'Can't say I have, my dear,' I answered, 'but as you know, I'm not exactly an avid ice cream eater.'

'Oh, James,' she sighed, 'you don't have to be, but from where we're sitting it's not too difficult to read their board. They have a brilliant assortment;' she continued enthusiastically, 'listen to this: strawberry, vanilla, chocolate, pistachio, caramel, raspberry and nougat!!'

'It all sounds quite delicious,' I said, 'and I can't wait to sample them all.'

'Honestly, James, there are times when you truly push my patience to the limit.' Mary said, with the exasperated expression on her face I'd become used to over the years, 'You are such an ass; for a donkey you would pass!'

'I don't think I like you when you're in one of your skittish moods.' I said.

'I'm not being skittish,' she was quick to get back to me, 'I'm merely being like Margaret Thatcher; I'm only a shopkeeper's daughter.'

'Did you know Mary that Margaret Thatcher scientifically invented *Mr Whippy* ice cream when she was practicing to be a chemist at Somerville College, Oxford University?'

'And correct me if I am wrong, James, but when Margaret was the Prime Minister she also sank the Argentinean battleship, *Belgrano*.'

'Alright, Mary, point taken.' I replied tongue in cheek. 'But it wasn't her who was responsible, it was the Royal Navy.' I added trying desperately to put the record straight.

'Did you know James, Harry Potter invented HP Sauce?'

'Now you are being silly, Mary.'

'Have you also noticed, James the British telephone kiosks and red letter boxes they have around here?' Mary said pointing to one on a corner next to Marks & Spencer.

'As a matter of fact, I have, my dear; they have been in and out of Republic Street more times than Dracula gets out of his coffin.' I put in before both of us began to laugh hysterically behind a disdainful Maltese lady who made it quite clear that she preferred not to speak or listen to us.

I can remember the background music; appropriately enough it was Burt Bacharach and his orchestra playing: "Raindrops keep falling on my head" as it started to rain torrentially.

'It's Burt Scratch my back.' I said to Mary teasingly, knowing she would remember we had a couple of his records back home.

'Oh, James, you know his name is called Burt Bacharach, you are only trying as usual to wind me up.'

The tropical storm was beginning to build up momentum and rainwater had gradually started to seep through the parasol on to the table and this was when Mary and I took shelter underneath an archway outside the Café Premier where we paid the bill to Manuel.

'Enjoy it.' Manuel said to us as we departed to make our way to St Lucia Street.

'Can you remember the other day, James,' Mary said, and reminding me again of another incident I would have much preferred to forget, 'the waiter in that little Italian bar in Old Bakery Street when he said there were two prices in there; one for the locals and one for the tourists and then going on to say that there was a little game they play and it was quite simple; you order the drinks we give you the bill and I then tear it up.'

'Yes, I can remember it all too well, as if it were yesterday.' I replied, as we sheltered once again, this time below a silversmiths' canopy in St Lucia Street.

'Well, it did happen yesterday, James.' Mary said, looking at what appeared to me like the most expensive item of jewellery in the window.

'I can also remember saying to the waiter that his little scam was very enterprising and we would be looking forward to visiting his bar again to sit amongst the members of Malta's notorious '*Cosa Nostra*'.'

'Now, James, you know you wouldn't have dared to say anything like that.' Mary said staring at my reflection in the window. 'They would kill you first.' she added, grinning like a Cheshire cat.

The rain had suddenly stopped and the water which had run along the side of the pavement into the gutter had ceased to flow and the deceptive dark clouds seemed to move quickly, heading towards a wild life conservatory park likened to an under-populated duck pond situated in an over-populated fishing village called Marsascala, south of Zejtun.

As we entered into Merchant Street I tripped over a Peruvian flute player who was standing next to an amplifier that looked like it had been chucked out by the Beatles sometime during the swinging sixties.

'He's from the *Andes*.'

'Where are they?' she asked.

'They're at the end of your wristies.'

'I can see it's going to be another one of those days.' Mary said, shaking her head slowly as I impressed her with my wealth of geographical knowledge.

It was eleven forty-five when Mary and I continued to make our way down St Lucia Street, taking our lives into our hands precariously walking down the well trodden steps passing by a confectionery and *patizzerija*, fashion boutiques; all adjacent to an artisan *chocolatier* and the side entrance to the Church of Saint Paul's Shipwreck which had a wooden board outside stating in large letters that all foreigners are welcome.

'Tell me James,' she said, in a puzzled sort of way. 'Why are you still wearing your Saint John's Ambulance Brigade sticker on your shirt?'

After convincing her that it was merely to impress the shop keeper of the jewellery store later that afternoon where I intended to buy her a silver bangle inlaid with different coloured stones, she stopped being inquisitive and this was when I continued to tell her I intended to receive good value for money.

Mary and I arrived at Ricardo's Café, Bar & Ristorante just as the bells of St John's Cathedral began to toll loudly heralding midday; other churches of lesser importance joining in with the noise.

'What a 'Hinge & Bracket',' I said to her as we walked into the restaurant where we were greeted by none other than Ricardo Bianchetti, the renowned chef and restaurateur from Milan dressed to kill in his black and white chequered trousers, white jacket, apron and red neckerchief; his pouty Maltese hostess of a wife, Tanya, lolling nonchalantly over the bar keeping a watchful eye on the till.

'Yes it is a bit of a racket.' Mary said looking around to find a table away from the open door.

The waitress, who was called Claudia, showed us to an idyllic little corner of the restaurant where the continental atmosphere continued with earthenware candleholders being placed on every table, and fabulous aromas of garlic and wine was wafting through from the open kitchen.

I ordered an aperitif consisting of two Maltese 'Rainbow' cocktails, a mixology of premium choice spirits, local syrups and exotic liqueurs and then asked Claudia to bring me an ashtray so that I could pollute what was left of the atmosphere by smoking a Rothman's cigarette.

'Tell me James, is this really necessary?' Mary said as she contemplated changing our warm surroundings for a table next to the door. 'You haven't had a cigarette all morning why are you bothering to have one now?' she added.

I remember mumbling something before placing the cigarette back into the packet and this was when she said:

'You know, James, I can see a time when the government will stop people from smoking in public places and, furthermore, they will increase the price of them so much no one will be able to afford them.'

'Yes, you are probably right, Mary,' I said to her knowing she had thought about it all in great depth. 'It does seem a little stupid,' I continued to say, 'to spend a lot of our hard-earned money on something which is to go up in smoke.'

We ordered our first course which consisted of crispy yet perfectly tender *calamari* and a bubbling dish of mushrooms baked in a creamy *mascarpone*, spinach and garlic sauce. The main course for me consisted of a *Spaghetti Bolognaise Napolitano* whilst, Mary, preferred the red-pesto based *pizza*, loaded with roasted red and yellow peppers, olives, a raw egg, cherry tomatoes, red onion, *mascarpone* and buffalo *mozzarella* cheese. The dessert was a mountainous creation of chocolate fudge brownie cake, vanilla and chocolate ice cream, with cream and a more than generous helping of our favourite chocolaty topping. *Ftira*, scrummy local bread resembling a huge sun-tanned Polo mint, soaked in pungent olive oil and chopped tomatoes was served with lashings of *Parmesan* cheese at no extra cost with all three courses. A small bottle of '*Marsovin*' Special Reserve red wine had been brought to our own little corner of the restaurant by Claudia; the cork which had been expertly extracted from the neck made a loud pop adding to the cacophony of noises coming in from outside.

It was when I was licking the last remains of ice cream from a dessert spoon I listened in to a conversation between two smart looking gentlemen sitting at a table next to us.

'What's afoot?' Mary asked.

When I said I didn't know, she replied by reminding me that a foot is below my ankle!

'Ah, very funny, Mary,' I said to her with caution, 'but can we not be serious for a minute; these two men are something to do with shipping arms, ammunition and rockets from Russia to Iran.'

'James, how many more times have I got to tell you, we are on holiday, not to spot Malta's regular spy guys.' she whispered. 'And,' she added, 'what was that noise?'

I told her not to worry as it was only my hip bothering me again.

'Listen, James, we will have to go now because we don't want to miss the premier audio visual show, 'The Malta Experience' do we?' Mary said, placing her spectacles in her handbag.

'No, I would hate to miss it.' I replied trying not to give the impression I couldn't have cared less.

'Now, James, don't be sarcastic,' she went on. 'I know how you have always wanted to see the ancient prehistoric temples of Malta's Stone Age.'

'Yes, Mary, I am really looking forward to that.' I replied seeing her revving up and raring to go.

I paid the bill to the hostess with the mostess, big boobs Tanya, who could just about manage to give us a smile after we had placed a two Lira tip in the poor box on top of the bar.

'*Grazie, arrivederci*; thank you and goodbye.' Ricardo said to us as we departed his restaurant.

I said to Mary as we walked down Barriera Wharf passing the Siege Bell Memorial and heading towards the cinema: 'Who is Harry Verderci? I bet you anything he plays for Inter Milan football Club.'

'Now you are being stupid, James.' she said walking at a slightly faster pace than me. 'The rain must have made you a little rusty; *arrivederci* means goodbye.'

We arrived at Malta's purpose built auditorium just in time to experience the forty-five minute multi-vision show of beautiful imagery and atmospheric sound-bite script and wholesome images of the complete history of the Maltese islands portrayed in eight languages. I can recall walking past a souvenir and coffee shop before going into the underground theatre where I just couldn't wait to relax and get my head down on one of their comfortable looking red velour seats situated around the curvature of the auditorium.

It was reminiscent of "Saturday night at the movies" when Mary and I were sitting in the back row of the Odeon in Leicester Square not caring which picture we saw. Mary and I immediately placed the headsets provided on to our ears; everyone in the audience looking like airline pilots waiting for take-off before the lights went down. The show had begun, the images starting to appear and the loud music which blared into my ears was beginning to disturb my sleeping pattern. I removed the headset and let it dangle over the seat and this was when I started to fall asleep and go back in time to continue my story.

Chapter Twenty-one

On the airfield Monday night 4th May 1942 at RAF Netheravon, Wiltshire

It was a quarter past eleven on that Monday night and within a week of a full moon and for Herman Klaus Schneider the time had arrived for him to jump the eight hundred feet from an RAF Whitley Mk.III long range bomber into a recently ploughed expanse of land near to Herford in Northern Germany where God, it seems, had refused to answer one of his prayers.

I was waiting at the side of the runway with Halewood and Greaves to watch the final checks being made to Schneider's parachute, the static line and personal baggage securely attached to his chest by an RAF jump-master prior to him boarding the aircraft. A de- Havilland Tiger Moth Mk.II was waiting for take-off directly behind the Whitley Mk.III and I couldn't help but notice how proud Wing Commander B.A Oakley, the Officer Commanding of 297 Squadron RAF Netheravon looked when he saw those two aircraft speed off down the runway, one behind the other to reach for the sky. Schneider was now going home to carry out his role as an MI6 double agent and to play his part in "Operation Cliff-hanger".

*

Tuesday 5th May 1942; the secret Special Operations Executive airfield in Newmarket, Cambridgeshire

The Westland Lysander Mk.III (SD) was waiting impatiently in the moonlight on the uneven and overgrown stretch of runway, known to the SOE, Special Operations Executive, as the 'Highway to Hell'; its forward propeller rotating noisily indispersed with the sound of a cuckoo singing its little heart out at the approach of summer.

Squadron Leader Keith Knowles, wearing his 'chocks away' regulatory brown leather sheepskin flying jacket, a white embroidered silk scarf and pilots helmet, complete with Halcyon goggles, glanced momentarily at his watch before closing the window of the cockpit; it was eleven fifteen precisely. The sinister looking "Lizzie" air plane with its matt black livery was carrying that evening enough weaponry, bombs and ammunition to sink an armada, silhouetted amongst the tall elm trees and again was within a week of a full moon. Squadron Leader Knowles was now ready to fly the rugged, short take-off and land the aircraft the three hundred miles into German-occupied territory; his mission primarily, to fly Captain Lorenzo Marino on to a short strip of land marked out by five torches in Fontainebleau, south of Paris and then with help from the French Resistance, Knowles was to recover a British agent; dangerously flying him back through a barrage of flak over Calais and then to continue with his mission to return home safely to an RAF station somewhere on the south coast of England.

Lorenzo, wearing a black woollen overcoat with the collar scruffily turned up at the back had the brim of an equally black trilby hat tilting down over his eyes; a 9mm semi-automatic *Beretta Modello* pistol which was bulging from the inside of his coat made him look like a Mickey Spillane character. He was carrying a medium size brown leather suitcase as he walked slowly towards the aircraft escorted by Warrant Officer Steven Smith, an RAF Loadmaster, seconded to the SOE; Colonel Woodruff; Commander West and Pauline Cox following on behind. Captain Marino, helped by WOII Smith, climbed the ladder to get inside the rear cockpit. It was when he was about to place one foot inside, he turned around and said to everyone: '*arriverderci*,' goodbye Great Britain, '*Bonjourno, Roma*', hello Rome, 'and a special '*Grazie, Ciau*,'; 'thank you and goodbye to Sergeant Shirley Pringle.'

'And just in case you are considering poking that canon of yours into the back of Squadron Leader Knowles,' Woodruff said to Lorenzo putting the fear of God into him for the last time on British soil, 'you will be making a big mistake and I will make life very difficult for your wife and family if you decide to do anything so stupid.'

'What's the matter you, you got a no respect and don't joke with me, you sonna ma bitch,' Lorenzo replied, waving his index finger at him, 'I am not a stupid boy!'

'And when you arrive in Rome, Donatello, give my kindest regards to Joey Macaroni.' Woodruff said to Captain Marino as he watched the RAF bag-handler, Warrant Officer Steven Smith, handing over his luggage.

Pauline Cox tried to compose herself giving him a discreet little wave and, turning away wiped the tears away from her eyes with a well used silk handkerchief.

Colonel Brian Woodruff, Commander Mark West, Pauline Cox and Warrant Officer Steven Smith stood back on the grass verge to see the aircraft manoeuvre into position in readiness for take-off. Captain Marino, after securing himself into the back passenger seat fastened his safety harness, slid down out of sight before Knowles pulled out the throttle and released the breaks enabling the aircraft to charge down the runway like the proverbial bat out of hell.

The Lysander touched down silently in a field where six members of the French Resistance had been waiting for the British air plane to appear in the night sky. Captain Marino was instantaneously whisked away in the back of a black Citroen van to begin a sixteen hour journey; the *'Jack Boot Route'* a regional train from Paris to Rome, calling at Lyon, Marseille, Nice, Ventimiglia, Livorno and Grosselo. The uncomfortable seat on which Lorenzo had been sitting for one and a half hours from Newmarket to Fontainebleau was now occupied by an Anglo French Resistance fighter called Valerie Kenny who was the proud possessor of a shapely pair of legs and kept on repeating: "Listen carefully, I will say this only once and I don't boil cabbages twice".

Squadron Leader Knowles courageously flying his aircraft back to base was confronted by three "Bandits", aircraft from the German *Luftwaffe*; a lone *Messerschmitt* 109 and two empty *Dornier* 287 bombers which were returning over the English Channel after successful missions over Margate and Ramsgate. He used his two forward firing 7.7 mm Browning machine guns to fiercely ward them off by flying directly in front of them and then much to the delight of his Station Commander when Knowles told him that one of them would be late in going for breakfast.

Meanwhile, Herman Klaus Schneider was nursing a broken ankle in his home town of Osnabruck after he had landed in a furrow of a recently ploughed field in Herford; he had been told on at least three occasions to bend his legs and keep his feet firmly together on reaching the ground.

He was to spend the rest of the war years hobbling around with a walking stick trying to emulate in later years, Herr Flik from the British television series "Hello, Hello".

I woke up just in time to see the end of Malta's Experience and this was when I said to Mary:

'Come on, Mary, let's go; the show is over; not that I saw any of it'. I added under my breath.

'Before we leave,' she said. 'I'd like to buy one of those tea towels.'

'If you must, my dear.' wanting to leave this dungeon of a place.

'It's the one about the Italian who came to Malta; you probably didn't see it.' she added, 'Anyway I know Carol would have a giggle when she reads it.'

'Italians, Mary! I have had quite enough of Italians during the last couple of hours to last me a lifetime.'

'Listen to this, James.' Mary said, as we perused through the souvenir shop on our way out, 'It says you have to read it with an Italian accent; those who don't suffer.'

> One day ima gonna Malta to bigga hotel
> Inna morning I go down to eat breakfast
> I tella waitress I wanna two pissis toast
> She brings me only one piss
> I tell her, I want two piss
> She say, go to the toilet
> I say, you no understand, I wanna piss on my plate
> She say, you no better piss onna plate, you sonna ma bitch
> I don't even know the lady and she call me sonna ma bitch!!
>
> Later, I go eat at a bigga restaurant
> The waitress brings me a spoon and a knife but no fok
> I tella her I wanna fok
> She tell me everyone wonna fok
> I tell her, you no understand. I wanna fok on the table
> She says, you better not fok on the table, you sonna ma bitch
>
> So, I go back to my room inna hotel and there is no shits onna ma

195

bed

I call the manager and tella him I wanna shit

He tell me to go to toilet

I say, you no understand, I wanna shit on my bed

He say, you better not shit onna bed, you sonna ma bitch

I go to the checkout and the man at the desk say: "Peace on you"

I say, piss on you too, you sonna ma bitch, I gonna back to Italy!!!

'Well, that is some tea towel,' I said to Mary, feeling the quality and not the width. 'And I'm sure Carol will enjoy reading it when she's drying the dishes back home.'

Mary purchased the tea towel, which, I may add, still hangs up against the wall in our small kitchen in Russell Court. I bought an eighteen-carat gold plated tie pin with the Maltese cross encrusted upon it and came nicely presented in a see-through plastic box.

On our way out through the door of this non-memorable experience we heard the sound of gun fire coming from nearby Fort St Elmo. I said to Mary: 'Come on, let's see what these jokers are doing now?'

'Oh, James can't you be reasonable.' Mary replied, with another sigh. 'Fort St Elmo is closed to the public and now houses the police academy who teaches them how to shoot people.'

'Well, that is very interesting, Mary,' I said, giving her a quick smile. 'But, how come some of them are wearing sixteenth century baggy trousers, banging on side drums and carrying halberds, tall axe-like weapons specially designed for getting rid of unwanted Canadians.'

'It's probably extra-mural activities they have in there, James.' she explained just as one of their percussion instruments fell on an actor's foot. 'And do try not to upset these super sensitive Maltese people.'

'Tell me Mary, are you looking forward to going to the Manoel Theatre tonight?' I asked, looking at my watch to see the time fast approaching three o'clock.

'Of course I am, James.' she replied, giving me a gentle nudge on my arm. 'You know I enjoy going to the theatres in the West End of London especially to see comedies being performed on stage with famous actors and actresses sharing the leading roles.' she added.

I told Mary not to get too excited because the tourist representative, Mrs Helen Azzopardi made a point in telling me that the Maltese International Stage Production at the Manoel Theatre for that evening's entertainment was to be 'George and Mildred' starring Carmen *Peroxide* Scicluna and *Dingli* Cliff Spiteri; both of whom should be residing in separate retirement homes in Msida Creek. During the finale with a little help from the audience participation, they sang "Keep young and Beautiful"; this was when I said to Mary: 'In their dreams.' Helen Azzopardi was absolutely spot-on when she made a comment about blonde- haired Carmen Scicluna from Senglea, whose appearance was enough to turn milk sour and when she spoke, she sounded like a noise coming from inside a metal bucket and Clifford Spiteri from Zabbar looking like someone who had just crept out from a metal box was as funny as a twisted ankle. Mary and I were told later that evening that Carmen Scicluna was the actress who was having it off with Helen's husband, George Azzopardi.

'Let's go for a refreshing gin and tonic at the Café San Giovanni in Saint John's Square.' Mary suggested, pulling at my shirt before we found a way back into the centre of the city by walking up the steep steps of Merchant Street. 'It is the Mediterranean siesta now and the shops don't open again until four.' she added.

'It doesn't look like siesta time to me, Mary; haven't the Maltese got any homes to go to?' and this was when I heard the distinctive sound of Scottish bagpipes in the distance.

As we were approaching Saint John's Square, Mary said: 'Oh look, James, there is a Maltese bagpipe band marching through Republic Street; this is really good, isn't it?' to which I replied: 'Yes, really good, Mary, but where is the bar and restaurant you are so keen to find?'

We found a suitable table beneath a parasol outside the Café San Giovanni and as she sat down she asked me if I was training to be a ballet dancer, to which I replied: 'No, dear, I just want to find the nearest toilet because I have just seen Howard Wilson heading in this direction.

'Hi, you guys, are you having a nice day?' 'Big Foot' from Canada called out, removing his recently acquired Polaroid sunglasses with the ticket still dangling from one of the stems.

'Well, I was until now...' I said, silently muttering the words under my breath and this was when Mary told me to behave myself.

'I went to see the old Saluting Battery from 'The Upper Barrakka Gardens'.' Howard told us in great detail. 'At precisely twelve noon, a gun is fired recreating the age-old tradition in trying to blow someone's head off.' he went on.

'And I was wondering at twelve noon this morning just who was responsible for making all that bloody noise.' I said to him, looking up at two tickets and not just the one.

'Well, sir, it wasn't me.' Howard replied, a serious look on his face.

'Don't worry, Howard,' Mary said to him, gently placing her hand on his arm. 'my husband was only joking.' she calmly explained. 'You do have to tell your pathetic little jokes, don't you James.' she added, kicking me in the shin with her size five and a half brown leather sandals and saying as the years go passing by I didn't improve.

'Well, folks, I have to go now; I have a number sixty bus to catch,' Howard said, momentarily glancing at his watch. 'I am going to Sliema this afternoon to do some shopping at the Plaza Shopping Complex in Tower Road.'

I was quite happy in the knowledge that Howard was about to disappear out of my sight into Zachary Street where he could take the opportunity to pester other tourists on his way to Valletta's bus terminus outside the City Gate.

Mary said 'Cheers, James,' raising a tall glass of gin and tonic with ice and lemon to her lips; I reciprocated by extending my arm to chink her glass.

The waitress, an English woman married to the Maltese chef, was called Sandra presented us with a plate of their delicious *bruschetta* ensemble, perfectly ripe tomatoes, capers and basil soaked in a pure virgin olive at no extra charge.

'This is food of the God's.' I said, squeezing the bread into my mouth and savouring every morsel.

'There is only one God, James; you should know that.' as the bells of Saint John's Co- Cathedral over the road began to toll loudly to bring to an end another Maltese wedding ceremony.

'There are a number of people in this world, Mary, who would argue that point and totally disagree with you.' I said to her in no uncertain terms, adding: 'also, I would suggest you keep your voice down because there are some peculiar looking characters lurking in St John's Square; some of whom are wearing bandages around the top of their heads. Can you see that chap over there looking in the window of the 'British Shoe Shop'; he looks as though he has just arrived from a war zone on the East coast of Africa.

'He is probably trying to make up his mind which shoes to buy before the shop opens at four.' Mary said to me, giggling with one of her cheeky grins.

'I shouldn't think so, Mary; it's an exclusive ladies fashion shoe shop.'

The clock on the wall of the Cathedral was fast approaching four o'clock and this was when we said our goodbyes to Sandra and the well fed-up pigeons before making our way back to *Triq Santa Lucia*, Saint Lucia Street via the charming old flower kiosk in St John's Square and Republic Street and for me to buy the silver bangle.

It was now dusk and light was fading rapidly as the Christmas lights came on to illuminate and brighten up the sad and tired streets of Valletta transforming them into vibrant walkways now that the shops and stores had at last reopened.

'Shall we go back to the hotel in a *karrozin*; one of those horse-drawn carriages?' Mary said, admiring and showing off her new addition to her jewellery box to everyone back in Republic Street and next to Great Siege Square.

'And, why not?' I said to her, looking over the road from the Law Courts to spot a Maltese mush to be our driver.

After several minutes of haggling with a man wearing a red scarf and flat cap we alighted the cab and climbed into the four-person canopied bench seats which were high up and a good way to see the sights and main tourist attractions in Valletta.

Side by side, Mary and I set off down Republic Street to the sound of a *karrozin* bell melodiously tinkling away passing by the famous Palace Square which sits directly in front of the Grand Master's Palace and, then, turning right into Archbishop's Street, we caught a glimpse of 'The Pub'; "Ollie's Last Stand", the late Oliver Reed's favourite watering hole.   It reminded me of a poem called "Ben Gunn" which goes:

> He lives on an island he's alive and quite well
> Reading the "Times" and still raising hell
> Among the palm trees he sits indiscreet
> In thin baggy trousers no shoes on his feet
> His spectacles hang loose on the end of his nose
> God only knows it's taken some blows
> With long greying hair a typical Saxon
> He sports a grey shirt with the words 'Glenda Jackson'
> He looks at his Rolex to check on the hour
> The battery for a long time has lost all of its power
> Looking down at "The Pub" he gazes at stars
> and wishes he could be with them to sink a few jars
> With a Vodka and Orange to add to the fun
> He is still on his island he's known as Ben Gunn

Contravening the cities one-way system, we circumnavigated Valletta, trotting along interesting little streets before drawing up outside the Broadlands Hotel just in time to freshen-up and to watch two of my favourite television programmes.

Mary, after taking a shower applied her make-up in front of the mirror as I switched on the television to see the end of the "Antiques Road Show" and the beginning of "The Weakest Link", with the delectable, Ann Robinson insulting everyone by saying: 'Goodbye'; it was a wonder there were any competitors remaining on the show to give her a black eye.

'Do you know James,' Mary said, 'tomorrow will be exactly one month until Christmas day?'

'Is that so, my dear; you do surprise me.'

'You can't fool me James Brown; you know how you love the festive season.'

At seven, Mary and I went up to the restaurant for our evening meal and when the doors to the lift opened we were greeted by Lawrence, Alfred and Salvo. We were both fortunate to be the first guests to arrive and Horatio, who was standing in the wings impatiently waiting to do something useful, showed us to our usual reserved table by the window. Salvo, after lighting the oil lamp presented us with the hotel's brown plastic folder containing the *Al a carte* and tourist menus; the evening's special culinary delights consisting of a choice, beginning with cream of mushroom soup or a *feta* cheese salad and the main courses; generous portions of lamb cutlets served with mint sauce, roast potatoes, broccoli and carrots or, alternatively, rib-eye steak served with a crushed black peppercorn sauce.

We started our meal by ordering two large gin and tonics and a bottle of local Marsovin Rosé wine. Salvo, holding a bread basket in one hand and his trusty corkscrew in the other said: 'Did you hear the one about the guy who goes fishing in Malta?' I replied: 'No, I haven't and I hope it won't take long because Mrs Brown and I have ordered a taxi for seven forty-five to take us to the Manoel Theatre.'

'That's no problem,' Salvo said with a big smile on his face. 'I will phone them up and tell them not to start until you arrive.' he added. He continued with his joke and this went as follows:

'An Italian guy wanted to know how a Maltese guy was catching more fish than he was.

He replied by explaining that when his wife puts her left leg out on the left-hand side of the bed when she gets up in the morning he goes into Sliema and catches lots of fish. And when she puts her right leg out on the right-hand side of the bed when she gets up in the morning he goes on to Manoel Island and catches lots of fish. And the Italian guy said to him:' 'Ah, but what happens if she puts her legs out on both sides of the bed when she gets up in the morning?'

'Well, in that case, I don't go fishing.' he replied.

'MAMMA MIA!' the Italian said.

Mary was laughing uncontrollably and it was exacerbated when Salvo said to us the *lampuki* fish was back inside the *A la carte* menu and then me saying to him: I wondered what that thing was flapping around on the table.

For starters, I ordered cream of pumpkin soup for Mary and for myself the *feta* cheese salad. For the main course I thought it wise for me to have the rib-eye steak and Mary to have the imported Aberdeen Angus Scotch beef at a small supplement of one Maltese Lira fifty.

I can remember me saying to her: 'Its Sandie Shaw again, singing: "Puppet on a Chain" and the cassette should still be inside it's plastic box, waiting for some nostalgia freak to come along and buy it from the flea market in 'Freedom Square'.'

'Now, James,' Mary said, waving a fork in front of my face. 'I think you've got the name of the song wrong, it's called "Puppet on a String"; it was Alistair MacLean who wrote "Puppet on a Chain.'

'If you say so, my dear, and I didn't know Alistair MacLean wrote songs.' I replied.

We started to eat our strawberry cheesecake just as an advance party of Maltese thespians came flurrying in after rehearsing their latest play at the St. James' Cavalier Centre in Valletta. The tables were all put together for them in the centre of the room and it seemed the attention had strayed away from our little corner of the restaurant towards the middle which was rapidly being filled with noisy Maltese 'Lovies' reminding the waiters to attend to them first in front of us foreigners.

The Wembley taxi arrived on time to take us the short distance to the *Teatru Manoel* in Old Theatre Street, Valletta. As we were leaving the hotel we witnessed Tony Galea being read his terms of employment by Gino, the manager which didn't include siphoning off whisky, gin and vodka from bottles in the coffee shop. We also clocked Doris who was peering out and listening to the indiscreet proceedings from behind a massive curtain; I said to Mary, it's better than seeing a Brian Rix bedroom farce, isn't it?'

'It certainly is, James.' she replied with a big sigh.

'Come on Mary, let's get out of here before Dominic the parrot and

Anthony Vella decide to open their traps and spoil our entire evening.'

As Gino opened the glass door to let us out into the street, the parrot squawked and I said to myself: 'here it comes.'

'Enjoy it!'

*

The Theatre Manoel that evening

This fascinating little purpose built baroque building is said to be the third-oldest European theatre still in use; all the delicate frescoes are of Mediterranean scenes and in 22-carat gold leaf. The *palazzo* Bonici a few doors away serves as a foyer and this was where Mary and I hob-knobbed and rubbed shoulders with the Maltese *cognoscenti* after making our grand entrance.

We were seated in the centre of the theatre's 650 seat oval-shaped auditorium and beneath the gilded ceiling and magnificent three tier chandelier.

Mary sitting on my left opened a box of Azzopardi Chocolates which I had just bought for her in the foyer and we began munching away starting with the strawberry cream fondant disregarding the hard nougat as we waited for the lights to go down and the plush green velvet curtains on the stage to be raised. Mary looked at the programme and the photographs of the cast and afterwards said:

'I think, James, Helen Azzopardi was speaking metaphorically.'

'Was she?'

'Yes, of course, look at the photograph of the actress in the programme,' Mary said, selecting another chocolate confection to add to our dentist's bill. 'Carmen Scicluna is a beautiful young woman and it will be many years before she'll be admitted to any rest home, but more importantly and I think this was what really upset Helen, she's a good ten years younger than her.'

The show began with a standing ovation when George and Mildred played by, Clifford Spiteri and Carmen Scicluna walked arm in arm down the centre of the auditorium to go on stage.

It was during the first act I fell asleep and this was when I continued dreaming were I had previously left off that morning.

Chapter Twenty-two

Roma Ostiense Railway Station in *Piazzale dei Partigiani*, Rome at 0800hrs Thursday 7th May 1942

The train which conveyed the "Condor" Captain Lorenzo Marino, alias Rolando Donatello, to Rome had stopped at nearly every station on the way, contrary to an unreliable wartime timetable, before arriving six hours late due to spontaneous passport checks by the German Gestapo, French and Italian police who were positioned on the borders between France and Italy.

Lorenzo, wearing his black overcoat and equally black trilby hat, stepped warily down on to the platform and was immediately confronted by Alfonso Bruciano, the British MI9 secret agent known as Joey Macaroni, who began his dramatic deception by kissing him on both cheeks to convince everyone they were more than just good friends.

During the arduous six hundred and ninety-four mile train journey from Paris to Rome, Captain Marino had his one-way ticket, papers and travel documents checked many times by the authorities and at one point he thought the multitude of names and fictitious addresses which had been given to him by MI6 could eventually lead to his arrest.

The now congested and over-populated steam-driven train pulled into the coastal town of San Remo at precisely four pm on Wednesday 6th May and this was when two thug-like characters both wearing black shirts, white ties and trench-coats climbed on board. Lorenzo, sitting in a dusty compartment became extremely worried when he saw the two bald-headed Benito Mussolini impersonators goose-stepping up and down in the corridor checking everyone's credentials. There was an air of sadness, albeit, quickly replaced by relief when he saw two members of Italy's Angry Brigade step off the train in *Alassio* following the arrest of two Jewish passengers who had given them their papers with false names and addresses; Monsieur and Madame Olivier from St. Denis, Paris.

Lorenzo, balancing a half-empty metal box on his lap containing a cheese and pickle sandwich, an apple, orange, several black grapes and a bar of dessert chocolate which had to satisfy his appetite for food until he arrived in Rome. The train pulled out of San Remo five minutes later to the excruciating sound of a whistle and it seemed all was good until... the silence became broken by gunfire being heard in the carriage next door. The German Gestapo who had boarded the train in Nice had shot dead an American Agent, a wanted enemy of *The Third Reich* who tried to escape from a door on to the track. Lorenzo, fluent in German and the English language had been supplied with a copy of the German newspaper, 'Frankfurter Allgemeine' by the French Resistance prior to his departure to confuse anyone who may be suspicious of him.

The train compartments were by now all full and Lorenzo, sitting next to the window had the benefit of seeing everything which was happening all around him. Seated next to him was a French woman with her three children, two teenage boys and a girl and, sitting directly across from him, were three Italian soldiers; all wearing the distinctive khaki army uniform. It was in Naples the door to the compartment was violently opened by a greasy sleuth wearing a dark green greatcoat and a pair of sunglasses firmly affixed to his ugly pockmarked face. He had every intention of checking everyone's travel documents but that was until a row broke out between him and an army sergeant seated next to the sliding door. The army sergeant, taking exception to this rude intrusion and with the aid of a hip flask containing one of Scotland's finest whiskies, was a wee bit worse for wear and desperately trying to drown his sorrows prior to him being shipped over to the waste lands of Egypt to join the *Italo-German* armies in Alexandra. The Italian policeman immediately, obviously anticipating a violent outcome of something which had every appearance of turning out quite nasty, turned swiftly out of the door neglecting to continue examining people's passports. Lorenzo, tired and frustrated, looked out through the window at the green and lush countryside in Genoa wishing he could be with his family but, all of his wishes had to wait until after British Military Intelligence and the Foreign Office based in London and Malta decided to allow him to go home. It was seven days later when Lorenzo passed by the Bay of Naples inside an Italian army truck en route to Sicily. Unable to go home to his village in San Giovanni a Teduccio to join his twenty-one year old wife, Francesca, and his two small children; three year-old Antonio and his one-year old daughter Anne-Sofia, Lorenzo had to accept he would have to wait until whatever he had to do was successfully carried out before he could see his family once again.

Joey Macaroni and Lorenzo walked swiftly along the platform heading towards a mustard Fiat 500 'Topolini' motor car parked on the forecourt in front of the station; its extraordinary and distinctive black wheel arches gave the impression 'Noddy' and 'Big Ears', the two cartoon characters were in charge. The driver, wearing a chequered flat cap was standing by the side of the vehicle with his arms and legs folded likened to a skein of wool waiting to be unravelled and made into a ball. He opened the nearside back door to allow Lorenzo to climb in and stretch out on a recently upholstered seat; the unmistakable smell of black Italian leather permeating all around him. The car with Joey Macaroni sitting on the right-hand side of the driver, Frankie Bivolli alias, Spaghetti Zanetti from Catania in Sicily and Lorenzo, sitting comfortably on his own at the rear sped off down *Piazzale dei Partigian*, heading towards Rome's famous Coliseum.

*

I was abruptly woken up by Mary prodding me in the ribs to tell me it was half-time; the intermission when alcohol revellers make a bee-line for fifteen minutes in the theatre's cosy little bar. Mary and I were unfortunate to be standing next to a British stage play production manager who was sufficiently disappointed with George and Mildred to warrant going back to London on the first available flight; a Maltese man and wife sitting at a table in front of the bar kindly offered to buy him the ticket. The much needed liquid refreshment and sustenance consisting of two large whiskies and a bowl of olives *pimento* before the continuous sound of a fire bell was heard to summon everyone to go back to their seats and fall asleep. I can remember a member of the audience asking me if the olives were pithed. I replied by saying: 'well they might be.'

I wasn't in any great hurry to go back to my seat in the middle of the auditorium next to the aisle and besides, having to leave half a bowl of the pithed olives and savoury popcorn on top of the bar, I couldn't wait until the lights dimmed to drift off once again into the past.

In a matter of moments I did just that and found myself standing inside the Town Hall, (*Rathaus*) in Osnabruck, Westphalia, listening to the interrogation of "The Rottweiler", Herman Klaus Schneider, by the *Gestapo*. Schneider under duress told them he had escaped from a maximum security compound in Brentwood, Essex and managed to find his way down to Folkestone in Kent en-route to Calais. He continued with his fairy stories by telling them a French fishing boat had run aground near to Dover and persuading the skipper to take him over to Boulogne from where he could profit by two-thousand French Francs. The "Hare" convinced the *Gestapo*, the *Abwehr* and the *Sicherheitdienst*, German military intelligence, that Britain is an island, not too difficult to get on but very difficult to get off. A member of the *SD* wanted to know how Schneider had broken his ankle. He replied by telling him he had tripped over a securing rope on the main deck of the fishing vessel when it was about to be tied up to the jetty in Boulogne. The *Gestapo* swallowed that one, hook, line and sinker, followed by the *SS* inviting him to their headquarters to receive the coveted Iron Cross for bravery.

Schneider's main brief now was to supply information to MI6 in London via Bletchley Park, the Communications, Observation and British Surveillance Headquarters. He was to keep 'C', the head of MI6, me and my colleagues informed when and where Nazi gold shipments destined for the Vatican in Rome were taking place and the exact amounts of bullion contained in their wooden boxes.

*

I was woken up by the sound of a clapping noise which seemed to become louder and louder as I adjusted myself back to a normal upright position in my seat. A member of the Maltese stage production team, who had walked down the aisle especially to see me, asked if I could be quiet because the noise of my snoring was playing havoc with the stage microphones causing feed-back and drop-off from the loudspeakers.

'If only they would and perhaps we could all get some sleep.' I muttered under my breath.

A screen had taken over from George and Mildred on centre stage and this was when the audience participation began with them singing: "KEEP YOUNG & BEAUTIFUL", sounding remarkably like the 'Ovaltineys' on a bad day.

"Keep young and beautiful
It's your duty to be beautiful
Keep young and beautiful
If you want to be loved"

The ball which was being projected on to this enormous flip-chart on stage bounced up and down on top of the words to help the audience with their reading; the music recorded sometime during the nineteen-thirties for me was a little over-the-top and I was fully expecting Fred Astaire and Ginger Rogers to dance down the aisle at any moment.

It was ten thirty-five when Mary and I stepped out into the moon-lit Old Theatre Street following on behind a line of people who gave me the impression they just couldn't wait to go home. We decided against taking a taxi back to our hotel and instead to do 'the walk' again up Republic Street, passing by Valletta's famous Operatic Ruins next to Freedom Square. It was when Mary and I were trudging up South Street; a steep and precipitous slope likened to a slate quarry heading towards the *Auberge de Castile et Leon*, she said to me:

'What was that noise I can hear? Don't tell me it's your hip bothering you again?'

To this I made no comment.

We arrived at our hotel hoping for a drink in the cocktail bar following the mountainous climb and a precarious abseiling exercise down the slippery steps of Saint Ursula Street.

I said to the receptionist, Tony Galea: 'How are things this evening?'

'It's very quiet' came the reply. I said to Mary: 'it's that bloody parrot again, if it doesn't learn to keep its big mouth shut he's going to end up wearing a black eye patch.'

'Shush.' Mary said 'you are so embarrassing; it's the receptionist who is talking to you.'

'Guess who's coming down the staircase, Mary?' I said to her trying to turn myself into stealth by hiding behind the curtain.

'He's limping, James.' Mary said to me as if she were a priest talking one-to-one inside a confessional box.

'I can see you, Sir James,' Howard said, leaning over the banister.

Mary and I came to the conclusion there was no hiding place in the Broadlands Hotel and we only had to suffer 'Big Foot' from Canada for one more day because he was going back home early on the Monday. I asked Hop-Along Cassidy why he was limping, to which he replied:

'Well man, this afternoon, I slipped and fell into some daw gore gunge on the side-walk outside the 'Burger King in Valletta and my ankle kinda gotten sprained. I spent the remainder of the afternoon in Saint Luke's Hospital, Gwardamanga.'

'Oh bad luck,' I said, feeling sorry for him and then continuing to say that it could have been worse, adding insult to his injury.

'Oh, James,' Mary said looking at me daggers. 'Howard has got to go all the way back to Canada on Monday nursing that foot, have you no compassion?' she added.

Being as I was in a rather benevolent and generous mood that night I offered to buy both of them a drink in the cocktail bar where I could sit down, relax and take the weight off my aching feet.

The bar again was pleasantly filled with people from all around the world. There were Japanese tourists, hell bent on bowing and scraping, French people kissing and slobbering over each other before going up to their rooms and then having to go through the same ritual again at breakfast. The German fraternity, tinkling away with tea spoons on the side of their glasses to summon Alfred, the waiter, to give them their bill; all adding to the voice of the lovely Petula Clark singing in the background: "Love, this is my song" and, "This is the song of my Life" followed by "So kiss me goodbye" and "Down Town". And, of course, the British holiday-makers discussing in great length how much they had saved since arriving on the island and how much they were going to take back home with them.

'Tell me Howard,' I politely asked. 'Where do intend to go tomorrow?'

'Well man, in the morning I'm goanna go on one of those Captain Morgan Harbour cruises from Sliema.'

'Well, in that case man, let me buy you another drink.' I happily replied. 'This is truly, music to my ears.'

'What is music to your ears, James?' Mary asked.

'Petula Clark.' I cleverly replied.

Chapter Twenty-three

'A Tale of Three Cities', Sunday 25th November 2001

It was Sunday and the start of a memorable day I would much prefer to forget.

Mary and I had just returned from breakfast and were so looking forward to visiting Valletta's main market which takes place on Sunday in St James's Ditch. Our intention was to buy some sticky nougat, Christmas album cassettes and the odd souvenir to remind us of our wonderful holiday in Malta. However, George Michael wasn't on our list for that morning's festive entertainment because of a major hiccup with us not being allowed out from our room. The lock on the door had suddenly decided to malfunction, ending up on the floor on the other side, thus making it impossible for us to get out.

It was eleven forty-five when Joseph finally arrived to rescue us: 'What a waste of a morning.' I said to Mary, who was now starting to laugh and making it blatantly obvious that she thought the entire situation was extremely funny.

Joseph incoherently murmured something through the keyhole which sounded like he was going to go away and fetch a ten-pound sledge hammer to break down the door. I can remember shouting at him and saying couldn't he find something a little larger before threatening him with extinction.

'I am very sorry, sir; sorry, sorry, sorry.' Joseph replied, before returning to his workshop on the roof to obtain the implement of destruction which by some strange metamorphosis had turned itself into a screwdriver. We were set free just as the bells began to toll to herald midday and to remind Valletta's citizens to wake up and realize that there could be more life on the planet Zog.

Mary and I had already decided to go to the Café Cordina in Republic Square for a much needed lunch-time drink before taking our lives in our hands, travelling along dangerous roads into Sliema where a Captain Morgan boat would be waiting to take us on a forty-five minute harbour cruise.

I insisted on buying a newspaper; a copy of Britain's version of '*The Sunday Times*' at a small newsagents in Merchant Street which had been managed by a dragon called Edwina since the beginning of the Second World War.

'It's a bit breezy today, Edwina.' I said to her having by this time discovered her name.

'Why don't you go back to England, then,' an elderly man said, when he nudged me out of the way with his elbow so that he could be served first. 'It's even colder there.' he added. The small bald-headed man wearing a pair of thick-lensed spectacles resting on his bulbous red nose had an attitude problem and because of this he gave me the impression he could have been in the Mafia or an active Member of Parliament for Malta's Nationalist Socialist Party in the House of Representatives.

'Do you know,' I told them, 'if it wasn't for us British you would still be eating water melon sandwiches and rubber cheese and peas cakes; chew on that one, good day.'

I left the man angrily scratching his head and Edwina entombed in her cavern; a poor apology for a news agency, without buying anything and muttering something to her sounding like: 'you can shove your newspapers up your arse.'

Mary and I hot-footed down Merchant Street with the speed of a thousand gazelles, passing by the Anglo Maltese League Café, Bar and Restaurant on our left as we made our way to Cordina's in Republic Square.

We were so happy to be alive sitting down at a table in front of the national library, the *Bibliotheca* in Republic Square with many pigeons to keep us company. Manuel, the waiter, greeted us as if it were for the first time and asked me what we would like to drink?

'I would like a Walther nine-millimetre pistol and a silencer.' I said to him jokingly.

'We don't have those cocktails on our menu.' Manuel replied with a strange and tired look on his face.

'Well, in that case,' I said sitting very close to Mary and holding her hand. 'Would it be possible to have two Harvey Head bangers instead?'

'We don't seem to have any of those either, sir.' Manuel said sighing.

'For Pete's sakes man, what do you have?'

'I will bring you two of our popular Maltese Rainbow Cocktails; they go down very well especially after it has been raining.'

'We would also like to order two of your savoury cheese cakes because they have become a favourite pastime and talking point when eating between meals.' I said to Manuel as I looked over at a table in front of us to witness a huge platter of cheese and peas cakes being devoured by a Maltese family.

The drinks, two colourful cocktails complete with umbrella and the oval *Pastizzi* made from delicious Maltese ricotta cheese wrapped in flaky pastry were brought to our table by Manuel; this was enough to satisfy our immediate requirements for a little while before venturing three sheets into the wind.

Mary and I said our final goodbyes to Manuel, thanking him for his effortless attendance and wished him well playing with his brand new ukulele.

We returned to the Broadlands hotel to change into our wet weather gear; two blue plastic capes and a sowester, just in case we ran into a violent storm sailing on the high seas. The door lock had been changed by Joseph Mizzi shortly after we had vacated the room that morning but, however, there was still a problem because the old key belonging to the door had been given to us by Frederick Mifsud by mistake enabling us to get in.

'Sorry, Sorry, Sorry, sir,' was his answer to everything, but I still wasn't convinced he was. On our way out, Dominic said his usual party piece, 'Enjoy it; it's very quiet', but this time I was smarter than he because I was quick to squawk at him first. I can recall saying to Mary: 'that's thrown him, hasn't it?'

At this point I saw Zahra Baldacchino; the hotel's secretary bobbing up and down from behind the reception desk with a big smile on her face and this was when I heard the parrot say: 'That's the way to do it.'

*

It was exactly two-thirty when we stepped off the bus directly outside Marks & Spencer at the Sliema Savoy bus stop in the Strand. We walked quickly over the busy road towards the Captain Morgan boats which were tethered to the quayside and this was when we heard:

'Hello, Mary love! Hello, Jim!'

It was her, the intrepid Hilda, standing next to her husband Stanley, the man from that awful den of iniquity in the North of England they call Liverpool. Beam me up Scottie was my immediate reaction when I saw him saluting me as I stood in the centre reservation of the road waiting to get knocked down by a bright red Sunday kit car chased by a Ferrari and a Lamborghini.

Standing by the railings and waiting to board the boat was the unavoidable Nicholas (knickerless) Bottomley; his wide-angle telephoto lens camera still hanging down from around his neck. There, standing at the quayside was Betty Ward and Vera Cruikshank, Frank and Mavis Riley and would you believe, Howard Wilson, wearing the biggest Stetson this side of Calgary, Alberta.

'I thought you were going on the harbour cruise this morning.' I said to Howard inquisitively.

'I kinda missed the boat this morning because of hobbling around in Valletta,' 'Big foot' from Canada said, sitting down by the side of the gangway nursing his wounds. 'I'm pretty sure with all of you guys I will make up for that delay.'

'Yes, I'm sure you will Howard.' I said again, tongue in cheek.

'Being on this boat today brings it all back to me.' Stanley Parry said.

'Yes?' I asked him, not really wanting to get into conversation with the man, but it would seem I didn't have a great deal of choice.

'You see, Jim,' he went on, 'a couple of years ago I dived from a jetty into the river Mersey in Birkenhead and rescued this little girl. She was only eight, you know, just a kid and don't ask me how she landed in the water. Anyway,' he continued, 'she was alright.'

'That was very brave of you Stanley.' Mary said.

'I didn't think of it like that, Mary; nobody else was around at the time. Hilda and I have kept in touch with the family ever since; they only live two streets away from us in Walton Vale, Liverpool.'

'You seem to have a certain affinity with water, don't you Stanley.' I said to him as Mary and I looked out to sea from the entrance to the Grand Harbour; the vast emptiness of the Mediterranean stretching as far as our eyes could see.

'Well, I did have the opportunity to get picked up by a Russian helicopter though, appearing on TVM, Television Malta, and making headline news in *'The Times'*.' Stanley pointed out in his eloquent Scouse Liverpudlian adenoidal accent, giving me the impression he was always suffering the strains of the common cold.

The detailed commentary on board unfolded the history of Valletta and the Three Cities connected with the two sieges of 1565 and 1942, as well as all the other places of interest, including the historical forts, battlements and creeks which can only be admired from the sea. Captain Morgan's Harbour Cruise is renowned for its detailed commentary, cruising into every creek and showing everyone the closest and most remarkable views.

'Tell me, Stanley,' Mary said to him as he leaned over the wooden rail on the starboard side of the boat, 'before you fall into the water, do you like my new bracelet? James bought it for me in Valletta yesterday.'

Stanley replied by saying: 'Yes, it's good gear that, do you like the silver pizza ring I bought for Hilda in Sliema? It cost me a lorra lorra dough.'

'Yes, that was very funny, Stanley.' I said, looking at his rather ugly and distorted reflection in the picturesque turquoise, green and blue-coloured water.

'Did you know Captain Morgan was a pirate?' Stanley said, adding to the history lessons on board the boat.

'Yes, I did.' I replied raising my eyebrows and shaking my head at the same time, 'Mary and I have been ripped-off by our lovely tourist representative, Helen Azzopardi, and even Dick Turpin had the decency to wear a mask.' I added.

'Well, I hope there are no holes in this boat,' Stanley said, wiping sea spray from his eyes. 'Hilda and I are about to take over the management of a pub called the 'Speckled Banana' in Kirkby on Wednesday, and that will be fun, won't it?'

'Yes, I suppose it will and stop you from continually getting yourself wet.'

'We are flying back to Liverpool tomorrow, leaving early in the morning.' Stan, the man said to me reluctantly. 'When we get off this boat will you join us lot for a farewell drink in Tony's bar because it would seem everyone is going home tomorrow.' he explained.

'That is very kind of you, Stanley,' Mary very bravely said to him. 'James and I would love to have a farewell drink with you all, wouldn't we, James?'

'Yes dear,' I somewhat reluctantly replied and then said: 'anything to keep you happy my darling.'

The time was ten-minutes to four when the boat was tied up to the quayside allowing us to step on to dry land once again. It had started to rain, but we didn't have far to walk to Tony's bar, it being very conveniently situated across the road from the quayside. Howard had found himself a new boyfriend, namely Nicholas Bottomley who had exchanged his 'Popeye' baseball hat for a Stetson when they sailed along Valletta's Grand Harbour.

Arm in arm we all walked across the busy road taking our lives into our hands lest we were knocked down by a Sunday driver; I should have been so lucky!

'Drinks all round everyone.' was the order of the day from Stanley Parry to a friendly waiter who was standing in front of the bar with his arms folded.

Mary and I were quite happy sitting down with a gin and tonic and plates of complementary peanuts, *Bruschetta* and butter beans to keep us occupied for a while but then Stanley, after drinking several pints of 'Hop Leaf', got up from his seat and began singing: "We'll meet again".

I said to Mary: 'Somehow, I don't think so.'

Chapter Twenty-four

Our last full day in Malta began by going up to the restaurant in the lift, packed to the gunnels with laundry sacks and Barbara, our busty chamber maid from the welcoming village of Zejtun situated close to the southern coast of Malta and once famous for its olive oil and spinach; sadly not one tree or plant remains, much to the delight of Popeye. I said good morning to Barbara before giving her a generous tip for meticulously cleaning our room and supplying us with extra blankets, a portable paraffin heater and OXO cubes when the central heating decided to malfunction early on Thursday morning. Barbara thanked us for our generosity and hoped she would have the privilege and honour to clean our room again when she decided we should return the following year; I suppose, everyone can live in hope I thought.

When the doors to the lift opened on the fifth floor I tripped over one of the laundry sacks and immediately fell into the restaurant, head first.

'Good morning, Sir James.' Lawrence said helping me to get up from the carpeted floor.

'Good morning, good morning, what's good about it?' I said, shouting at Lawrence unnecessarily.

'Sorry, sorry, sorry.' he replied, meaning he wasn't sorry at all.

Salvo was the next person to arrive on the scene, carrying a basket of sliced *Hobz Malti* from the kitchen. I can remember seeing a bright red fire extinguisher by the toaster waiting to put out a fire and Lawrence standing at ease in front of the guests just in case one of them had an idea to electrocute themselves by poking a knife inside the appliance to retrieve their burnt offerings.

'Good morning, Sir, Madam,' Salvo said to us when he delivered a pot of coffee to our table.

'Is it?' I replied, pouring fresh coffee into Mary's cup and knowing what was going to come next.

'Do you know who the patron saint of Bugibba is?' he asked

I said to him, it is probably Saint Paul because he gets around most places on the island.

'You're right, but how did you know that?' Salvo said and then continued to enhance my somewhat limited religious knowledge by saying: 'If it wasn't for Saint Paul, the small town of Bugibba wouldn't have any tourists.'

'And do you know who the patron saint of Gzira is?' I said to him jokingly.

'No, who is it?' Salvo replied, giving me a curious look.

I told him it was Colonel Saunders because if it wasn't for him Gzira wouldn't have its Kentucky Fried Chicken.

Salvo wasn't amused in my attempt to be the hotel's resident comedian and went away scratching his head. I told him another joke later which confused him even more after I had said that a colleague of mine asked me when I last had sex? I replied by saying 1945. He said that was a long time ago, wasn't it? I said, no not really, it is only twenty hundred hours now. This was when Mary piped up and said: 'just shut up James and eat your cornflakes, you know it was around five-thirty yesterday afternoon.'

The joke became famous throughout the hotel because I overheard Salvo repeating the same one to an elderly German couple that evening.

It was just after nine when Mary and I departed from the restaurant having escaped from Salvo who was about to tell us another one of his pathetic little stories that seem to last for hours. I said to Mary: 'Do you realize, all those people, including 'Big Foot' from Canada have all gone home.'

'Yes, I do realize that, James.' she said with wicked smile on her face. 'It looks as though we are going to have a *very quiet* and pleasant day, doesn't it, so *Enjoy it.*'

'And we are going home tomorrow.' I replied becoming more, or less excited by the minute.

'Tell me James,' Mary said, holding on to my arm as we walked down the stairs to go to reception. 'Just how did Edward Greaves, you're stable mate in the 'Circus', lose an eye?'

'Well, it was at the Battle of Trafalgar.' I replied.

'James, really, you know very well that's a load of eye-wash.'

Down in reception George Attard had just printed the menu for the evening meal; the starter being deep fried *Gozitan* goats cheese parcels served on a bed of lettuce or alternatively the hotel's speciality, an extra thick pumpkin soup. The main course consisting of Lamb Stroganoff or *Bragoli*, a Maltese dish made with rolled beef stuffed with bacon, parsley and hard boiled eggs; grilled swordfish being another alternative at 1.50 Maltese Lira extra.

'I shall be looking forward to my dinner this evening; the menu seems to be quite interesting.' I said to Mary putting my arm around her shoulders as we stood in front of the small wooden easel.

'Yes, the food sounds delicious,' Mary replied enthusiastically.' and because it is our last night in the hotel we can order a bottle of Maltese Chardonnay.' she added.

Doris suddenly appeared from behind her favourite hiding place, the full length wall hanging tapestry in reception, to take up her position in the coffee shop. I said to Mary: 'no one is called Doris today,' and this was when she cleverly replied: "Perhaps, perhaps, perhaps".'

I said to her: 'can you remember British Rail having their 'Have it away Day'?'

'You always have to have the last word, don't you, James? You are so guttural.' she sighed.

As we were taking steps to make our way out of the hotel, Dominic did his usual loud squawk and said 'Enjoy it'.

I looked back and waving a finger in his direction said: 'you have only a few hours to live now Dominic so don't push your luck.'

Mary said to me: 'Do you know, James, I was thinking about taking Dominic to London with us tomorrow,' to which I replied: 'You cannot be serious.'

It was to be the start of a warm and sunny day when Mary and I walked along the esplanade, Gerolamo Cassar Street into Floriana from Valletta's Castille Square, to catch a number sixty-seven bus to take us to the stop near to the Preluna Hotel in Sliema. Mary and I had decided earlier that morning to visit Balluta Bay in St Julian's with its quaint triangular grassy mound, the *Piazza*, surrounded by shops, restaurants and a kiosk serving the best cheese and pea cakes in town; their *Hobz-biz-jejt*, small pieces of local bread rubbed with tomatoes until it turns pink, and then topped with tomatoes, capers, olive oil and seasoning is complementary when one has a cup of coffee or a glass of beer sitting leisurely outside their café.

Balluta Bay features a Neo-Gothic Carmelite Parish Church, 'Our Lady of Mount Carmel' and has its own associated monastery conveniently located next door. The limestone built Carmelite Church, with three bells and a series of electronic bells which tinkle jolly tunes at midday, stands resplendent on a slope facing the water and it is best viewed in the evening, especially during the *festa*; the powerful orange glow of the light casting spectral shadows and dazzling highlights conjuring up dreamy images of Maltese families gravitating slowly along the coastal promenade between *Ghar id-Dud* and St Julian's, making frequent pit-stops for nuts, seeds, nougat and ice cream. Balluta Bay has become unashamedly Malta's *Costa*; Marbella without the villains and during the month of August it could be described as Blackpool with its illuminations.

The rickety old yellow and white British Leyland bus we had the misfortune to alight had travelled all the way from Valletta's bus station minus a metal plate on the floor and sitting on a brown leather bench seat which had been cobbled to death many times, Mary and I could see the tarmac on the road passing by underneath us.

When the bus approached our stop in Tower Road I alerted the driver by cautiously giving a gravitational pull on a length of string to ring the bell. The inevitable happened; the string broke and we ended up travelling along the promenade towards the Preluna Hotel, the stop where we wanted to get off in the first place. I managed to convince the driver that his bus was in urgent need of repair and required a new floor because he could have lost a couple of passengers. 'Sorry, sorry, sorry.' he replied without batting an eyelid.

Mary and I walked along Sliema's High Street from the Preluna and this was where we stopped to look in the window of Malta's Unique Leather Shop, the place for original leather wear, Italian handbags and briefcases. There was a soft leather jacket in a warm shade of red in the centre of the window which Mary found difficult to make up her mind to buy as a special Christmas present for our daughter, Carol. However, we didn't buy it and continued with our walk along the promenade towards Balluta Bay. We made a pit stop at one of Malta's favourite ice cream parlours, the *Gelateria* Lungomare next door to the Tower Palace Hotel; the two homemade pistachio flavoured cornettos were out of this world and could be a weight-watcher's nightmare.

Passing by the Water Polo Club – The Neptune's, we saw the oldest pub in Malta called the 'City of London' bar in Main Street, Balluta and this was where Mary and I, after crossing the busy Tower Road, made our second pit stop for a cool and refreshing gin and tonic. The atmosphere was tremendous, sitting outside on the terrace taking in the sea breeze, the fumes from the traffic and listening to two local women having an argument in the street. To compensate for this, the owner, Julian Borg, gave us two attractive tee-shirts with the words 'City of London Pub', established in 1914, printed on them and then after he had wished us a sincere *bonjourno*, we departed his establishment profiting by his generosity.

It was ten forty-five when we walked back along the promenade with the aim of sitting underneath the Judas trees by the little kiosk in the *Piazza*. As we walked by the sea wall, trying to avoid the spray Mary and I were approached and accosted by a Scottish Time Share pest from Lennoxtown, one of the towns on the periphery of the city of Glasgow who would insist on trying her best to take us back to a hotel in Sliema where she could make in-roads to extract money from our bank account. I later, said to Mary: 'They are like rubber balls, you bounce them against a wall and they keep coming back.'

I asked the woman if she had any idea who she was talking to.' And after I had insisted on telling her who I was, she then said: 'And why are ye no black?'

It was during this unfortunate and unpleasant experience we threatened to chuck her over the sea wall and go play with the sharks. I said to Mary: 'If she doesn't go away, I will certainly kick her in the nuts.'

'But she hasn't got any nuts.' Mary replied, looking around to see who was listening.

'She will have at Christmas.' I angrily pointed out to them both in no uncertain terms.

We eventually sent her running away in tears and then watched as she disappeared into the Carmelite Church to seek sanctuary.

'Listen, James,' Mary said, sounding out of breath. 'Why don't you go over to the kiosk and get yourself a well deserved cup of tea and a cheese cake because I am going back to the Leather Shop to buy that beautiful jacket for Carol.'

I emphasised to her, it was a lovely gesture and it will be a complete surprise for Carol at Christmas.

'Don't be away for long, Mary,' I said looking at my watch to check on the hour. 'The bells of the Carmelite Church chime at midday and play a sad tune and I wonder what it will be?'

I bought a cup of coffee at the little kiosk and sat down at one of their tables beginning to miss her because this was the first time during our holiday we had been apart. It was when I observed the cruelness of the Mediterranean crashing against the sea wall and the surf-like spray going on to the road, I thought about Captain Marino and Carmelo Borg Pisani rowing ashore from an Italian motor torpedo boat to scale the cliffs at *Ras id-Dawwara* to the north of *Dinghli Cliffs* and the events leading up to them secretively landing on the island of Malta.

It was the morning of Thursday 7th May 1942 Captain Marino was given his orders in the gardens of the Villa Borghese, Rome, by Alfonso Bruciano alias Joey Macaroni. His orders were to befriend a student of the Faculty of Literature and Philosophy at the University of Rome called Caio Borghi, also known as Carmelo Borg Pisani; a Maltese fascist sympathiser from the City of Senglea situated to the south of Grand Harbour Valletta. Together they were to be transported inside a truck, driven by the Italian double agent, Frankie Bivolli alias Spaghetti Zanetti, to the port of Reggio di Calabria to take the fifteen kilometre journey over to Messina, Sicily. They were then to travel down the eastern coast to Pozallo in the south, passing through Taormina, Catania and Syracuse on the way.

At 0100 hrs on the night of 18th May 1942 Operation "Cliffhanger" had begun. A flotilla of Italian S100 fast attack E-Boats, known as *Barchiono Esplosivo*, a tame sounding Italian name for a speedboat packed full of explosives delivered by four torpedoes which were waiting in Pozallo harbour to take the "Condor" Captain Marino, alias Rolando Donatello, and Carmelo Borg Pisani over the ninety-three kilometre shallow channel of water to the island of Malta.

I thought about when I was informed recently that the Royal Navy fired torpedoes at the island of Comino for practice; the waters being so clear the unexploded projectiles could be retrieved from the seabed by Maltese/Italian civilians, surreptitiously and secretly aligned to the Order of St. John of Jerusalem.

It was at precisely 0200 hrs on the night of 18th May 1942, three Italian E-Boats fired twelve torpedoes into Anchor Bay; the explosives having been replaced by several tons of Nazi gold. A contingent of Maltese and Italian partisans were waiting on the rocks for a signal from one of the boats to enable the torpedoes to accurately reach their target. It had taken Captain Marino, the "Condor", nearly a week to report his findings to the British Government inside the Castille in Valletta. Meanwhile, Carmelo Borg Pisani was captured by the Royal Navy whilst trying to scale the cliffs at *Ras-id-Dawwara* and was subsequently hanged as a spy, aged 28, on the 28th November 1942. Captain Lorenzo Giovanni Marino returned home to Naples to join his wife and family none the wiser for his experience and the disappearance of all that gold after it had been made into bells.

*

Mary came back, carrying in one hand an exclusive carrier bag containing Carol's Christmas present; a creamy red leather jacket and in the other a rum and raisin ice cream cornet. She informed me Carol had phoned her on the mobile to tell her that she had just read in the *Daily Telegraph* about Colonel Brian Woodruff who had mysteriously thrown himself off Chelsea Bridge and Commander Edward Greaves had died from a heart attack, also Rear Admiral, Sir Steven Halewood, had walked in front of a No 52 bus in Notting Hill, West London, in the early hours of yesterday morning. Carol had also told her that my book had arrived from the publishers and in my absence had taken the initiative to sign for them.

The three bells of the Carmelite Church in Balluta Bay had begun to chime melodiously, sounding like echoing voices from heaven heralding midday; the synchronized bells then continuing to play an early seventeenth century children's poem "Oranges and Lemons".

> Oranges and Lemons say the bells of Saint Clements
> You owe me five farthings say the bells of Saint Martins
> When will you pay me say the bells of Old Bailey?
> When I grow rich say the bells of Shoreditch
> When will that be say the great bell of Bow?
> Here comes a candle to light you to bed
> And here comes a chopper to chop of your head
> Chip-chop, chip-chop; the last one is dead.

Looking into my cup of Italian cappuccino I had a chill running down my spine not knowing what to expect when I returned home. Mary, who was now sitting cosily by my side said: 'You know, James, you have only smoked nineteen cigarettes since we arrived in Malta.'

'Well, you never know, Mary, this may be the last nail in my coffin,' I replied giving her the reassurance she probably wanted to hear. 'And what shall I do with the last one, Mary?'

'Oh, really, James, why do you always have to be so dramatic; just smoke it, James, just smoke it.'

Footnote:

Alfonso Bruciano, alias, Joey Macaroni, born in Palermo, Sicily and a British MI9 agent based in Rome – executed; shot by the German Gestapo in June 1943, Age 42.

Frankie Bivolli, alias, Spaghetti Zanetti, born into a Sicilian Mafia family in Syracuse, Sicily; died mysteriously in the forever nervous city of Catania, Sicily in 1945, age 37.

Also by Michael Alty:

The Guildford Boys - ISBN 978 1 84549 428 5

The Ghost of Latchford Hall - ISBN 978 1 84549 528 2

Published by Arima Publishing.

The poems: 'The Piper', 'The Grouse', 'Soap on a Rope' and 'Ben Gunn' in this book are from "Mirror Images" - copyright Mike Alty 2002

"Oranges and Lemons" - an early seventeenth century children's poem, origin unknown.